IRON CROSS AMERIKA

ERIC MEYER

First published in the United Kingdom in 2011 by Swordworks Books

ISBN 978-1-906512-80-4

Typeset by Swordworks Books
Printed and bound in the UK & US
A catalogue record of this book is available from the British Library

Cover design by Swordworks Books
www.swordworks.co.uk

IRON CROSS AMERIKA

ERIC MEYER

CHAPTER ONE

'I speak in the name of the entire German people when I assure the world that we all share the honest wish to eliminate the enmity that brings far more costs than any possible benefits... It would be a wonderful thing for all of humanity if both peoples would renounce force against each other forever. The German people are ready to make such a pledge.'

Adolf Hitler - 14th October 1933

She was beautiful, in the mysterious way that only French girls know how. I didn't know any French, at least, nothing that I could use outside of a brothel, so I tried her with English.

"Mam'selle, don't you know it's dangerous out here?"

She smiled a warm, dazzling smile. "I know that, but I wanted to see all of the excitement. You are English?"

"American, Miss. Paul Schaffer, from Chicago, Illinois, Ma'am."

"I am Anne-Marie Dubois. Tell me, what is an American

doing fighting with the Germans?"

I pulled her out of the way, as a shell exploded in the next street. The British were still trying to delay the advance but their efforts were getting weaker. I sometimes wondered what I was doing here, in the middle of a war. My parents were German, Werner and Charlotte Schaffer, both from the city of Koln where I was born, the city the English call Cologne. After the war ended in 1918 they tried to escape the poverty and famine of a collapsed Germany by emigrating to the US in 1921 to try to make their fortune. We'd arrived in time for them to have their dreams cruelly shattered by the Great Depression, all I could remember of my childhood was poverty and more poverty. Yet according to the newsreels everything had changed in Germany after a new leader had brought an exciting new hope to that country. My job on a local Chicago newspaper was going nowhere so I returned to Germany to see for myself the brave new world that Adolf Hitler had created. Yet as a young journalist I wanted to do more than just see it, I wanted to write about it, to record it and let the world know about the German miracle. When Germany went to war, I immediately enlisted. I was fluent in German, a gift from my parents, there was much talk of possible alliances with the US and I hoped to become involved in the creation of a dynamic new nation that would be the envy of the world. They allowed me to join an SS Kriegsberichter-Kompanie, the War Correspondents.

I brushed the dust off my uniform. Unlike the Waffen-SS in the new field grey, we still wore the original uniform of the Allgemeine SS, black tunic complete with the twin lightning runes on the collar tabs and the cuff title of my unit, SS-Kriegsberichter-Kompanie. Regulations demanded a peaked officer's cap, black riding breeches, high, polished jackboots and a red swastika armband on my sleeve. I had a Walther PPK pistol holstered on my belt, the standard issue officer's firearm, released in 1931 from the Walther factory in Thuringia. It had a double-action trigger mechanism, a single-column magazine, and a fixed barrel firing the military 7.65mm round, or so they told me during my short military training at Lichterfelde outside Berlin. I had other weapons more suited to my work. Instead of a rifle, I carried a Leica II rangefinder camera, issued to me by Dr Goebbels' Reich Ministry of Public Enlightenment and Propaganda. My unit didn't possess artillery, instead I used a solid, reliable Swiss Hermes typewriter to fight my particular war. Another shell exploded, nearer this time, caking us both with dust.

"Miss Dubois, you really should get under cover."

She shrugged. "I'm sure I'll be fine, there doesn't seem to be many shells exploding."

She reminded me a little of Lisl, my girlfriend in Berlin. She worked in a nightclub as an exotic dancer, Lisl von Schenk, the beautiful, blonde daughter of an aristocratic Prussian family. The clients loved her haughty, spirited performance, as did I after many nights spent in her apartment. Whenever I called in to see her, she had one thing on her mind, sex, which suited us both perfectly.

A half-track clattered along the street, a Demag Sd Kfz 10, laden with troopers of the Der Fuhrer Regiment, SS-

Verfugungstruppe or SS-VT, Himmler's Nazi party combat troops. Berlin had attached me to the Regiment to send reports and photographs back to Berlin for publication in Volkischer Beobachter and Der Sturmer, both Nazi party publications. So far it had been an exhausting assignment, our troops had sliced through Belgium and France, all the signs were that they were about to drive the British into the sea. Except that here the fighting had stalled, the Blitzkrieg was halted and the British Army was making a stand in the nearby Nieppe Forest. To break the deadlock, Generalfeldmarschall Wilhelm Keitel's Oberkommando der Wehrmacht (OKW) had ordered Der Fuhrer in to smash through the stubborn British Tommies. The half-track rumbled past, the troops waving happily when they saw my camera and the commander, Obersturmfuhrer Willy Braun, gave a cheerful wave. I'd interviewed him two days ago for a feature in Signal magazine and written a piece that had painted him and his unit in blood-stirring rhetoric, for which he still owed me a favor or two. Then a machine gun started to chatter and bullets zinged all around us, Braun's half-track swerved away to deal with the enemy as I pulled Anne-Marie into cover.

"Miss Dubois, you have to get inside now and keep your head down, the battle is getting worse," I shouted to her. Silly bitch, she'd get her pretty head blown off.

She shook her head, her eyes were blazing with that ferocious intensity that you see in women sometimes, as if the presence of extreme danger and death is some kind of aphrodisiac. I'd like to have helped her out with her obvious arousal, but

I had an urgent job to do and my people were due to arrive at any moment to take me up to the front. I pulled her inside the building and shouted at her to stay under cover, making a mental note to come back after the fighting to see if she was still in the same frame of mind.

We had a good view of the action through the open space where the window had once been. It was definitely warming up, streams of machine gun fire crisscrossing as Der Fuhrer fought their way forward and the British stubbornly defended the town. Behind them was the thick, dark expanse of the Nieppe Forest, the vast expanse of woodland outside of Le Touquet. Braun had said that if the enemy dug in there it would be a bitter fight to get them out and it looked to me as if they were doing exactly that, the battle was curving inexorably towards the thick, dark forest. Max and Karl-Heinz came running down the road, Max still managing to look elegant and immaculate despite the swirling smoke, dust and debris of war that left us all looking like vagabonds. Like me, he was a non-German, in his case he was Swiss, born of wealthy ethnic German parents. The war had seemed to him like an ideal opportunity to escape the stifling boredom of middle-class Swiss life, he'd said. What he didn't need to say was that our SS-Kriegsberichter-Kompanie was by far the best way to participate in the war, glamorous uniforms, the excitement of being near the front without the dire necessity of carrying a weapon and actually having to shoot at anybody. Unless of course it was with the Leica II still camera. Other members of our platoon even had a movie camera and sound equipment with which to record our SS Legions for posterity, as well as for Reichsfuhrer Himmler, our boss. They saw me in the window and ran over, Max spotted Anne-Marie at once and immediately drew himself up to his full height. He was six feet tall, slim, blonde and looked every inch the Neo-German Prussian Nazi aristocrat that he harbored ambitions to be. Karl-Heinz Brandt, an SS Scharfuhrer, was our driver and general assistant. A Rhinelander, he was as different from Max as it was possible to be. Short, muscular, dark and swarthy, he provided the energy and muscle that hustled our unit along from battlefront to battlefront.

"You managed to find the local talent, I see," Max said sarcastically. "We were covering the battle, maybe that was too risky for you!"

He was always sarcastic and I thought he was probably born to be supercilious, weren't all middle-class Swiss that way? He disliked me intensely because my first language was English, the language of the enemy. He often said that I was only one short step from being a traitor, apparently owing allegiance as much to England because of my accent, as to Germany because of my heritage. Fortunately, I was as tall as he was and had learned to fight in the tough Chicago High School, where kids had to learn fast or spend their lives being kicked around by the ever-present bullies. The hard lessons I learned in that school I put to work when Max became too obnoxious on one occasion, to his astonishment I sucker punched him and put him on his back. Since then we'd enjoyed an uneasy truce, agreeing to put our dislike on hold until after the war. Max, however, found it difficult to remember our gentlemen's agreement, I guessed he enjoyed holding a grudge. I didn't rise to his bait.

"I got my story, Max, Der Fuhrer had a hell of a fight on their hands taking this town and I managed to shoot some good pictures. It looks as if they'll be attacking the wood soon, Nieppe Forest, they say it'll be a total bastard."

He snorted. "The English will probably run like rabbits when they see us coming, I wouldn't be too scared of fighting in the forest if I were you, Schaffer."

A salvo of shells came over, British, probably two pounder anti-tank guns, they smashed into a school further along the street, another cloud of dust and smoke enveloped us. The two-pounder was largely obsolete, only effective against thin armor, but they seemed to have large numbers of them and best avoided as they could still cause havoc when used against unarmored troops in built up areas. As far as our High Command knew, the Tommies had no high explosive shells for these guns and so they were not terribly effective except when they struck a vehicle or building, sending showers of fragments whistling through the air to shred flesh and bone. And, of course, when they scored a direct hit. I pushed Anne-Marie away from the empty window.

"You need to take cover, the firing is getting more intense, the British are shooting back because they think our soldiers are positioned in the town."

"Don't worry, I'll take care of you, Miss," Max said with a confident smile.

She laughed at him. "I bet you would, pretty boy, but I don't need taking care of."

He scowled as she abruptly twisted away and went out through the back of the building. Well, she was an adult, she was entitled to get herself killed if she wanted to.

I looked across at Karl-Heinz, "Scharfuhrer, where is our movie unit?"

"Der Fuhrer is almost ready to renew the attack, the film crew is planning to cover it as they move into the wood. They say there'll be some good footage, a lot of fireworks."

"Yes, it's going to be a nasty one, there'll be a lot of casualties in there."

"The enemy worries you, Schaffer?" Max sneered.

"Fuck off, Max," I dismissed his comment. "Karl-Heinz, let's find the Der Fuhrer forward observation point, we'll see if we can get some good pictures as they go in."

"Yes, Sir."

I climbed out of the empty window frame onto the street and we started walking in the direction of Der Fuhrer's last known position. Stray bullets knocked chips of stone out of buildings all around us, but I steeled myself to ignore them, I wouldn't give Max the satisfaction of proving him right. Scharfuhrer Karl-Heinz Brandt had no such qualms, when a storm of bullets rattled around us or a shell knocked a hole in a nearby building, he just ducked low to avoid the fragments that showered around us. He was right though, we were here to take pictures and write articles, not to be killed. We found the Regimental HQ outside the town, a chaos of SS troopers, armored half-tracks with mounted MG34 machine guns and Kubelwagen jeeps. The Commanding Officer, SS-Oberfuhrer

Georg Keppler was shouting at his men to hurry. Max went away to find our own Kubelwagen, Keppler caught sight of Karl-Heinz and me.

"Who the hell are you?"

I saluted, "Sir, Untersturmfuhrer Paul Schaffer, SS Kriegsberichter-Kompanie. We're covering your advance, is it ok with you if we go up to your forward OP?"

He looked at me coldly. "You're the American, aren't you?"

I nodded, "Yes, that's right."

He sneered. "Jesus Christ, SS Amerika has arrived. Did you come here to show us how to fight the war? You'd better keep out of the fucking way, Schaffer, while we show you how Germans fight this war. We've got a real fight on our hands, the Tommies are well dug-in in that wood and it's going to be a swine to force them out. They've got every approach covered with machine-guns and snipers, we're going to lose some men going in there. Go up to the OP if you wish but I warn you it's going to be a real fight, you may get that pretty black uniform a little soiled."

I nodded and saluted again, he moved away to shout at some harassed mechanics to get the half-tracks repaired in time for the battle. I found a staff officer and discovered that another regiment, SS-Germania was spearheading the attack on the right flank. Der Fuhrer was covering the left flank but he told me that the attack had been postponed until the following morning. That gave me some time, I collected Karl-Heinz and Max and we found the cookhouse heating up a monstrous pot of evil looking stew even so our mouths watered with the spicy smell. The advance had gone so quickly that food was often the last thing brought forward. The three of us sat on a fallen log in the warm twilight, drinking hot coffee to wash down the meal.

"Max, how do you want to play this tomorrow morning, split up or stay together? If we do stay together Karl-Heinz will be on hand to assist us both, we'll need him to help carry the gear if it gets really hot."

He was the motor that drove us along, he always seemed to know the best place from which to capture a good action shot, the most interesting trooper to question for a good story and when we turned around for a spare camera, replacement film or typewriter and paper, he simply handed them to us. He also knew when to push our heads down when shells and machine gun fire threatened to put an early end to our war reporting careers. The Scharfuhrer had fought in the Great War after he'd lied about his age to join up as a fifteen year old private in the 1st Westphalian Infantry, he'd subsequently earned promotion to Gefreiter, Corporal, and been awarded an Iron Cross, Second Class. He had many talents including how to keep warm and dry in the teeth of a howling rainstorm and where to find the regimental cookhouse and shelter from heavy gunfire. This last skill was one we especially valued him for and would probably have foregone all of his other skills as long as he kept that one. Not all of our SS-Kriegsberichter-Kompanie had fared as well as we had, we'd left the corpses of more than a dozen of our journalists and photographers on the battlefield during the advance through Belgium and France.

"Why don't we search out our film crew and see what they are planning?" I suggested.

"I haven't seen them around lately, Sir," Brandt said. "It would be a good idea to look them up. We don't want to cover the same ground as they do tomorrow."

"They've probably moved well back from the fighting," Max sneered.

It wasn't a fair comment, the film unit had suffered just as many casualties as the rest of us.

"If you're so keen on fighting, why don't you grab a rifle and join Der Fuhrer tomorrow?" I said to him quietly. "I'm sure they would value the extra help."

Even in the dim light, I saw him flush.

"Don't think I wouldn't, Schaffer. But you know they won't let us foreigners fight with the regular SS-VT units."

I heard Karl-Heinz mumble something about 'why don't you go and fight on your own then?' but Max chose to ignore it. I rummaged in my pack and found a bottle of schnapps and passed it around, even Max seemed to unwind a little.

"Here's to a victory tomorrow," he said, raising his tin mug in a toast. We followed suit.

"Look, I saw Obersturmfuhrer Braun earlier," I said to them, "he was driving along the main street with a bunch of his lads in that half-track of his. I'll ask him if we can follow his troops in, right behind the first wave, how does that sound?"

They both nodded their agreement and I got up and went to find him. I asked one of our sentries and he pointed to a patch of ground fifty yards away. I thanked him and walked over to find Obersturmfuhrer Willy Braun.

"Paul, you Yankee bastard, how's the dirty magazine trade going?" he asked me with a smile. Like the rest of them he was dirty and unshaven, tired and stressed, but there was a crackling undercurrent almost like electricity that hung over the whole camp, these men knew they were going out tomorrow morning to win a decisive victory.

"I wish it was the dirty magazine trade, it'd be more interesting than taking pictures of your ugly mugs."

He laughed, we were on good terms after I'd done a good feature on him.

"Willy, when that article comes out I'll get a copy of Signal to you, it should have your ugly photo on the front page, you know, 'How I Won the War by Obersturmfuhrer Willy Braun'."

The men around him laughed. They were a hard, tough looking bunch, I didn't pity the English troops who had to face them in the morning. Like Willy, most were tall, blonde and muscular, the Aryan ideal, naturally. Unlike them, I was quite dark, but then again, so was Adolf Hitler, so who was complaining?

"Piss off, Paul," he smiled. "What do you want?"

"We want to follow your first wave in tomorrow, three of us, me, Karl Heinz and Max."

"That fucking Swiss-Prussian ass-licker, why are you still traveling with him?"

"Because like you I have to follow orders, Willy. How about it?"

"You'd better stay out of our way then. And watch out for

snipers, the wood is rotten with them, they're like lice."

"We'll wear our tin helmets then."

"You'd be better off with a Panzer III, Paul."

I smiled, the Panzer III was a medium tank, well armored and had become the spear point of our armored thrust through France and the Low Countries. The crews swore that the three-man turret was the tank's best feature, it meant that the commander was not distracted with either loader or gunner's tasks and could fully concentrate on maintaining situational awareness. They'd certainly swept the enemy before them and earned a formidable fighting reputation.

"They didn't issue one of those, I'm afraid," I smiled. "I'll have to manage with my helmet. We'll see you first thing in the morning, Willy, thanks."

He waved as I walked off. I got back to our camp and settled down to sleep for the night. Karl-Heinz had parked our Kubelwagen in the shelter of some trees and had rigged up a shelter tied to its side so we were able to sleep under canvas. We had no need of an alarm clock, in the morning the uproar was deafening, shouts, whistles, engines roaring. The Regiment was not concerned to hide their intentions from the enemy, their next move was so obvious that there was little point in trying to conceal it.

Willy's platoon had orders to attack at eight-thirty, so we had time for a hurried breakfast from the cookhouse. We sat eating amidst the cheerful soldiers of Der Fuhrer, they were buoyed up, bright-eyed and bristling with confidence, which was not surprising. So far, they'd swept the Belgian, British and French troops aside like confetti. They looked fearsome enough in their dusty, battered field-grey uniforms, leather webbing straps festooned with spare ammunition and stick grenades, some already had their steel helmets on. After all, they were the SS-VT and considered themselves the elite, the best, bravest, fittest soldiers in all Europe. While they chatted, we sat silently watching them. I gave Karl-Heinz my Leica and he stood up to walk around and take some background shots. Then a whistle sounded and they scrambled away to join their respective units ready for the start of the battle. They were not using the half-tracks, it was going to be a long, hard slog on foot to prize the English from their fortified positions inside the forest. It would be man against man, there was no room for armor. While they were still assembling, we shouldered our packs, put on our steel helmets and stood ready to follow them.

"Gentlemen, watch the snipers," Karl-Heinz said solemnly. "That's the real danger. Artillery, well, you won't see it coming and there's nothing you can do about it, but snipers, they're the real bastard so keep your heads down."

Max laughed. "Do you want us to dig trenches as well, Scharfuhrer, like the ones you used to hide in during the last war?"

"No, Sir, they already have trenches dug in the wood, the English I mean. They're in there waiting for us."

His smile faded and he tightened the strap on his helmet. There were three blasts on a whistle that were repeated along the lines of troops and the men started forward.

The tree line was two hundred yards away, for the first

hundred and fifty yards they walked forward steadily, nothing happened. Fifty yards from the trees there was a long, stone boundary wall about four feet high. They paused behind the wall and peered over the top, officers checked the wood with their binoculars but gave no sign that they had spotted the enemy.

"Why don't they use an artillery barrage?" I asked Karl-Heinz.

"I doubt there are any spare guns for this battle," he replied. "They're all deployed elsewhere, they've got to do this the hard way."

"I told you, the English will run like rabbits when they see our men coming for them," Max said. I ignored him, the English I'd seen up until now, as well as the French and Belgians, were anything but cowards. They were just outnumbered and outgunned. Then the whistles sounded, three blasts and the Der Fuhrer troopers vaulted over the wall and started to charge towards the wood. They got halfway there when all hell broke loose, rifle and machine gun fire broke the calm of the morning as a hail of British lead swept through our lines. Men were falling all over the open space in front of the wood and our troopers broke into a run, hurtling towards the trees to get to grips with the Tommies that they couldn't even see to shoot at yet. By the time they got there, they must have lost fifty of their original number of two hundred, the rest charged into the wood and I heard the shouts and screams, the gunfire and explosions of grenades as the two sides came together. We waited.

It took half an hour of vicious fighting before our men were able to progress deeper into the wood.

"What do you think?" Max asked.

Karl-Heinz nodded. "That should do it, they've cleared the first defensive line, and we should be safe to go in now."

We shouldered our packs, climbed the wall and started walking towards the trees. We passed men whimpering in pain, corpses, their uniforms shredded with machine gun bullets, broken equipment and everywhere, the stench of the battlefield, the metallic smell of blood mixed with cordite fumes and vomit, the foul smell of excrement. Death was never pretty, as we'd come to realize during this campaign. None of us took photographs, our instructions were clear, our masters wanted so see victory, not the bloody price that had to be paid for it. When we reached the trees, we saw the first of the English bodies, they had dug a trench line just as Karl-Heinz had predicted. The trench had now become the grave of many of these men. They were piled in bloody heaps where our machine pistols and stick grenades had made short work of them. I bent down and picked up an English sub-machine gun, they called it the Sten Gun. I checked the clip, it still had a full load of bullets. Cheap looking, hastily made of pressed steel, they were still capable of spitting out a lethal volley of bullets. I shouldered the gun and looked around for spare ammunition.

"What do you want that for?" Max sneered. "Going to fight for your friends the English?"

"No, I'm looking out for snipers, just in case some of them are still hiding in the trees to blow your stupid head off, Max."

He looked up quickly at the tops of the trees.

"You think there may still be some here?"

"If there are, it might be an idea to be ready for them," I said, smiling inwardly at his sudden attack of nerves.

"That may be not be a bad idea," he said. He took his pistol out of its holster and clicked the safety catch to the fire position.

"Lead on, Schaffer, you've got the machine pistol."

I heard Karl-Heinz mutter 'Hail the conquering hero', somehow he always managed to pitch his voice so that Max could never quite make out what he said.

Before we moved on I took some photographs with my Leica and made some notes, it seemed we were up against the Royal West Kent Regiment, judging from the shoulder flashes on the uniforms of the English corpses. Ahead of us, we could hear the sounds of the battle as our troops swept further forward, dislodging the English. Several times, we passed corpses lying at the base of trees where our soldiers had killed them, but they hadn't died in vain, there were many German casualties littered over the forest floor, many moaning in pain. Oddly there were no English wounded, I wondered how our men could be such good shots. We pushed on further until we came to a stop, a group of around fifty of our troops had bunched in a clearing. In the middle of them was a group of English prisoners, about fifteen of them, lined up cowering against the side of an old stone building. They were covered by two of our light machine guns, MG34s, each manned by a grim faced trooper. It was exactly the kind of material we were looking for, our victorious men holding a shivering bunch of English Tommies prisoner, just what the soldiers' mothers and fathers wanted to see back in the Reich. We pushed through the ring of our troops until I found the officer in charge, a Hauptsturmfuhrer, a captain.

"SS-Kriegsberichter-Kompanie, Sir, may we take a couple of photographs and take some details, we're sending material back to Signal in Berlin, possibly they'll be syndicated to Der Sturmer as well."

"I don't want anyone taking photographs, Untersturmfuhrer, why don't you go and find someone else to film."

"Look, Sir, this is exactly what we're looking for, you've beaten the Tommies, the readers go crazy for this sort of stuff."

Then I played what I thought was my trump card.

"The Fuhrer reads through Signal, you know, and I'll be sure to mention your name and unit."

It always worked, catching the eye of Adolf Hitler was the passport to fame and fortune in Nazi Germany. Except this time.

"No photographs, why don't you just fuck off."

I could hardly believe it.

"But why, Sir? What's the problem?"

"Look, these men have been sentenced to be shot, we don't want any records of it, not everyone takes kindly to this kind of thing."

"Come on, Schaffer," Max said, pulling at my sleeve. "This is not our kind of story, let's move on somewhere else."

I shook him off. "What have these men done, Sir? Why were they sentenced to death?"

The officer sighed tiredly. "I really don't have time for this.

They were sniping at us through the trees when we advanced, they got a lot of my men, the troops are boiling with anger, they've lost friends, one of my people lost his twin brother."

"Schaffer, come on," Max said again.

"Shut up, Max. Sir, you can't shoot prisoners out of hand, they fought a battle and lost, that's all. You can't shoot them for that!"

"And who says so, you?" he sneered as he said that, then shouted to the machine gunners. "Achtung!"

They moved the safety catches to the fire position and aimed at the Tommies. I couldn't believe what I was seeing.

"You men, stop, don't do that!" I took hold of the officer's tunic, put my face next to him and shouted, "You do that and it's a war crime, you could wind up in a concentration camp!"

Everything went silent for a few moments, the troops looked incredulously as a mere journalist dared to threaten their commander. The officer lost his temper.

"Take your hand off me, boy. I'll give you three seconds and then I'll shoot you myself!"

Max was still pulling at my sleeve, trying to get me away. Karl-Heinz looked on in astonishment at the sight of two officers about to come to blows. The Captain started to reach for his pistol and I knew he was about to shoot me, but I couldn't back down, I hadn't joined the SS to condone murder. I swung the Sten Gun around and pointed it at his stomach. I had no idea if it was functioning or whether it had a safety catch and if it did, was it on or off? But the metal barrel pointing at him was a sufficient threat Abruptly his troopers swung their weapons up and pointed them all at me, an assortment of MP38 machine pistols and Kar 98k rifles. He smiled.

"You'd better stand down, my friend, or they'll fill you with more holes than a colander."

I was shaking with adrenaline, anger surged through me with the thought that this arrogant bastard thought he could murder prisoners with impunity.

"You try it and you'll die first, I want you to give the order to your machine gunners to stand down," I shouted at him.

He smiled a cold, arrogant smile. "No."

"You'd better, Sir, or I'll kill you!"

He shook his head. "I do not take orders from junior officers, especially," he looked at my unit badges with a sneer, "especially from journalists who are not even soldiers. Now fuck off, sonny, before you get hurt."

"Tell them to stand down!" I shouted again.

"No, Untersturmfuhrer, you will stand down, now!"

An officer had come up to us, unnoticed. SS-Oberführer Georg Keppler, surrounded by his staff, all armed with MP38s, all pointed at me. Keppler had not un-holstered his own pistol, he just put his hand out to me with total confidence. "Give me the machine pistol, now."

"Yes, Sir."

I gave him the Sten Gun.

"And your pistol."

So I was really in the shit. At least I was for now. When the authorities knew about him shooting unarmed prisoners, I knew that I'd be vindicated. I took out my Walther and handed it to him. He turned to Max and Karl-Heinz.

"You are with this officer?"

"Well, yes," Max started to bluster, "but it wasn't my idea, I didn't want him to do this."

"Both of you give me your weapons."

They went white with shock, it could only mean one thing, arrest. Arrest on a field of battle, just the fact of it happening to a soldier was serious. They took out their pistols and gave them to him.

"What else do you have, cameras, pencils, typewriters?"

We all nodded, he smiled thinly.

"That should really frighten the enemy." His men laughed loudly, enjoying the morning's entertainment, a break from the bloody battle.

"You're all under arrest. Scharfuhrer," a tough looking sergeant stamped forward, "Yes, Sir."

"Take two soldiers and remove these men. You can hand them over to the Feldgendarmerie, they're to be placed in the cells. The charge is treason on the battlefield."

Max was shouting, almost crying that he was innocent, he hadn't been involved, he was nothing to do with it but he may as well have been talking to a brick wall. Karl-Heinz was quiet, the old soldier knew when it was useless to protest and you just had to resign yourself to your fate, rather like being in the wrong place at the wrong time when an artillery shell struck you. The Scharfuhrer led us away to the rear, we were forced to put our hands over our heads. We had only gone fifty yards when we heard to two MG34s open fire and the Tommies' screams as they were riddled with bullets. So it was all for nothing, I may as well have kept silent, except that I couldn't stand by and watch innocent men murdered. Our guards didn't even slow as the guns fired, they kept pushing us forward and marched us out of the wood. They took us out to the road, then along to the SS Feldgendarmerie post set up to control the battle area. They were known by their nickname of Kopf Jaeger, Head Hunters, an obvious referral to the SS Totenkopf, the Death's Head skull emblem embroidered on the front of their caps. But its deeper meaning lay in its reference to their severe reputation as efficient military policeman and strict enforcers of military law. We were not expecting to be treated well while we were in their hands. My only hope was that our unit CO, SS-Standartenfuhrer Gunther d'Alenquen would hear of our plight and intervene for us, although the last I'd heard of him was that he was still at our headquarters in Berlin Zehlendorf. It was a long way from Nieppe Forest. They had appropriated an old police station as their temporary base and we were pushed roughly into a cell, all three of us together. The door slammed shut, there was no water and no toilet, just a filthy, stinking bucket on the floor that was obviously what we were supposed to use.

"You're a fucking idiot, Schaffer," Max said. "We could all be shot for this, you know."

"So you were prepared to stand by and watch those men being murdered?"

"Bullshit, we're fighting a war, that's the way things happen sometimes, I expect they were moving on too fast to take prisoners and had to shoot them quickly to get rid of them."

"Max, the reason doesn't matter, what they were doing was murder. In fact what they did do, I assume they shot those poor devils after we were arrested."

"That's tough, you'll probably find out what it's like if they shoot us. Christ, I wish I'd been able to get into a real combat unit instead of this bunch of cowards."

"It is wrong to shoot prisoners," Karl Heinz suddenly spoke up. "If we do it, they will start to do it, then everyone will shoot all their prisoners and wars will become no more than butchery."

We were both surprised and looked at him.

"So that's what you think, is it, Brandt? And what would you know?"

"I know a lot more than you do, Sir. I was an infantry Gefreiter, a corporal, in the trenches. Believe me that was butchery enough, but at least we did not slaughter the prisoners."

"That's fucking crap, we haven't got time for every single prisoner, we've got a war to win and we don't want to get bogged down in the trenches like your lot did the last time," Max said.

"You won't say that when you're underneath an artillery barrage from a thousand heavy guns, Sir."

Max grunted and turned away.

"Guard, I need to speak to someone," he shouted. "This is all a mistake."

He shouted for several minutes, but no one came.

I sat down on the hard bunk and thought about what I'd

done, but no matter how I re-ran the events through in my mind, I knew that I couldn't have allowed them to shoot those prisoners.

As the day wore on I got thirsty and hungry, but no one came to bring any food or drink. By the early evening, we'd all had to use the bucket and it stank worse than ever. As it started to get dark there was a rattle of keys and a soldier brought in three metal bowls of stew and a pail of water. There was a flap in the bars and he managed to push it all through to us, we tried to ask him questions but he clearly had orders not to speak to us. We ate the stew using our hands, there were no spoons, we washed it down with water out of the pail and then waited through the long evening. Just when we thought we'd have to sleep there without knowing our fate, the outer cellblock door opened again and an officer came in, I recognized him as Sturmbannfuhrer von Gehlen, the second in command of Der Fuhrer Regiment. He stood outside the bars and looked at us. His face was thunderous.

"You have interfered with the progress of a military operation, put the lives of my men in jeopardy and treasonously threatened the life of a senior officer. You will be taken to Berlin under guard where you will be tried by a court martial at RSHA Headquarters, I expect the tribunal will be looking for the death sentence. Personally, I hope they shoot the three of you. Good night, gentlemen."

He spun on his heel and walked away. I felt numb, RSHA headquarters in Berlin meant Prinz Albrecht Strasse, home to the Sicherheitsdienst, the SS security service, and of course the

Gestapo. I'd never felt so far from home, at that moment all I could see were visions of Chicago, my childhood home, the home that I would probably never see again.

Our journey back to Germany was not comfortable, we were handcuffed and made to travel in a locked goods compartment. It was dark, unventilated and the only furnishing was the ubiquitous bucket. By the time we arrived in Berlin, I would have cheerfully volunteered for the firing squad option just to get away from the smell. We were herded into a closed truck by a troop of SS who watched us with loaded machine pistols. The truck bumped through the busy Berlin streets until it stopped at our destination. We climbed out, pushed and shoved by the guards, and went up the steps into the building. A hard faced Gestapo man carefully wrote our details in a record book.

"I hate you fucking traitors," he said, looking up at us. "If I had my way I'd shoot the fucking lot of you, then I wouldn't need to waste my time down here. Bastards!"

"Kriminalassistent Mischer, do you want them on the lower level?"

He smiled. "Yes, I think that would be very suitable accommodation for our new friends, take them down there."

They pushed us down to the dark, dank sub-basement where a hard looking jailer again wrote our details in a book and nodded to the escort to push us into our cells. They were individual cells this time, stinking of sweat, urine, sewage and fear. The floor was damp, we were so far underground that something was leaking inside the cell, constantly leaving the floor damp and ice cold. They left us in solitary confinement to consider our fate. We languished in those cells for three days, only seeing the jailer twice a day when he brought food, normally stale bread and water. Once a day another prisoner came around and emptied the shit bucket, but the sewage smell was so bad that it made little difference. At the end of the third day, the keys rattled in the lock and the Gestapo escort dragged me out of the cell and back up the steps, past a grinning Kriminalassistent Mischer. We went along a maze of corridors until finally I was pushed through inside a courtroom and up into the dock, where Max and Karl-Heinz were already waiting. Max looked terrible, filthy, unshaven, pale and gaunt, quite unlike the arrogant dandy I had come to know and dislike. Brandt was no better. Before we could talk there was a flurry of movement at the front of the court and the judge came in.

"Untersturmfuhrer Paul Schaffer, Untersturmfuhrer Maximilian Hofstetter and Scharfuhrer Karl-Heinz Brandt, you have been found guilty of treason. Do any of you have anything to say before sentence is passed?"

I looked at him shocked.

"Excuse me, don't we get a trial before we're found guilty? It's not that simple, those men were unlawfully trying to execute prisoners, I only tried to stop them. They should be on trial, not us."

He looked at Max. "Do you have anything to say, Hofstetter?"

"It was nothing to do with me, I tried to stop him."

"Karl-Heinz Brandt, what do you have to say?"

Brandt realized with the weary understanding of a veteran soldier that there was little point in saying anything. He just shook his head.

"Very well. I have taken into account the fact that you two officers are volunteers from outside the Reich, also that you, Brandt, were not in a position to stop these men from committing treason, although that doesn't alter the fact that you were with them and responsible for their safety and security. Normally, you would all be sentenced to death by firing squad. However, I have decided to be lenient and sentence you to ten years hard labor in a concentration camp. You will be taken to Mauthausen Camp in Austria where I understand they have an expansion project about to start, so your efforts will not be in vain. You may all think of it as serving the Reich in a different way while you work your sentence. That is all. Heil Hitler."

IRON CROSS AMERIKA

CHAPTER TWO

'In the course of my life I have very often been a prophet, and have usually been ridiculed for it. During the time of my struggle for power, it was in the first instance only the Jewish race that received my prophecies with laughter when I said that I would one day take over the leadership of the state and with it that of the whole nation and that I would then among other things settle the Jewish problem...but I think that for some time now they have been laughing on the other side of their face. Today I will once more be a prophet: if the international Jewish financiers in and outside Europe should succeed in plunging the nations once more into a world war, then the result will not be the Bolshevising of the earth and thus the victory of Jewry, but the annihilation of the Jewish race in Europe.'

Adolf Hitler 30th January 1939

The main gate of Mauthausen-Gusen concentration camp was the entrance to hell. We were transported there in a closed railway container packed with other prisoners from a variety of nations recently conquered by Germany. There were French, Dutch, Czechs and Poles, Jews of course as well as German citizens including foreigners like Max and me, convicted of a variety of crimes. When the train eventually stopped in Austria, the guards fitted shackles to our wrists and fastened us together by a chain connected to our ankles, making it extremely difficult and painful to shuffle along. We marched along a narrow road until we came to the camp, high, barbed wire fences, guard towers and inside the huts that were the prisoner accommodation. Next to the camp was the quarry, the reason for the site of the camp so that prisoners could work the quarry and supply granite to Austrian and German towns and cities. We marched in and they forced us to parade in the main square of the camp. Armed guards surrounded us, wearing the distinct uniform of the SS-Totenkopf, the Death's Head battalions. They were armed with Kar 98k infantry rifles, all cocked and pointed at us in such a way as to leave no doubt of their intentions if we failed to follow orders or tried to escape. Four prisoners arrived wearing patched, ragged trousers and striped jackets. They looked half-starved, thin and they were covered in spots and sores. They started to unlock our manacles and we were made to stand at attention, waiting for God only knew what. In front of us was a set of wooden buildings, presumably the administration offices. The door opened and the soldiers leapt to attention as a burly SS officer stepped out and stood on the verandah looking down at us. When he started to speak his voice was oddly high-pitched, but no one laughed.

"My name is SS-Sturmbannfuhrer Franz Ziereis, I am the Commandant of this camp. You are here for one reason only, to work. All of you will be given suitable work assignments, you will obey the camp personnel without question. Anyone who disobeys, will be shot! If you try to escape, you will be shot! Anyone that does anything that may disrupt the good order of my camp, will be shot! Remember, the motto of our prison system, Arbeit Macht Frei, work will free you. That is all!"

More prisoners came and directed us to a long hut. The guards clustered around so that we had no alternative but to go where they told us to go. Inside, the hut guards shouted at us to strip to the waist, they took our shirts and tunics and issued us with striped jackets, there was apparently a shortage of striped trousers so we had to wear our own. More shouting and we were led out, split into groups and taken to our barracks huts. They herded us inside and the door slammed shut, we heard the lock fastened from the outside. Inside it was gloomy but we could make out long rows of bunk beds, three high. At first, I thought the hut was empty but then I saw a man laying on one of the bunks. I walked over to him, he looked ill, emaciated and filthy and as far as I could see, near death.

"I'm Paul Schaffer, we just arrived."

"Wilhelm Mott, welcome to hell, my friend."

His breath hissed out, he was finding it difficult just to breathe.

"Can I get you anything, some water perhaps?"

He stretched his lips in a ghastly semblance of a smile.

"There is no water in here. They only issue water twice a day. There is nothing you can do, I am dying."

I wasn't sure how to respond to him. The others had clustered around in a fearful group, desperate to find out anything about the strange camp we had been brought to.

"Do you need a doctor?"

Again his lips moved but he didn't manage a smile this time.

"Yes, I need a doctor, but there are no doctors to treat us here."

"What do you do here when you fall ill?" I asked him.

"You die."

The other prisoners murmured in dismay. "That's ridiculous," Max said. "Everyone must be entitled to some basic medical care, this is the Third Reich!"

Wilhelm Mott turned his head slightly to see who had spoken, even that tiny movement exhausted him.

"No, you are no longer in the Third Reich. You are in hell, you are here to die."

They went silent, I couldn't think of anything to say. Mott fell into unconsciousness.

"What do we do now?" Max said.

"I suggest we find ourselves a bunk and get some rest, we may need to use our energies later," Karl-Heinz said, ever the practical old soldier.

It was a good idea, we threw ourselves down on the bunks and tried to rest, I found a top bunk, but it was difficult. We were hungry, thirsty and terrified. Each bunk only had one thin blanket, which was the extent of the bedding, no mattresses on the wooden beds, nothing. The hut itself was empty of any furnishings except for the inevitable bucket in the corner at the end of the hut near the door. The stench from it was foul, but it wasn't the only smell we had to contend with.

Inside the hut itself there was a foul odor of unwashed human bodies, a stink of filth, sweat mixed with the thick, malodorous stench from the bucket. And yet, over and above that was a thick stink that we had noticed long before we reached the camp, a sweetish smell almost like rancid meat. I wondered what they could be processing here to make such a disgusting smell. As it started to get dark, the door flung open and a horde of men crowded into the hut, which was our first practical introduction to the realities of Mauthausen. I was half-dozing, the shouts and screams brought me fully awake. A filthy, stick-thin and ragged prisoner was shouting at me.

"Who the fuck are you to lie on my bed? Get out of it now before I break your fucking neck!"

I sat up and watched him warily. "If this is your bunk, where is mine?"

I had a suspicion that this was going to be some kind of test. We'd all heard that prisons had a hierarchy, if you didn't stand up for yourself you could sink to the bottom of the prison system and get the worst treatment, the hardest work assignments and the least food.

"You want somewhere to sleep, you fight for it like I did for this," he snarled.

All around us fights were starting, there was more and more shouting and screaming as the existing occupants of the hut fought us newcomers for the rights to occupy the bunks. I looked around and made a rough calculation, there were about sixty bunks and at least eighty men crowded in here. So I would have to fight, even as the thought crossed my mind his arm came up and he swung at me with a thick piece of timber that he'd had hidden inside his jacket. I put up one arm to block the blow and hit him, a hard punch to the jaw that split his lip and sent him reeling back, he staggered before he fell on the wooden floor. Two teeth fell out and rolled under the next row of bunks. He looked up at me, his face furious but he was beaten, the one blow had taken all the fight out of him. He staggered off, presumably to find another place to sleep with someone easier from whom to take it. I felt tremendously guilty, but I suspected that anyone that didn't fight and claw for every advantage in this place would quickly succumb and die.

"You did the right thing."

I looked around. It was the prisoner occupying the top of the next row, another ragged, emaciated scarecrow.

"I didn't want to hurt him."

He laughed, more of a cackle. "You'll find that you'll have to kill sometimes to survive in here."

I ignored him. He looked half-crazy.

"What's that smell that surrounds the camp, I've never known anything like it before?"

"It's the ovens, where they burn the bodies, they keep them going day and night."

"That's a lot of bodies, why are there so many deaths?"

I noticed that some of the men that had arrived here with

me had clustered around to listen.

He tried to laugh again, but this time it became a coughing, wheezing fit. He'd probably been a big man once, he was as tall as I was, but he was stooped, very thin, his teeth missing and much of his hair had fallen out in clumps. He managed to get his breath back.

"You don't understand, do you? This is a death camp, men that are too ill to work are killed, and then their bodies cremated in the ovens, sometimes as many as five hundred in a single day."

"That's crazy, how could five hundred people just fall down and die in a day?" someone said from the crowd clustered around my bunk.

"My friend, I've seen prisoners being beaten to death by the SS guards, sometimes they force them to take an ice cold shower and leave them outside in cold weather. They shoot the prisoners when they feel like it, use them for medical experiments, hang them, starve to death those who are sick, they've even been know to inject Phenol to kill the unwanted. They beat us to death, throw prisoners on the 380 Volt electric barbed wire fence, even force prisoners outside the wire and then shoot them on the pretence that they were attempting to escape. Believe me they have many, many ways of killing five hundred a day, no problem for them. Recently they brought in a gas van, they re-routed the exhaust so that it flows into the closed back of the van and kills the occupants."

He slumped back, tired from speaking so much.

"What the fuck have you got us into?" Max snarled at me.

He'd managed to hold on to a middle bunk in the next row, underneath the prisoner that had been talking. I looked across and made out Karl-Heinz who had taken the lower bunk.

"It was that judge in Berlin who sent us here, Herr Hofstetter, not Paul."

"He should have let those troopers kill the Tommies, that way we'd never have got into any trouble."

"But the Tommies would have," Karl-Heinz added quietly.

There was no food or water issued to us. I spent the night listening to men's sobs, their gasps for breath, low murmuring in the dark. Once, someone called out, "It's no use, he's dead."

I didn't bother to find out any more, I tried to get some sleep but the best I could do was an uneasy doze. I tried to send my mind to a better place, I was in Berlin, in Lisl's apartment, we were making love, no, it was more than that. It was a primeval urge to impregnate and be impregnated, an energetic, raw fuck, we sweated and pawed at each other, pulling our bodies tighter into each other for erotic pleasure. But even as I neared an orgasm, she started to slip away into the night, her face seemed to melt and I was looking at a skull, I recoiled in horror and woke in a sweat. In the morning, the shutters were opened with a loud bang that woke anyone who wasn't yet awake. Amidst the groaning and cries of pain, I heard several shouts for orderlies to remove bodies of those that had died during the night. We were bullied out onto the parade ground and forced to line up with thousands of others from the other huts, there we stood in the dawn chill while guards went up and down the line to count us. The bodies had been laid out to one side, there were more than twenty of them that had died overnight from all of the huts. After the count we were sent to line up for breakfast, lukewarm potato soup with a lump of coarse, stale bread and water from a bucket. Then we went back to the parade ground to receive our work assignments.

"Schaffer, Hofstetter, Brandt, you're in the quarry, hurry, they're leaving now."

The three of us looked around, confused, until a guard came and clubbed Karl-Heinz with his rifle butt.

"Over there, fool, by the gate, hurry!"

Brandt stumbled away and Max and I followed, I nearly fell when a heavy boot kicked me in the rear but I managed to keep upright and join the group of emaciated and worn out scarecrows who were lining up to go out through the gate to the quarry. The gate opened and forced us to march out along the road to the nearby quarry. They issued the three of us with pick axes and we were set to work breaking huge lumps of granite, separating them into more manageable-sized pieces.

The quarry had ripped away part of the mountainside. We worked right at the bottom of the quarry, at the end of a steep ramp that we'd marched down. There was another way up to the top, a flight of steep steps that had been cut into the rock. Every time a prisoner tried to ease up a guard came along with a whip and slashed them bloody for a punishment. Once, the prisoner being whipped didn't get up, two trustee prisoners were ordered in to cart him away. The man working next to me made a cutting sign across his throat, and then looked up into the sky. We got the message, he was destined to go up the chimney of the crematorium.

We'd worked solidly for three hours without any sign of even a drink of water. My legs felt rubbery, I felt dizzy and even worse, this was the first day of the next ten years. Halfway through the morning, two guards rushed into a mass of men, we immediately stopped, glad of any excuse to take a break. I never knew what the prisoner had done wrong, but the guards strapped a canvas bag to his back into which two other prisoners carefully placed a large piece of granite, I estimated it must have weighed over a hundred pounds. One of the guards drew his pistol and pointed at the steps. I heard him shout an order.

"You carry it up to the top, and then come down for another one. Be quick about it or you'll carry two up next time!"

The poor wretch started plodding up the steps. It looked as if he had a mountain to climb, which I imagine was the way he felt. Like most of the others he was painfully thin, struggling up the steps and I knew he wasn't going to make it. He battled almost to the top, and then looked at the quarry below. He stood there for a moment and I saw the guard with the pistol take aim. Then he simply stepped over the side and fell to the bottom, landing thirty feet away from us with a heavy thump, the granite slab he was carrying accelerated his fall his body literally split apart when he hit the ground.

What happened next astonished us, the prisoners turned away and carried on working, the guard shouted to two men to take the body away and everything went back to the way it had been.

"This place is a lunatic asylum," Max said desperately. "We'll never survive this, we won't last ten days, let alone ten years."

"Shut up, Max," I whispered to him, "we're not supposed to talk."

"I don't care, these people are animals," he whined, "there must be something..."

He stopped as a guard approached him, then he screamed shrilly as he felt the lash on his back, the guard struck him repeatedly until he fell to the ground sobbing.

"Get up and work, quickly," the guard shouted, "unless you want to climb the steps, like that other prisoner."

"No, please stop, I'll work," he murmured hurriedly as he climbed to his feet.

He snatched up the pickaxe from where he had dropped it and started swinging it at the hard granite. He kept his head down and worked through the day as we all did, there was a brief break at midday for water and a slice of stale bread and then we worked on. By the time they marched us back to the camp at the end of the day for the evening roll call, I was convinced that anything would be better than this. I even envied the man who had thrown himself off the steps. At least his misery had ended. We reported to the cookhouse for food and they issued us with another bowl of thin, watery potato soup with a couple of vegetables and one lump of rancid meat floating in it. Together with a tin mug of water, it was all we were given to eat.

We sat together, the three of us. I looked at Karl-Heinz.

"How do you feel, do you think we can make it?"

He shrugged. "Some of these men here have survived for more than a year in this camp. But ten years, I don't know. I don't think so."

"Max, what do you think?"

"No, that whipping nearly killed me, if they'd done it again I was ready to run up those steps and jump off. Fucking bastards!"

"So what are we going to do? How can we hope to survive this?" I asked them.

"You don't hope to survive your sentence," a voice said from the next row of bunks. We looked around, he was one of the scruffiest, most ragged and emaciated looking men I had yet seen here, where skeletal men wearing rags was the norm. He swung his legs down off the bunk and walked over to us.

"I've been here for eighteen months, there's only one way to survive the camp. You live for each day, every day you just have to get through, worry about tomorrow when it comes."

"Eighteen months!" Karl-Heinz gasped. "You must have seen more death and misery here, than most men see in a lifetime. You poor bastard," he held out his hand, "Karl-Heinz Brandt, pleased to meet you."

He shook Karl-Heinz's hand, it was almost laughable, the everyday pleasantry in this house of horrors. "Gerd Rundheim, don't feel sorry for me, my friend. If you want to survive you look out for yourself."

"Haven't you ever tried to escape?" I asked him.

His eyes widened with horror. "Don't even mention that word. There are men in this room that would sell you out to the guards for a slice of bread. Besides, there is only one way out of here."

We all craned forward to listen. "Which way is that?" I asked, but I already knew the answer.

"You saw it this morning. You are here to work and starve until you die, nothing more."

"How long is your sentence?" I asked him, wondering if he would survive this hell.

"They gave me twenty five years for distributing leaflets protesting against the war."

Twenty-five years! He was a dead man and obviously knew it. He was just eking out his last days and months until the inevitable arrived. I went back to my bunk and lay down to conserve energy. In the morning, I had already begun to accept the inevitable, I was never going to leave this place. I lay awake much of the night, I thought about Lisl, my girl in Berlin. Was she laying in bed now, between silk sheets, her stomach full of good food and wine? I thought again of my home in Chicago, of America, of everything I had left to come to this cruel pit of torture and death. Why on earth had I come to fight for people who were sadistic enough to shoot prisoners of war? To fight for a regime that used such inhuman methods to imprison and eventually kill prison inmates. And yet, I had heard of similarly brutal prisons in the US, especially in the Deep South where inmates were worked and starved until they died. I had little doubt that some of our own troops had resorted to killing prisoners who were inconveniently in the way during the heat of battle. None of that helped me out of my particular predicament and I sympathized with Karl-Heinz and Max, in spite of Max's constant complaints and moaning. My own actions had brought them here, without me they would have been happily taking their pictures and filing articles to Signal and Der Sturmer. I had to think seriously about this. All of us here had an option, at any time we could choose death, there were many ways to die in this hellish place. I made up my mind that I would only take so much, if I found my strength going so much that I became like one of these coughing, wheezing scarecrows, I would make that choice and take the only exit from the camp that was open to me.

We shuffled out for the roll call and the breakfast that did little to satisfy the raging hunger that was starting to dominate my mind. All of us were expending massive amounts of calories carrying out heavy manual labor in the quarry, we only got a fraction of the food we needed to keep our bodies healthy. The inevitable consequence was that we would get weaker and weaker until we could no longer work and were chosen to be killed.

Then we marched out to the quarry. The backbreaking work started immediately and I had the feeling that it wouldn't be long before another example of the sadistic cruelty that was so rampant in this place manifested itself again. I was right, even more so than I would have believe possible. A second group of prisoners appeared at the top of the quarry but instead of being marched down they stood at the top, dangerously near the edge of the fatal drop to the quarry face below where we worked. The guards were looking up, grinning and Gerd Rundheim who was working nearby whispered across to me. "Watch out where the bodies fall, if one hits you you're finished so try and keep away from the quarry face."

"Surely you can't mean the guards are going to push them off?"

"Just wait, and keep well back."

He could see I didn't understand. "Look, when they want to reduce the numbers even more, maybe they want to make room for more prisoners or possibly stretch the food supplies out, they kill off some of us. The guards make a sport of it, you'll see, just keep clear."

I pretended to keep working while I watched what was happening at the top of the cliff. I could hear what the guards were shouting, they'd pushed one prisoner near to the edge, and another stood behind him. With great ceremony, they offered the man behind the choice. He could push the prisoner in front of him off the cliff and to his death, or he could refuse and the guards behind would shoot him. One of the guards shouted the word, 'Los!' for them to begin.

For a few seconds nothing happened, I waited, as did the rest of us. Then there was a hoarse shout from a guard and the next moment a man came plummeting down the cliff, screaming all the way to the bottom. Even more sickening were the guards, who laughed and cheered at the fine entertainment they were being given that morning. One by one the bodies plummeted down, I was waiting for the crack of a bullet, surely one man would refuse to push his neighbor to his death. What was there to survive for in this camp, starvation, sickness, brutality and death? There was no other way. But even that terrible reality they chose to cling to, more bodies fell screaming to the quarry floor until the edge of the cliff was empty of prisoners, the guards had pushed them all over. I turned away and carried on chipping at the stone with my pickaxe, the guards would be checking soon and anyone not working hard would face the whip. By the end of the day I was beyond exhaustion, after the evening potato soup and water I was ready to fall asleep in my bunk. Gerd must have recognized the symptoms in my face, perhaps by the resigned slump of my shoulders.

"Paul, you need to hang in there, the first few days are the worst."

"You cannot be serious, how can anything get better? You were right, all of you, it's a death camp, we're here to work until they can't get any more out of us and then they kill us. What's the point?"

"The point is life, my friend. There's always hope and always the possibility that things may change. This war, for example, Germany could lose."

I laughed at that. "Gerd, I've been at the front filing reports and taking photographs. There's no way we're going to lose, our armies are unstoppable."

"Perhaps, but they once said that about Napoleon's armies. You never know what's around the corner, just survive each day."

"Yeah, leave me alone, Gerd, I need to sleep," I mumbled at him. In truth, I needed to be alone to think about whether I wanted to take the quick way out of this place.

We did survive, all three of us for a year, until the news swept the camp that Germany had invaded the Soviet Union. It was the 22nd of June 1941, Germany and its allies had sent four and a half million men over the border into Russian territory. It was scarcely believable. Gerd Rundheim, who was still alive after all these months, was ecstatic.

"See, I told you when you first came, anything could happen, now it has."

I looked at him, he was just a skeleton with a thin covering of flesh. Quite how he'd survived I had no idea, he should have been dead long ago. I imagined that I didn't look much better myself, I was always cold, always desperately tired and hungry.

"How the hell does that help us, Gerd?"

"It's easy to work out, they'll never beat the Russians, the war will be over and we'll be free."

I thought about our formidable forces smashing through France and Belgium. The Panzer Divisions, Reichsmarschall Goering's Airfleets, thousands of aircraft. Then I thought about the Russians, their armies decimated during Stalin's purges, the officer corps all but eliminated by the feared NKVD secret police, hostages to the communist leader's paranoia. It would be best not to mention any of this. Survive for today Gerd had advised almost a year ago. It wouldn't help him to know the truth.

"I hope you're right, my friend, it would be nice to look forward to our freedom."

"I'm looking forward to getting a huge, juicy Wiener Schnitzel," Max said.

Everybody groaned and someone threw a piece of wood at him. Thinking of such luxuries as a good meal could easily lead to despair and that led to death, one way or the other.

The following Austrian winter was vicious, freezing cold and during the night the numbers of prisoners who succumbed to the bitter chill rose dramatically, every morning more and more corpses were dragged out to be counted in the roll call. In the very depths of winter we struggled to keep alive, constantly pulling our jackets around our thin, starved bodies, the jackets were the same ones we wore summer and winter, there was no issue of warm clothing. We were hacking at the granite in the quarry as usual when some prisoners did something that upset the guards. We never knew what it was. Maybe they didn't do anything, perhaps the guards were cold and bored and just wanted some entertainment. Twenty prisoners were loaded with slabs of granite and made to start climbing the stone steps that led to the top. Even from fifty feet away I could hear them wheezing to drag air into their lungs, their rib cages rising and falling with the effort that was all but impossible for them. Survival was the only thought in every man's head, nothing else. Get to the top of the steps without falling, live for the next day, don't give up, and keep some hope alive. They struggled up one after the other, a snake of men plodding higher and higher. We watched fascinated, pretending to work.

"They won't all make it," Max said. "There's no way, most of them are living on borrowed time already."

Was it sympathy, I wondered? He had mellowed under the brutal camp regime, but on the other hand, he might just be thinking of an extra portion of soup if some of them fell to their deaths. Even as I thought it, my mouth watered and I felt ashamed. I looked up again, some of them were wobbling, I looked again, no, they were all wobbling as they tried to keep going. The first man was almost at the top when disaster struck, whether he missed his footing or perhaps even had a heart attack, he was so weak, who knows what might have happened. He fell backwards, just collapsed and fell against the next man down, who fell backwards too.

It was like watching a row of dominos. Each man was so weak, so burdened by the heavy slab of granite he carried on his back that he fell back against the next man and the quarry filled with the shrieking sounds of falling, dying, broken men. The crash as they hit the bottom of the quarry, their limbs askew, their lifeblood leaking out onto the dusty ground. Of the twenty men who had started up the steps, only three had survived, managing to move out of the way as the man in front of them fell backwards. The guards were laughing hysterically, their shoulders shaking with mirth. How could these people be part of the cultured German race that my parents had told me so much about? The race of doctors, musicians, philosophers and writers, that was the envy of the civilized world. We worked through the rest of the day in silence before we were able to shuffle painfully away and eat our soup. We got a little more than usual, the dead men's rations were shared out, none of us refused. Survival was all that mattered.

We managed to last through the winter, growing weaker and weaker, then it was spring and the weather got warmer, summer arrived and the three of us managed to avoid the daily attrition that kept the numbers of prisoners that constantly arrived from outgrowing the camp. At the height of summer, we stood to attention as usual at morning roll call, swaying with exhaustion and sickness but trying to avoid selection by the guards as too unfit for work. 'Up the chimney' was a macabre camp saying for those unlucky enough to be taken out by the guards to a special holding centre. It was a windowless hut with sign outside that said 'Medical Centre' but we knew that no medical aid was ever given inside. Instead, sick prisoners were held there until after we'd marched away to work and then killed in the endlessly imaginative ways that the camp authorities devised.

This morning was different. A black Mercedes limousine was parked outside the administration hut, together with a smaller Opel saloon car, also black. When the door opened, a stranger came out with Ziereis, the Commandant. He was another SS officer, but his uniform was different, more like the field-grey of the Waffen SS. He stepped forward to speak.

"My name is SS-Sturmbannfuhrer Doctor Oskar Dirlewanger. As you know, the Reich is expanding into a number of occupied territories, new lands that will give us Germans the living space that we need to survive as a race and to spread our culture. I have been honored with the command of a new unit of police, it is named the SS-Sonderbattalion Dirlewanger. The purpose of this unit is to protect our people from terrorists and partisans. I need men, people who wish to fight, to defend our glorious Reich from those who would attempt to destroy it from within. I am therefore able to offer some of you the possibility of having your sentence commuted in return for service in the SS Sonderbattalion Dirlewanger. All those men who are interested, may remain on parade, while the others march away for work. I am only interested in fit men who have previous military service. That is all."

The whole camp erupted, a chance to get out of here! Max came over to me, his face elated. "Christ, this could be it, Schaffer, we'll be out of here!"

I nodded. "Let's hope so, it all looks possible. Karl-Heinz, it may almost be over."

He was half smiling, but not quite as enthusiastic as I would have thought.

"Yes, it could be our way out, but a way out into what? Why do they want us to do their dirty work?"

I laughed at his continual caution. "Cheer up, my friend, what could be worse than this?"

He gave me a very serious look. "That is the question I am asking myself, I think the answer may be one we would not enjoy."

"Rubbish," Max said, clapping him on the back, "we're out of here, that's all that matters."

Gerd looked somber. "What the hell's the matter with you, Gerd?" I asked him.

He stretched his lips into a ghastly half smile. "Look at me, Paul. Who the hell would want me? I'm unfit, almost dead with starvation and overwork and I have no military service."

"In that case, Gerd, we'll have to help you along. Don't you want to get out of here?"

"Of course I do, but it's not possible."

"Stay with me, Gerd, we'll do what we can. Karl-Heinz, remember when we were on the Western Front, the soldier that stormed the enemy machine gun post and saved our lives?"

He was puzzled for a moment, and then his expression cleared as comprehension dawned. "Of course, Gerd Rundheim, bravest soldier I've ever met."

"Exactly! Max, you'd better support us, we need to help Gerd and get him out with us."

He looked doubtful. "I'm not sure they'll take him, you know. He's pretty far gone."

I took hold of his jacket, put my face next to his, and whispered. "You'd better make sure you say the right things, Max, or I might have to tell them about your night-time excursions into other men's beds. Do you think they'll be keen on having a homosexual in their ranks?"

He went a ghostly shade of white. "No, for God's sake, don't say anything. I didn't think anyone knew."

"You should know that you don't do anything in this camp without someone knows about it, Max. Just bear it in mind when it comes to supporting our old friend, Gerd Rundheim."

Half the prisoners marched off to the quarry. I imagined that they were ones like Gerd who thought they had no chance of being selected for service in this SS Police unit. Probably some were communists and political objectors, who would prefer a death in this camp rather than give their service willingly to the cause that had enslaved and imprisoned them. I wasn't sure whether to admire them for their principles or despise them for not making the effort to get out. It was their funeral. The rest of us were formed into a long line, the head of the queue was the door to the Commandant's office where they were interviewing the men in twos. Gerd and I were halfway back in the queue, Max and Karl-Heinz were immediately in front of us.

"Gerd, listen to me, I'll quickly explain how the military works and we'll work out a career for you in the army. You'd better remember, you were seconded to the SS to escort the war correspondents, you carried a machine pistol, an MP38. You know anything about the MP38?"

He shook his head. I racked my brains to remember all that I'd been told about the machine pistol.

"Try and remember this, the MP38 machine pistol is a blowback-operated automatic weapon. It can only operate on full automatic fire, but it has a relatively low rate of fire that will allow for single shots with controlled trigger pulls. The cocking handle also serves as a safety mechanism. The MP38 is generally very reliable, although the 32-round magazine can cause problems. The single-feed in the MP38s magazine can result in increased friction against the remaining cartridges moving upwards towards the feed lips, sometimes it can cause feed failures. Keep the weapon and magazines clean, dirt will cause it to jam, another problem is that the magazine may sometimes be misused as a handhold. That can cause the weapon to malfunction when pressure on the magazine body causes the magazine lips to move out of the line of feed, since the magazine well does not keep the magazine firmly locked. Grasp the weapon either on the handhold on the underside of the weapon or the magazine housing with the supporting hand to avoid feed malfunctions. Is that clear, Trooper Rundheim?"

For the first time, he smiled. "As clear as night and fog, Paul."

"Untersturmfuhrer Schaffer to you, Schutze, got it?"

He clicked his heels and gave a passable Hitler salute. "Jawohl, Herr Untersturmfuhrer."

I thought it might work, if the recruiting officer was half-blind, but we had to try.

"Your uniform was the black Allgemeine SS uniform, I'll explain the badges to you. Have you got that?"

"I'll do my best," he replied shakily.

"You'll do better than that, Trooper. Smarten up, back straight, head up, you're in the SS now. Remember that, 'Jawohl, Herr Untersturmfuhrer, Heil Hitler', got that?"

He nodded.

"No, say it, Gerd, as if you mean it. Your life depends on it, man."

He repeated it ten times until I felt he sounded a little convincing. He'd been here a long time, which could explain why he looked so emaciated and ill. The rest was up to luck. They'd brought in the new gas van, I noticed that the prisoners who weren't selected for the SS police unit were quietly led to the gas van and locked inside. Max and Karl-Heinz went forward, we watched carefully but neither appeared in the group for the gas van.

"Rundheim and Schaffer!"
We marched forward.

IRON CROSS AMERIKA

CHAPTER THREE

'I've had my fill of Hitler. These conferences called by the ringing of a bell are not to my liking. The bell is rung when people call their servants. And besides, what kind of conferences are these? For five hours I am forced to listen to a monologue which is quite fruitless and boring'

Mussolini June 10th, 1941

Inside the hut, a lean, older man was sitting behind a desk. He was flanked one side by an elegantly uniformed SS Obersturmbannfuhrer, on the other by a tough looking SS Scharfuhrer. He was a paunchy looking guy, who looked like one of the old veteran stormtroopers, a bullet head covered in scars, broken nose and tiny eyes that seemed to be permanently screwed up in suspicion. They were all wearing field grey, the standard for all new SS uniforms these days, except of course for the rather more ceremonial Allgemeine SS, the old guard's drinking clubs. The officer who was seated, looked at us keenly. His eyes were empty, cold, rather like many of the camp guards, except that there was something different in those eyes, in the expression. This was no prison warder, he had the look of challenge in that glance he hit us with, as if to say, 'I am a fighting soldier, have you got the guts to do the same?'

He spoke suddenly. "I am SS Sturmbannfuhrer Doctor Oskar Dirlewanger. I have the honor to command the SS-Sonderbattalion Dirlewanger, our job is to police the rear areas after our troops have passed, to deal with criminal activities, partisans and undesirables. I am looking for men who can follow orders to the letter and have the strength and determination to eliminate the enemies of the Reich, regardless of their status. Are you prepared to volunteer for such a mission or not?"

I almost forgot myself, I was so fascinated with the strange man in front of me. It was like confronting the Angel of Death, he even appeared to reek of death, or was that my imagination? But I caught myself in time.

"Jawohl, Herr Sturmbannfuhrer," I shouted, coming to attention. Next to me, Gerd snapped to attention as I'd coached him and stared six inches about Dirlewanger's head. He nodded in satisfaction.

"Very well, can you both shoot straight with rifles and machine-pistols?"

"Yes, Sir."

"What about killing enemies of the Reich, communists, partisans, Jews, does that present any problem for you? After all, you're an American, I understand."

"I was an American, yes, but I am here to obey whatever

60

orders I am given, Herr Sturmbannfuhrer. My loyalty is to the Reich."

"Very well."

He asked details of our military service, I told him about the war correspondents' unit, it would be in my records anyway. I embellished it with hair-raising tales of being caught up in action and having to shoot my way out of a battle. Gerd convinced him he'd been an SA street fighter, breaking heads of anyone who decried Adolf Hitler, as well as extensive training in the secret SA and SS camps that had been set up to circumvent the restrictions of the Versailles treaty. It was the best he could do, his records made it clear that he hadn't seen any real action and when he talked glowingly of the qualities of the MP38, Dirlewanger nodded approvingly. He looked at his watch, he was obviously running short on time.

"Very well, I'm prepared to accept both of you. Schaffer, you may retain your SS rank of Untersturmfuhrer, Rundheim you will assume the rank of Schutze, a private soldier. Go out of that door and join the other new recruits, we're driving straight to Berlin to get you kitted out. There's food outside too, you all look as if you need some building up before you can do justice to your new unit. Welcome to the Sonderbattalion Dirlewanger."

I clicked my heels. "Thank you, Sir, Heil Hitler." I saluted and Gerd managed a ragged salute too. Then we marched outside to where the other new recruits were clustered around a table where there was the most magnificent sight I'd seen in a long time. Food! Loaves of bread, meat, fruit, I felt as if we'd arrived in heaven. We dived straight into it, the previous recruits were munching away, two men had already been sick, eating too much food after living for so long on a starvation diet.

"You'll make yourself ill," Karl-Heinz said, coming to stand next to me.

"I don't care, I just need food. My friend, how can we deal with this assignment? You know they want us to be little more than executioners, I'm not sure if I can handle it."

"Be careful, someone may hear you. There is only one way we can handle this job and live with ourselves afterwards."

"What do you mean?"

He looked around again to make certain he wasn't overheard. "It's either go along with them or die in this camp. All we have to do is make sure that we aim to miss, it's quite simple."

"And if we're told to hang someone, Karl-Heinz! What then?"

He looked uncomfortable. "I don't know, but for God's sake, just keep your head down and survive."

"You're right, I will."

Gerd joined us. "I want to thank you, Paul, for helping me with this."

"You may not thank me later, my friend, we don't know yet what we're getting into."

He smiled. "I don't care, whatever happens now, it was worth it for this food, I don't care what happens afterwards."

That was Mauthausen thinking. Survive only for the day. While we were eating, another man came and stood watching us. My heart sank, surely not. Mischer, Kriminalassistent Mischer of the Gestapo.

The Gestapo, the Geheime Staatspolizei, the Secret State Police, was the official secret police of Nazi Germany and held ultimate power in Hitler's Germany. It was in the iron grip of the SS leader Heinrich Himmler in his position as Chef der Deutschen Polizei, Chief of German Police. The Gestapo was administered by the Reichssicherheitshauptamt, the RSHA or Reich Main Security Office and was considered a sister organization of the Sicherheitsdienst, the SD or Security Service and a sub-office of the Sicherheitspolizei, SIPO, the Security Police. There may well have been people I'd less liked to have seen than Mischer, but it was hard to think of anyone. I recalled the dank, stinking cell underneath Prinz Albrecht Strasse with a shudder.

"It seems we meet again, Schaffer."

I looked at him without replying, the food in my belly congealing into an ice-cold lump.

He smiled, obviously delighted with the terror that his appearance had caused.

"Don't worry, my friend, I am only here to confirm the identities of Sturmbannfuhrer Dirlewanger's recruits and make sure there is nothing in their records that requires further investigation. I don't think that your simple-minded act of American bravado counts against you. But remember, Schaffer, you and your friends will be watched every second. The Gestapo never sleeps, never. You would do well to follow orders this time and stay out of trouble."

He stared at me for a moment more and then walked into the hut.

We arrived at the SS training barracks just outside Berlin. Formerly a Wehrmacht officer training school, Lichterfelde Kaserne, southwest of the Berlin downtown area, was an old Prussian cadet training school. The SS took it over in 1933, and it became the headquarters of Hitler's bodyguard regiment, the Leibstandarte-SS Adolf Hitler. We weren't there for training. They issued us with uniforms, boots, steel helmets, winter camouflage uniforms and weapons. Our field grey SS tunics had the embroidered cuff title 'Dirlewanger' on the sleeve. As an officer, they issued me with a pistol, a Walther PPK in a leather holster and an MP38 machine pistol. Like me, Max had kept his rank and they issued him with the same weapons, Karl-Heinz had also remained in rank as an SS Scharführer and was given a machine pistol. Gerd was issued a Kar 98k, he looked at it dubiously.

"How the hell does this thing work?"

I tried to explain to him the working of a Mauser Kar 98k, at least as far as my limited knowledge from basic training went. The Kar, Karabiner 98k, was a controlled feed bolt-action rifle based on the Mauser M 98 system. It fired a 7.92mm bullet over iron sights, and was considered to be a reliable, accurate if somewhat bulky and heavy weapon. The rifle was designed to be used with an S84/98 bayonet. Gerd looked at it with dismay.

"How does this fit on?"

"Just make it look good," I told him. "Karl-Heinz will show you how it all works later."

The SS had allocated a disused factory building on the outskirts of Berlin for our use as sleeping quarters. Dirlewanger had organized heaps of blankets, the officers were allocated camp beds too, set up in the factory offices to give us some privacy. The NCOs and private soldiers slept on blankets on the old factory floor, there were almost three hundred of us in all. I was appalled, three hundred men who for the most part were the absolute scum of the earth, the dregs and sweepings of Germany's criminal underworld. There were constant fights, the officers seemed content to let the men slug it out. Discipline was virtually non-existent, frequently men pulled weapons, knives and once a rifle was pointed, but each time their comrades managed to persuade them to stand down. Those of us who had been recruited from the Mauthausen concentration camp spent most of the first full day eating and recovering from our ordeal, but on the second day we were marched to Lichterfelde for shooting practice.

The march was shambolic, the men had no idea of keeping in step and the NCOs had to constantly shout and cajole them to get in order. I could see bottles being passed around, by the time we arrived at the barracks at mid-morning some of the men were well on the way to being drunk. Dirlewanger was an enigma, he marched proudly at the head of his men, smartly uniformed, stiff backed as if he was at the head of an elite Leibstandarte battalion instead of the vicious misfits that trailed along behind him. On the range, there were targets set up in the shape of British Tommies as well as a few classic, hook-nosed Jews. We blazed away, the shooting was truly awful. Halfway along the line an argument started amongst two troopers as to which one had fired through the centre of a particular target. Suddenly, one of the men whirled around with his rifle shooting the other man in the chest. He fell over dead. We all stopped shooting, Dirlewanger walked over and we waited to see how he would deal with him.

"Well? How the hell did this happen?" he shouted.

"The man was insulting the Fuhrer, Sir. He said that he wished that we were shooting at Adolf Hitler at the other end of the range. It was treason, Sir, I couldn't listen to it any more."

Dirlewanger nodded. "I couldn't agree with you more, Schutze Froebel. I'd have shot him myself."

He turned to his adjutant. "Obersturmfuhrer Kraus, detail some men to take the body away. The rest of you, carry on."

We turned away and reloaded, then spent the rest of the morning blazing away at the targets until the blessed break for lunch. The barracks' cooks had prepared a blissful stew full of meat, dumplings and vegetables. Already I could feel my strength beginning to return. Max seemed very happy. "They certainly dealt with that schutze who was rubbishing the Fuhrer, damned traitor deserved what he got. I think I like this unit, they've got the right attitude."

"Max, he didn't say anything of the sort, it was a simple argument," I said to him.

"He must have said something or the CO wouldn't have been happy about him being killed. I should watch what you say, Paul, these people mean business, they don't take kindly to traitors."

"He wasn't a traitor," I said tiredly.

Max shrugged, he obviously wasn't interested. "Well if he wasn't, he was definitely unlucky," was all he said. He walked back to the stew cauldron to get another helping. So that was the man's epitaph, he was unlucky. Maybe he would have been better off if he'd stayed in the prison or concentration camp he'd been recruited from. Karl-Heinz had been watching, he joined me with Gerd.

"Untersturmfuhrer, you should be careful, Max will report you if you say something he doesn't think is appropriate, he's got it in for you."

"Karl-Heinz, he'll do that anyway, do me a favor and watch my back."

"Don't worry about that, we'll keep an eye out for you. This bunch is trouble, Sir, the whole battalion is like a bomb waiting to explode."

We went back to the range after lunch for more shooting practice. I kept well away from the main group of men, Karl-Heinz and Gerd stayed with me, and I pretended to supervise their shooting. It was fast becoming obvious that the Dirlewanger unit had more than its fair share of psychopaths. Some of them had been drinking all day and I didn't want to be near a drunken soldier while he held a loaded weapon. We got through the afternoon without anyone killing one of the men and marched back to our sleeping quarters. They had arranged for food to be set out on a huge table and we munched away happily, still regaining our strength. I noticed an officer staring at me and wondered what kind of mental illness he suffered from, most of the battalion seemed mentally ill in one way or another. He came around to speak to me, my mind was put at rest by the fact that he wasn't carrying a loaded weapon.

"I heard you're a Yank, is that right?"

"Yes, Paul Schaffer from Chicago."

We shook hands. "Heinrich Weiss from New York, I used to be Henry White in the US but Heinrich Weiss seemed more suitable when I joined our German friends."

He told me his story, he'd been a financial dealer, buying and selling stocks and bonds. He came to Germany hoping to make rich pickings but got himself caught up in some kind of a fraud in Munich involving trading stocks in a non-existent company. Sentenced to ten years in prison for fraud and theft, he'd taken the opportunity to volunteer for Dirlewanger's outfit.

"How have you found them, the Sonderbattalion Dirlewanger?" I asked him. "This is all new to me."

"They're good men, Paul, really good men. Some of them are a bit wild, like that one on the range, I know, but when they're given a job they know how to do it. We had one only last month, a bunch of communists that the Wehrmacht had rounded up in Poland, they call it the General Government these days. The regular soldiers refused to shoot them so we were ordered in to take care of them. You should have seen it, my friend. The commies were locked into a stone barn, the men climbed on the roof, knocked holes in and threw stick grenades down on them. They weren't all killed outright, of course, so we went in and finished them off afterwards. A couple of the men even used their combat knives. My God, that was something to see."

It was astonishing to listen to an American talking about such barbarity, but I recalled that not long before he would have been in the ranks of the cavalry slaughtering the American Indians. Nations always bred their share of psychopaths and serial killers, it was a pity that so many of them seemed to have been herded together in this one unit.

"It sounds like a bloody business, Heinrich," was all I could say in reply. "Do we ever get assigned to more conventional military action?"

"You mean at the front? A couple of times, yes. You ought to see the CO, he's like a demon, absolutely fearless. Always leads his men."

"Dirlewanger?" I asked incredulously, thinking of that elegant, slim but definitely more elderly officer. I afterwards found out that at that time he was forty-seven years of age.

"Damn right, Dirlewanger. He sets a great example to the men, just goes charging in and they follow him."

"Doesn't he ever get wounded?"

"He does, yes, always getting wounds from bullets and shrapnel but somehow he manages to survive. The luck of the devil, I guess."

"It must be that, yes."

Later that evening I managed to slip out of the barracks on the pretext of going with a vehicle to collect food from the central SS warehouse in Berlin. The driver was unusually decent, he agreed to drop me off in the city and pick me up later for no charge, but we both knew that he would call on me at some time in the future to return the favor. I walked up the street and found the familiar entrance to the nightclub. The lighted sign shone brightly in the Berlin night, the Blue Goose. Around the corner was the familiar stage door, I went in and even the doorman hadn't changed, Rolf Biermann, a former artilleryman from the Great War, a veteran of the trenches who now spent his time guarding the girls as if they were his treasured daughters.

"Can I help you, Untersturmfuhrer? You shouldn't be here, this entrance is only for the performers."

"Is Lisl in the back, Rolf?"

He looked puzzled. "Do I know you?"

"Paul Schaffer, the American, have I changed that much?"

"Paul!" he looked embarrassed. "No, you've changed, well, no more than anyone has changed since this war started. It must be the uniform," he said, but it wasn't what he meant. I knew that I still bore the scars of the camp, indelibly etched on my face.

"It's ok, Rolf, I know I look like shit, but three days ago I looked a lot worse. I was in Mauthausen."

"Dear, God," he breathed, then looked around to make sure that no one else was listening, "it must have been bad."

"It was. Take my advice, Rolf, if they ever try to send you there, shoot yourself first. Tell me, is Lisl in the back?"

"She certainly is, the usual dressing room. She goes on in thirty minutes."

"Thanks."

I went through and knocked on the door. Lisl opened it and her mouth dropped open.

"Paul, this is amazing. What are you doing in that uniform? Come in, my God, I thought you were in prison."

I went in and we fell into each other's arms. "It was a concentration camp, Lisl, not a prison."

She nodded. "Don't talk about it, I can see what it did to you, it's quite clear from you're your face, you've aged, you know. How long can you stay, I have to go on stage soon and I get off about three in the morning."

"It's just a quick visit, my love, to let you know I'm still alive. Are you seeing anyone?"

She grinned. "On and off, but now that you're back they can go to hell."

I had a lot to talk to her about in such a short time. While I held her in my arms, I told her about the Sonderbattalion Dirlewanger, the reputation they had to cruelties inflicted on people in the occupied territories.

"I'm not surprised that such people exist," she replied. "The things that go on in Berlin these days are terrible even here in the middle of the Reich. We all live in fear, Paul, the Gestapo is everywhere, no one dares to say what he or she thinks about anything, where has our culture vanished to? Then we have the bombing, it's quiet tonight but the Americans come over by day and the British by night. I sometimes think Germany is going straight to hell, it's not the place that we used to know."

"It'll all be over sooner or later, Lisl."

She grimaced, like most people she expected the war to go

on for many, many years. She could have been right, too.

"Listen, I have to get back, we're due to report for training tomorrow at Lichterfelde. I don't know when I can get back, we may be posted soon to the Eastern Front."

She paled. "The Eastern Front, it's just a slaughterhouse, my darling, you'll be killed. The trains come in every day to Berlin Hauptbahnhof, the Central Railway Station, full of casualties, thousands and thousands of them. Can't you go home to America? She smiled. "You can take me with you if you like."

I shook my head. "We're watched carefully, it's a miracle I got out of the camp. I'll be ok, I think we'll be posted well back from the front, my darling, it's an SS police unit, hunting down partisans, not front line soldiers."

In fact, we'd be hunting anyone that Sturmbannfuhrer Dirlewanger decided was an enemy of the state. I said goodbye to her then, she was due on stage and I had to get back before I was reported for desertion, but it was worth ten lifetimes to see her again. We agreed to make up for lost time when I was given some leave, then I left while she began to prepare to go out on stage. I waited on a street corner for five minutes until the familiar sight of the ration truck appeared.

"I owe you one," I said to the driver as I got out at our quarters.

"You do, Untersturmfuhrer, I'm sure we'll sort something out sooner or later."

We spent the next two days training at Lichterfelde, shooting practice on the range, knife fighting, at which some of the men really excelled, thank God the knives for practice were only made of rubber. Unarmed combat, mine clearing and basic military skills were covered in rapid succession, I doubt that anyone learned anything much of value. On the third day, the officers were called into a conference room with Dirlewanger and his adjutant, Obersturmfuhrer Kraus.

"Good news, men, we're going back into action," Dirlewanger said. Most of the officers cheered, after only a few days with them it was clear that what it meant to these soldiers was the chance to slake their thirst for blood and more importantly to take the opportunity for pillage and looting.

"We're going into Belorussia," he continued. "Our armies are pushing on towards their objectives, Army Group North for Leningrad, Army Group South for Stalingrad and the Caucasus and of course Army Group Centre for Moscow. Our job is to cover their backs, to make sure that their supply lines are not interfered with. We'll be hunting out partisans, communists, Jews and any other riffraff that stands in the way of the Third Reich's expansion to the east. Our base of operations is the city of Minsk, there've been a great number of problems there that they need our special skills to deal with. Sonderbattalion Dirlewanger has been assigned to the command of Obergruppenfuhrer Erich von dem Bach-Zelewski, the Higher SS and Police Leader for Russia Center who I'm sure you've all heard of. It is indeed an honor for all of us, the Obergruppenfuhrer is a man who wholeheartedly agrees with the methods we employ to cleanse the rear areas of the enemy, so let's make sure we don't let him down. That's all, men, departure by train at six am tomorrow morning."

They gave another cheer and we left the conference room to pass on the 'good' news to the men.

Heinrich Weiss, my fellow American, was ecstatic. "I've heard of this von dem Bach-Zelewski, he's a man just like the CO, the partisans are terrified of him. They reckon his outfit killed thirty thousand partisans in the city of Riga alone."

"Heinrich, how could there have been thirty thousand partisans in one city?" I asked him. "It's a ridiculous number. He'd had to have killed off innocent civilians too, in their tens of thousands, to make up those numbers."

"Well, I don't know about that, but there aren't any partisans there now, von dem Bach-Zelewski sure finished them off, the Reichsfuhrer was said to be extremely impressed."

He left me and went to speak to his men. Karl-Heinz had overheard the conversation. "Sir, don't take any notice, there's nothing you can do about it now. It's pointless getting upset about it."

"I know that, Scharfuhrer, but it's not something any of us could forget about easily, is it? We're being sent out with a pack of psychotic killers to commit murder."

He nodded. "I know that, Sir."

We spent the evening supervising the packing and checking of supplies and equipment. I slept badly that night, a vision of prisoners being butchered haunted my thoughts. It was during one period of wakefulness that I had the idea of how I could fight back against the terrible brutality of the SS, that I served. I would keep a diary, starting with my recollections of the incident in France that had led to my being sentenced to the concentration camp and including everything that I had witnessed since at Mauthausen. I would continue keeping the journal, until such time as I was killed or until the war was over. It would be my secret, something too dangerous for the men to know about. I would need somewhere to keep the documents as I wrote everything down, Lisl, of course. Would she be prepared to help? Probably she would. She was as brave as a lion, I knew that for certain and she had little love for the Nazi regime. I only had time for two hours sleep, then it was stand to and we were hastily throwing everything into the trucks ready to take the short journey to the railway station.

It was already chaos when we got there, the worst sight of all was the casualties, hundreds, thousands of them being de-trained into ambulances that were shuttling backwards and forwards. We were directed to board a long train, the men were loading our heavy equipment into box cars, most important were the three anti-tank guns. The Soviets were known for making sudden, lightning attacks with their armor and it wouldn't do to be caught out by a squadron of T34s. The T34 was a Soviet medium tank produced from 1940, it was regarded as the most effective, efficient and influential Russian design of the war and was taken seriously by our own armored regiments. During the winter, the T34 often defeated our German tanks through its ability to move over deep mud or snow without bogging down. Our armor could not move over terrain the T34 could handle, our Panzer IV used an inferior leaf-spring suspension and narrow track, and tended to sink in deep mud or snow. They were fast becoming the most feared weapon in the Russian armory.

I wondered if we had well trained anti-tank gunners or were they as ill disciplined and useless as the troops I'd been with on the Lichterfelde range. It could be an interesting experience finding out. I soon would, at last the guns, the endless wooden cases and bales of equipment were loaded, the men were aboard and the train left the station bound for Belorussia. I was in a compartment with several officers including Max and Heinrich Weiss, my American compatriot. The walls and upholstery were smeared with fresh blood that no one had bothered to wash away, it served as a ghastly reminder of where we were going. Heinrich watched me staring uneasily at the bloodstains.

"Paul, this is nothing, you wait until we get there," he said. "We'll repay them in kind for all of this blood, we'll give them blood by the bucket load, their streets will run red with the blood of all the people we'll kill."

Max moaned, a weird but contented sound that was almost sexual. Perhaps it was sexual.

"I can't wait, Heinie," he said enthusiastically. I'm looking forward to showing these Slav peasants how the Sonderbattalion Dirlewanger deals with them."

"You'll love it, Max. Not all of the men do, mind. Some of them find that after the first few bodies they lose their nerve, the will to keep going. I don't know what the problem is with them, we get the prisoners to dig a mass grave, line them up on the edge and then shoot them so that they drop neatly in. Simple, secure and we don't even need to put a finger on their filthy bodies."

"Fantastic," breathed Max.

"It is, truly an awesome spectacle, you have to see it. Even then, some of the men get still get squeamish, silly bastards. We've tried dynamite, too, get them to jump down into the grave and then ignite the charges, but it didn't work well, it made a hell of a mess and we still had to go down and finish them off."

"They used a gas van at Mauthausen," Max offered.

I was staggered that he could even suggest it, having come so near to finishing-up in the death van himself. I gave him a hard look, but he just shrugged.

"Gas vans are too slow," Heinrich shrugged offhandedly. "They're experimenting with a new type of gas chamber but I don't know if they'll be using them in our area. No, I'm afraid we have to make do with the old-fashioned tried and trusted methods, bombs and bullets. What do you think, Paul?"

What I thought was I'd like to throw the pair of them under the wheels of the train, but it wouldn't have been clever to say it.

"I think that captured partisans should be questioned before we even think about death or imprisonment, they could possess large quantities of valuable information."

"Partisans? They're not all partisans, some of them are just civilians taken in reprisal raids. When their partisans kill a couple of our men in the rear areas we round up a hundred civilians and kill them to deter them from doing it again."

"Does it?"

"Does it what?"

"Does it deter them, Heinrich?"

He looked puzzled. "I haven't got a clue, Paul. Maybe, maybe not."

"So why do it if you don't even know that it works, why kill hundreds and thousands of people when maybe it's all for nothing?"

"Because those are my orders, of course, I'm a soldier," he looked even more puzzled. "Look, Paul, we've got a few Hiwis helping us in the Regiment, they don't seem unduly worried about rounding up their people. Maybe you Americans are too soft."

"Hiwis, what the hell are they?"

He explained that Hiwi was the abbreviation of Hilfswilligen, or volunteers. They were made up of Soviet deserters, prisoners and volunteers from among the local population. These so-called Hiwis were employed as sentries, drivers, storekeepers and workers in depots. A few were active soldiers within SS regiments, including the Dirlewanger. The experiment surpassed all expectations. There were already two hundred thousand of them in the rear of our German armies, as well as the few that were active in SS regiments, by the end of the year the plan was to raise that number to over a million. I reflected on how the Germans appeared to be so good at getting foreigners to fight their wars. Imprison, or threaten to imprison them, and offer them the chance of fighting instead of dying of starvation in a death camp. Machiavelli would certainly have approved. I had no choice but to appear to agree, at least for the present.

"You're right, of course, Heinrich. Listen, I need to check on the men."

I got up and started along the corridor of the railway carriage. I couldn't take another minute of their stomach churning conversation and Max especially shocked me, having been so recently released from Mauthausen death camp.

I found Karl-Heinz and Gerd in the corridor two coaches along. They were trying to avoid a group of our men who were practicing throwing combat knives against the woodwork of the carriage. Most were very drunk.

"Any problems?" I asked them.

"With the enemy or our own men?" Karl-Heinz asked.

I smiled. "Not much to choose between them, Scharfuhrer?"

"No, Sir. We're trying to stay out of their way."

"Good plan. I want to check out the equipment further down the train, make sure it's secure. You'd both better come with me."

We went along to the end of the train, there was a goods car where much of our weaponry, ammunition and supplies were transported, but no one guarded it.

"I think here would be a good place to take a rest, I expect they prefer to avoid this place in case there's an attack that ignites the ammunition, I think we'll be safe. If anyone comes along, we're mounting guard on the ammo. In fact, we are mounting guard on the ammo."

They gratefully slumped down on a pile of old sacks and I found some shabby blankets and made myself comfortable.

"Sir, do you know how to use that machine-pistol?" Gerd

asked me. "I gather you were a reporter with the SS, not a soldier."

"They showed us how to point and shoot, yes, all SS officers had to learn, so I'll be ok. Same with the pistol, I'm not sure I'd be able to strip it if it jammed, though. I'll just pray it never happens."

"Like I said, we'll watch your back," Karl-Heinz said. "If you get a jam, I'll free it for you."

I had little doubt I would have need of their help in the near future.

We had to stop twice on that journey, the Soviets had a habit of sending in single engine fighters and bombers to attack our supply trains and when the warnings sounded, the train stopped. During the hours of darkness, all of the lights were doused and we sat and waited while the aircraft went over. One problem we had been warned about, but so far had no defense against, was the U-2. The Polikarpov U-2 was adapted as a night ground-attack bomber, fitted with bomb carriers beneath the lower wing, to carry one hundred or two hundred pound bombs. They were also armed with machine guns in the observer's cockpit. Our troops nicknamed it the Nahmaschine, the sewing machine, for its rattling sound. Intelligence reported that the 588th Night Bomber Regiment, composed of an all-women pilot and ground crew complement, flew the U-2. They had already become notorious for daring low-altitude night raids on rear-area targets, such as this train. The Soviets made great play of using women pilots in order that our troops suffered a further degree of demoralization, simply due to their antagonists being female. The pilots earned the nickname Night Witches. All we could do was watch and wait until the sound of the droning aircraft engines had receded into the distance and thanked God that we'd been spared their attention this time around.

Once one of our wandering foot patrols stopped us when they found dynamite strapped to the line. It was a simple booby trap, the explosives laid and left to wait for us to roll over them, when the contacts would be bridged and the mine exploded. But on this occasion, they defused it and we were able to continue on to Minsk unscathed.

We detrained and marched through the streets in an untidy column, most of the buildings bore all of the signs of the battles that had battered this town, they were all missing their glass in the windows and many of them had lost roofs and walls. A few civilians were hanging around the streets watching us with dulled, lifeless eyes. I doubted that any of them were partisans, they just looked tired and hungry, but it would be unlikely to dissuade the Dirlewanger from rounding them up and killing them if they were ordered. The guns and supplies were due to be loaded onto a truck and sent to our new base, a building that had once been a luxury hotel. The four-star Karl Marx Hotel was a sorry sight, most of the furnishings had been pillaged and the paintwork was peeling badly, but at least it was a roof over our heads. The Wehrmacht NCO in charge of billeting allocated the rooms, they'd given the entire second floor to the officers. I had the benefit of my own room, for which I was thankful, I couldn't stand the company of my psychotic brother officers for longer periods than were strictly necessary. I unpacked, it was mid-evening and Dirlewanger called the officers to the hotel bar for a planning meeting.

"My friends, for most of us it is our first visit to Minsk. I want to make sure that none of the residents of this shithole of a town ever forgets the name of the Sonderbattalion Dirlewanger. There is an industrial complex to the north of the city, my information is that there is a group of partisans sheltering there. We're going in tomorrow at first light, I'm afraid we won't have time to settle in here first. Units of 1 SS Infantry Brigade are taking up blocking positions around the perimeter to stop anyone escaping and I've instructed our gunners to hitch up the anti-tank guns, we'll use them to flatten any buildings where we meet resistance. Any questions?"

"Are there any civilians we need to take into account, Sir?" I asked him.

"Probably, yes, Schaffer. There are quite a few houses there, probably for the workers."

"What do you want done with them, Sir?"

"Good question. 1 SS Infantry Brigade will obviously shoot anyone that reaches their perimeter, but if you see anyone trying to escape, shoot them."

"And the ones that don't try to escape, Sir?"

He looked irritated. "Damnit, shoot them too, of course. We need to show these communist Jewboys that we mean business. The bullet is the only language they understand. Any more questions? No? Dismissed!"

"That's what I call action," Max gloated as we walked out.

Heinrich walked alongside him, smiling at the prospect of bloodshed. I was sickened that a fellow American could be so depraved. And yet, the German race was reputedly a far more ancient and noble civilization than that of America, it was what had brought me to Germany in the first place, to defend the culture of my ancestors. What were they doing butchering innocent people and behaving in a way that would have made their Visigoth and Ostrogoth predecessors proud?

"You mean killing unarmed civilians, Max?" I taunted him. "That's a really brave thing to do."

"Unarmed communists and Jews, enemies of the German State, Schaffer, there's a difference. Too much for your stomach, is it?"

I had to be extremely careful with him, with all of the Dirlewanger men. They would relish reporting me for any kind of squeamishness over the murderous duties we had to perform. I could be killed for any reason, summarily executed. It would be no problem for them, as they'd probably even enjoy it.

"No, it isn't too much for my stomach, not at all. If those are our orders, that's what we'll do. I haven't forgotten how we got here, Max, or where we came from, none of us want to go back there."

He nodded, satisfied. "Good man. We'll have some fun tomorrow, Paul, a chance to hit back."

Hit back at who, I wondered. As far as I was aware, the only people who had ever done anything bad to Max Hofstetter were the Nazis, he'd never even seen a Russian up until now.

I went to brief the men of my squad, I had ten troopers in all including Karl-Heinz Brandt and Gerd Rundheim.

"Just remember, we don't want to get ourselves killed so keep your heads down. And don't forget, either, we're not war criminals, we're just here to stop ourselves from dying a nasty death in a concentration camp. Be as lenient as you dare to be."

"We'll fire over their heads, Sir, don't you worry," Gerd said.

But it wouldn't be enough to save the poor devils we were going to attack, the slaughter tomorrow was likely to be terrible. Were there really any communists in this factory complex, any partisans? Or was it just a reprisal raid, perhaps not even that, just a horrific way of warning the locals not to even think about becoming partisans. Many of them would be old people and children, but it was not in my power to spare them. All I could do was aim high and record what happened for a later war crimes investigation.

I slept fitfully, in the morning the shouts of the NCOs roused me and I dressed hurriedly and strapped on my weapons. The troops were excited and noisy, they were going to war against an enemy who would be largely unarmed, civilians who couldn't shoot back. There was a line of Russian trucks waiting outside and we climbed in. They drove for three miles until we were outside of the city and stopped at a suburb. When I looked back, I saw we'd passed through a cordon of SS troops, their faces were oddly familiar. Heinrich saw me glancing at them.

"They're the SS Infantry Brigade 1, Paul. A vicious bunch of bastards, they were all recruited from the SS-Totenkopfverbande, they used to guard the concentration camps. I guess some of them may have been at Mauthausen, that would be a coincidence, wouldn't it?"

That was the look I'd recognized, the empty-eyed gaze of men who'd seen so much death and human devastation that they no longer cared. Concentration camp guards.

"Yes, it would be a coincidence, Heinrich."

"They're bringing up our artillery now, it looks like we're going straight in."

The trucks towing our three guns stopped and Dirlewanger gave orders for their deployment. When everything was ready, he put a whistle in his mouth ready to begin the operation. I looked around, there were at least two hundred of the SS Infantry Brigade 1 soldiers on the perimeter, many of them armed with MG34 light machine guns. The Maschinengewehr 34, MG 34, was an air-cooled machine gun that had gone into service in 1935. It fired the 7.92x57mm Mauser cartridge and normally mounted on a bipod or tripod. The ammunition was belt-fed making for an impressive rate of fire. It was a classic medium support infantry weapon, or so they'd told me at officers' training school. They'd said nothing about it being intended for use against civilians.

There were three hundred of us in the Sonderbattalion Dirlewanger, including several machine gun crews. The rest of us armed with machine pistols, rifles and grenades. Each of the anti-tank guns was ready, manned by a crew of four who looked as if they knew their business. Our target was a collection of miserable looking factories, perhaps half a dozen of them, not one of them much bigger than a two car garage.

Surrounding them were about twenty small houses, not much more than huts. It seemed to be a huge force to deploy against such a small target, but it was not my decision. The whistle blew. Immediately, the three artillery pieces fired, two of the factory buildings were hit, flames and smoke erupted from them. One of the small houses disappeared, blown to rubble by high explosive. Dirlewanger blew three short blasts, the signal to stop.

"Damnit, men, I told you not to fire those guns until I gave the order."

He looked around wildly. "Where's the artillery commander, Obersturmfuhrer Durst?"

A sheepish looking officer stepped forward. "Sir!"

"What's going on, Durst, why did you open fire?"

"I'm sure I saw movement, Sir. I thought we were about to receive fire from the enemy."

"Did you? Very well, but they'll be alerted now. You'd better finish the job, destroy the buildings and we'll go in and mop up the survivors. Ten minutes, no more, make it quick!"

Durst barked out an order to his gun crews and the quick firing guns shattered the quiet morning as they started the task of destroying the factories and houses. We waited, relaxing, taking sips of water from our canteens. The fragrant smell of spirits, schnapps, wafted across to me, some of the men were already starting to get drunk, it seemed to be the norm for the Sonderbattalion Dirlewanger. The CO shouted orders.

"Two more minutes, men, then we go in. Platoon commanders, get your men ready. Stand by."

I pushed the men into a ragged semblance of a line, I felt nervous, this was my first real action leading men into the barrels of the enemy guns. Neither did I have much confidence in the men I led, I had no idea how they would react when the Russians opened fire, would they turn and run, dive for cover or press home the attack? Suddenly, Dirlewanger blew his whistle and started to run, I had no option but to follow.

He was shouting manically as he ran, "Kill the bastards, come on men, get in there and finish them off, don't leave anyone alive!"

He started to fire his MP38 machine pistol and all along our line almost three hundred men started to fire ragged volleys at the buildings we were charging towards. A head appeared in the window of one of the factory buildings, disappeared, then a gun barrel pushed through and a light machine gun started to fire back at us. Several men fell before the battalion poured fire down on the Russian gun.

"That's a Degtyarev DPM, shoot the bastard. Where's our fucking artillery?"

The Degtyarev was nicknamed the 'record player' because the pan shaped magazine resembled a gramophone record with its disc-like shape and its top cover that revolved while the weapon was fired. The bipod mounted DPM had a reputation as an effective light support weapon, having a slow but sufficient rate of fire. A reputation that was enough to make us all dive for cover.

Durst had obviously seen the danger and three rounds cracked out from the anti-tank guns, the machine gun disappeared in a cloud of smoke, flame and dust.

"Come on, men, let's kill these fuckers!" Dirlewanger shouted.

He was like a man possessed, as if slaughtering every Russian in the area was his holy mission. More of the enemy were firing and a few of our men fell to their bullets, but the enemy fire was sporadic and thin, every time one the partisans popped up to take shot at us a hundred guns fired at them and they were blasted into bloody ruin. We reached the buildings and split into groups to sweep through every room, I took my platoon into the small workshop we reached and we searched it thoroughly but there was only a bullet-riddled corpse lying askew on the floor beneath a window. We walked carefully back outside, the other units were coming out of buildings they'd searched, occasionally a shot was fired, once I heard a short burst of fire from a Soviet light machine gun that was quickly cut off and then everything was silent. The CO looked around cautiously, and then his gaze alighted on the tranquil cottages and shacks.

"Go through the houses, if you see anyone I want them brought out immediately, kill any person that resists, be careful, there may be partisans still hiding in there."

We ran towards a small house, two of my troopers, more experienced in this kind of brutal police action ran ahead and kicked the door in. Two more men ran into the house and before I reached it, there were several bursts of gunfire. I then reached the house and went in, two corpses were on the floor in the living room, a middle-aged man and woman, both unarmed, both dead. The rest of the ground floor was clear, I went up the stairs, on the landing two young children were lying dead on the landing, their bodies riddled with bullets. I heard a scream from one of the bedrooms and ran in. A teenage girl was lying on the bed held down by two of my men, her skirts hoisted over her head and her underwear ripped off and lying on the floor in shreds. Another trooper had his pants down, his penis stuck out brutally in front of him, he was about to rape the girl. Her face looked up at me, but she didn't see me, I was sure, her expression was frozen in resigned terror. I wanted to be sick.

"Stop that, you men, at once! I will not condone rape, and I want to know who killed the civilians."

One of the troopers holding the girl down had a machine pistol in one hand, he spun it around and pointed the barrel straight at me.

"Untersturmfuhrer, you don't get it do you? This is one of the fringe benefits of belonging to this battalion, if you don't like it, why don't you fuck off!"

We all stood frozen for a few moments. I was carrying my MP38 but my finger was not near the trigger. I had no doubt whatsoever that the man would kill me if I didn't back down. To my shame, I nodded and left the room. As I went down the stairs, I heard a scream and then the whimpers of the girl as they took it in turns to rape her. Karl-Heinz and Gerd were waiting in the living room, staring down at the bodies.

"What's going on up there, Sir, anything we need to take care of?"

"Just a brutal rape, my friends, nothing more."

I told them what was happening. Their faces showed their disgust, but we were concentration camp survivors, we had to tread very carefully.

"Come on, there's nothing left for us in here, let's get outside and see if we're needed."

While we waited outside the house, there was a single shot from inside. A few moments later, the three troopers swaggered out of the front door. One of them leered at me.

"All dead in there, Sir. Sorry about that little misunderstanding, but she was a tasty piece, just asking to be screwed. She was a virgin too, how about that?"

The CO came bustling along, his eyes crackling with excitement. "We've taken care of all of them, I believe, anyone left to deal with here, Schaffer?"

"No, Sir, they're all dead. But I must protest, these men murdered a number of innocent civilians and raped a young girl."

He looked surprised. "What do you expect them to do, Schaffer? These people are Russian scum, the only way to deal with them is to kill or terrorize them so that they don't start shooting or knifing our troops in the rear areas. It's all part of the job, believe me, Reichsfuhrer Himmler has told me personally that he fully approves of my methods. You'd better get a grip, my friend, you need to learn to adapt to the methods that we use if you want to stay with the battalion, I can always have you sent back to Mauthausen. Is that what you want?"

"No, Sir, I'll make sure that I don't make any more errors

of judgement."

"Very well. Torch the houses, we don't want the partisans using them again."

I wanted to tell him that the partisans hadn't been using them, they'd just been civilians, but I kept quiet as the men found paper and wood and piled it up inside the cottages and huts. As we marched away to the waiting trucks, I could smell the smoke mixed with the sweet, sickly sweet smell of burned flesh. I thought of the girl on the bed, all I'd seen was her pale body, her genitals exposed, she'd been visibly shaking with fear. I made a mental note to remember the names of the three troopers who participated in her rape. That would be the first entry in my Dirlewanger diary. I noticed Karl-Heinz and Gerd watching me carefully as we drove away through the cordon of SS troops that waited in vain for the chance to join in the slaughter of the innocents. In my mind I was thinking of that girl's face as my troopers held her down. I wasn't staring at the face of a young Belorussian peasant girl. It was Lisl lying there, waiting to be raped and brutalized by her captors.

IRON CROSS AMERIKA

CHAPTER FOUR

'Nature is cruel; therefore we are also entitled to be cruel. When I send the flower of German youth into the steel hail of the war without feeling the slightest regret over the precious German blood that is being spilled, should I also not have the right to eliminate millions of an inferior race that multiply like vermin.'

Adolf Hitler.

"If you get us sent back to Mauthausen we're all dead, Sir," Karl-Heinz said. "You need to be more careful." He'd seen my confrontation with Dirlewanger and was justly terrified about being sent back to the camp.

"What do you want me to do, condone the rape of innocent girls, Karl-Heinz?"

"That's not what he means at all, Sir," Gerd said hurriedly. "We're just trying to survive, you know that we're only here on sufferance. Whether we're sent back or not won't make any difference at all, they'll still kill, rape and pillage, it's the way the

93

battalion fights."

"You call that fighting, Gerd, hacking at innocent civilians?" I snorted.

"No, it's not fighting. But it's the way they are and you won't change anything. Look, Sir, remember what they're like and stay away from the worst of the nastiness, try to survive, remember the way it was in the camp. Survive just for one day, each and every day."

I felt very old and very tired. The Sonderbattalion Dirlewanger had three hundred men in its ranks whereas the German armies had upwards of three million men on the Russian Front, we'd heard plenty of anecdotes of the brutality they inflicted on people in the occupied areas. They were right, I couldn't fight them all.

"You're right, both of you. It's about survival, I'll keep my mouth shut, don't worry."

They smiled with relief. Karl-Heinz brought out a bottle of schnapps. "Let's drink to that, then."

"We may as well, my friends, it seems that the rest of the unit does."

But the taste of the fiery spirit could not take away the thick, oily smell of burning wood, oil and corpses that seemed to have stuck to our clothes. I'd thought to have experienced the last of that in Mauthausen, it seemed that I was wrong. That night I found a quiet spot, away from prying eyes and began to write the entries into my diary.

In the morning Dirlewanger was ecstatic, burning with fanatical enthusiasm.

"We've got another mission on the books, it's set for tomorrow. We've been asked to help out one of the Einsatzgruppen, my friends."

The Einsatzgruppen were SS and SD paramilitary death squads that like the Sonderbattalion Dirlewanger were charged with the mass killing, typically by the shooting of Jews and partisans, although non-Jewish or otherwise innocent civilians often became caught up in their operations. They operated throughout the territory occupied by our armed forces following the invasions of Poland, in September 1939, and later the Soviet Union. The men of the four Einsatzgruppen came from the SD, Gestapo, Kripo, Orpo, and Waffen SS. A disproportionate number of them were former concentration camp guards. Each Einsatzgruppe was under the operational control of the Higher SS-Police Chiefs for its area of operations. The brutality of these uniformed butchers was legendary, astonishing and awesome in its profligacy.

"Obersturmfuhrer Kraus, which unit have we been ordered to assist?"

The adjutant checked a piece of paper on his clipboard.

"Einsatzgruppe Special Commando B, under the command of Standartenfuhrer Walter Blume, Sir."

"Just so. Blume is a very dedicated officer and this mission is one that is perfectly suited to this battalion. A bunch of Jewboys have taken refuge in railroad cars, they're refusing to come out and if we're not careful they could be dangerous, there are sure to be partisan fighters hiding amongst them. Damn it all, these fucking Jews, they always cause trouble for the Reich. We're driving out to Mogilyev, departure at six am. It's a two-hour journey, I want us to get there as fast as possible, deploy the troops and kill them all, with luck we can be back here in time for evening dinner. We won't need the artillery for this one, the Einsatzgruppe already has enough heavy equipment. Any questions?"

I couldn't be sure, but I felt that he looked in my direction, waiting for me to object. But this time I kept quiet, like the other officers.

We spent the rest of the day checking equipment and carrying out the tasks that are ever present in an infantry platoon, even one as irregular as this one. The men drank alcohol, played cards and resolutely ignored me when I went around checking their weapons and ammunition. The best response I got was 'fuck off', most didn't even bother with that. I noticed the soldier who'd threatened me with the machine pistol, Schutze Hoffman. He was sitting on his own, staring into space.

"Is everything ok, Hoffman?" I asked him, deciding that building bridges might be the best way to survive amongst this group of criminals and psychopaths. He gave me a hard stare.

"What do you want to know for? What business is it of yours, American?"

"Schutze, I'm only doing my job, making sure that the platoon doesn't have any problems. If you don't like it, I'm sorry."

He kept staring at me, as if to trying to decide whether to speak to me or not.

"I have something of a problem, you can help if you want."

"If I can I will, yes. What is it?"

"I got a letter from home last week. I want to know what it says."

"I see. So you haven't read it?"

He looked around carefully to make sure that there was no one in earshot. "I can't fucking read, can I? I wouldn't be asking you otherwise. Are you going to help me or not?"

I spent an hour reading and explaining to him, helping an illiterate soldier understand what his parents had written and what they meant, even though the day before he had raped at least one girl, murdered several other innocent civilians and threatened to shoot me. I finished reading the letter to him and tried to get some kind of common ground between us.

"You know I came from a camp, don't you?" I asked him.

He nodded.

"Did you also come from a camp?"

"Yeah, I did, Dachau, it's a death camp near Munich. Dachau was the first concentration camp opened in Germany, it's in the grounds of an old munitions factory near the medieval town of Dachau. Munich isn't far away either. They said it was the first regular concentration camp established by the Nazi Party. Heinrich Himmler was Chief of Police of Munich, which had responsibility for that area," Hoffman said proudly. "They said it was the first concentration camp for political prisoners, whatever they are. I wasn't political, that's for sure, I was a moneyman."

"I thought you were a thief, Hoffman?"

He laughed. "That was just a misunderstanding."

"Was it really bad, this Dachau death camp you were in?"

"There were plenty of deaths, they killed Jews, gypsies, communists, yeah, it was pretty fucking bad," he said it as if to say, what a stupid question. I suppose he was right.

But in spite of everything, I still found it hard to believe that they were the norm in Germany rather than the exception.

"In Mauthausen where I was they deliberately put thousands of prisoners to death, most of them were just Germans."

He shrugged. "I'll remember to stay out of it, then. But I expect you're mistaken, most of them were probably just Jews."

I shook my head. "Not really, I'm not mistaken. The Jews were German. They were all Germans, all of them, Jews, Christians, communists, most of us were just in the wrong place at the wrong time."

He laughed. "Those poor bastard Jews tomorrow are certainly going to feel they were in the wrong place at the wrong time."

"What do you mean?"

"Don't you get it, Untersturmfuhrer from America? They won't be partisans, they'll just be women, children and old men, most of them starving to death. I've been here a year and those half a dozen partisans we saw yesterday were unusual. Most times we get called out and we never even get shot at."

"You're saying that our mission here is just to kill civilians."

He clapped his hands ironically. "Well done, Untersturmfuhrer. That's exactly what we're here for, to kill civilians and spread terror, the CO thinks it's the best way to control the territories we conquer. Spread fear, he says, and they'll be too frightened to cause trouble."

"Do you think it works?"

He laughed again. "I couldn't give a damn one way or the other. They pay me to take orders, although sometimes there's a bonus, like when there's a juicy piece of Russian tail just begging to be fucked. It was nothing personal, Untersturmfuhrer, just a bit of fun."

"I see." I walked away from him before I was either sick or I pulled out my pistol and shot him.

Max was with Heinrich Weiss, they were chatting excitedly about the forthcoming mission.

"The CO wasn't too happy with you yesterday, Schaffer," Max said. "You find soldiering a bit too tough for you, do you?"

I was about to tell him the truth, that it was butchery, not soldiering, but I remembered Gerd's warning. Survive for each day, if I told them what I thought they'd almost certainly report me to the CO for the sadistic pleasure of seeing me disciplined, even returned to the camp.

"It was nothing, just a misunderstanding. You're wrong, you know, soldiering is a good and honorable profession. I can't wait to meet the enemy in battle."

They both looked taken aback, they'd obviously been expecting something else They both missed the irony in what I'd said. To them, shooting innocent civilians was real fighting.

"Good for you," Weiss said. "We thought you had something of a yellow streak."

"No. Heinrich, I'll bet you would have loved fighting the Indian wars, ripping through the villages, slaughtering the women and children."

His eyes blazed with enthusiasm at the thought of it. "God, yes, that would have been something. Leading a cavalry troop, a saber in one hand and a Remington revolver in the other, seeing the Indians being cut to ribbons. You're right, Schaffer, I was born in the wrong time."

"I'm sure that's true, Heinrich."

I left the two psychotic officers to their conversation and went to find the camp bed that had been erected for me. I needed to get some sleep, to send my mind away from this band of lunatics. I thought of Lisl von Schenk and went to sleep feeling the soft, warm touch of her beautiful body. My dreams that night were about her, but she was inside a house being raped by a gang of bloodthirsty soldiers, I was trying to help her but I was trapped outside the house by rolls of barbed wire that stopped me getting near her. She was calling out to me, Paul, screaming my name and I suddenly came awake. "Lisl!"

I was staring at the amused and slightly embarrassed face of Karl-Heinz Brandt.

"It's me, Sir, time to get up."

I remembered where I was and slipped out of one nightmare into another.

"Thank you, Scharfuhrer."

I was fully dressed, I only needed to put my jackboots on and I was ready to face the day. We were all unshaven, one of the men told me that the only time they bothered to shave was when they found a town with some nightlife, then they got themselves cleaned up. If necessary, they would kidnap a barber and keep him prisoner for the whole time the battalion was stationed in a town, to be their personal groomer. The sergeant major, Sturmscharfuhrer Mintel ran around shouting, "Breakfast in five minutes, we move out in twenty so get your asses into gear, you idle swine."

We ate a hurried breakfast and washed it down with ersatz coffee. The trucks were already waiting outside and the men cursed and grumbled as they were shoved into them ready to leave. I climbed into the back of our vehicle and a few minutes later we were driving along the bumpy Soviet track that passed as a road in this desolate, destroyed country.

We arrived at the outskirts of Mogilyev, a dusty little industrial town that had the distinction of having a railhead. We bumped through the town, the troopers looking out keenly for bars, women and loot but they were not likely to find much of any of them in this broken, destroyed place. We reached the railway yard and the trucks stopped, we jumped out and assembled in a rough formation. A hundred yards away there were a dozen railway boxcars, halted in a siding. Surrounding the boxcars was an SS unit, I assumed they were the Einsatzgruppe that Dirlewanger had mentioned. The CO called for us to listen.

"I'll have a word with Standartenfuhrer Blume and find out where he wants us to deploy. Kraus, make sure you deploy sentries just in case, although with the SS here already I doubt there'll be much partisan activity."

He marched over to the other SS unit and we stood waiting. Some of the men sat down in the dust and a few pulled out the inevitable bottles of schnapps. Max came over to me.

"What do you think is happening, Schaffer?"

He seemed nervous for some reason, I couldn't imagine why. Apart from our own troops, there was at least a company, if not more of the Einsatzgruppe B waiting to go into action. I shrugged.

"I haven't got a clue. I imagine that some poor sods are being lined up for the chop."

"As long as they're not too heavily armed, I can't see any sign of the enemy yet."

He fidgeted some more, swapping his machine pistol from hand to hand, he turned away from me at one point and took a swig from a hip flask as if I couldn't see what he was doing. I ignored him and went over to join my platoon. We watched as the Einsatzgruppe started to knock the locks from the railway boxcars. Inside they were packed with people, ragged, starving men, women and children who fell out of the cars, pushed by the pressure from those inside trying to get out into the fresh air. Dirlewanger came back to us and started to issue orders.

"It seems there's been a misunderstanding, they're not very dangerous, just Jews for the most part, maybe a few communists but it's the same thing. The Einsatzgruppe is getting them out and assembled for inspection, they just want us to keep an eye out for any partisans trying to slip away. Spread out and form a perimeter, make sure that none of the prisoners escape either."

The men ignored him and stood around chatting, taking sips from their bottles of schnapps. Dirlewanger shouted and Sturmscharfuhrer Mintel dragged men around and put them on sentry duty. The rest of us watched the activity around the railroad cars. More and more people were disembarked, a pitiful looking group of people resembling the worst of the inmates of Mauthausen, I wondered how on earth they'd got into such a state. Starvation and brutality was my best guess. As they fell out of the boxcars they were forced into a growing mass of humanity, many of them clutching their children, babies, some of them with small suitcases and bags. I couldn't believe how so many had been packed into such a small space, by the time the cars were emptied there were around three thousand people in a huge group, some standing and some sitting on the beaten earth midway between us and the railway line. The Einsatzgruppe had set up four MG34 machine guns to cow them into submission, many of their troops were standing watching with machine pistols pointed at the wretched crowd. A soldier suddenly ran over to Dirlewanger and spoke to him.

"Move behind cover, men and over to our left, we're standing directly in their field of fire, I want everyone to take cover when we reach out new position."

We moved fifty yards and took cover in a culvert that was about five feet deep, it made a perfect trench. Still we waited, another soldier ran across from the Einsatzgruppe, he was an officer, an Obersturmfuhrer. He spoke to the CO and then ran back.

"Listen, men," Dirlewanger shouted. "Standartenfuhrer Blume has asked for volunteers to fill out his firing party, apparently there are partisans and saboteurs mixed in amongst these prisoners and he's taking no chances. They are all to be executed. Fifty men should do it, I'm going over there myself. Sturmscharfuhrer, bring the volunteers and follow me."

There were more than enough offering to join the killing squad. Mintel brought them after the CO and assigned them to positions near to the MG34s. Still we waited while Blume stood and shouted at the group of prisoners, haranguing them, I couldn't hear what he was saying, but what difference would it have made? Suddenly, the firing started, light machine guns, machine pistols, some rifles, a few officers drew their pistols and fired individual shots. The ragged, terrified crowed tried running, but each step away from a group of gunners took them nearer to another group. They were cut down like cattle, it was a slaughterhouse of blood, filth, screams of dead and dying, the wounded trying to shelter underneath the corpses of the dead. After only a few minutes half of the prisoners had been cut down, still the survivors ran here and there, trying to escape, except for a few who stood frozen with either fear or fatalism to be cut down in the hail of bullets.

I should have done something, I know, should have tried to stop it, perhaps shot the commanders, the Lords of Death, Blume and Dirlewanger, but I did nothing, just prayed for a miracle. And my prayers were answered. A ragged fusillade of rifle and sub-machine gunfire spat out at the executioners, some fell, and the rest took cover. Partisans!

I shouldn't have been relieved to see the enemy, but I felt a surge of pleasure that someone at least was standing up against this murderous band of thugs. But I shouted to my men, I still had a responsibility to them.

"Platoon, keep your heads down, machine gun crew, swing around to cover the enemy, quick men!"

We moved quickly to the other side of the culvert, some of the men started firing but there was little to see. There was a line of nearby wrecked railway trucks, a cargo of heavy logs had spilled onto the ground and it seemed that they were firing from under there. At least it would keep their heads down. Once my men were all under cover, I looked around to see what the CO was doing. He was rushing back towards us, leading the fifty volunteers into action against the partisans. He was either very brave or he had a death wish, some of the enemy started to fire at them and several men around him fell, but he ran on, seemingly with a charmed life. Just before he reached us, he flinched and I saw scraps of his uniform fly off where he'd been hit, but he ran on and ignored the wound. He threw himself down next to me.

"What's the situation, Schaffer?"

I told him where the partisans were sheltering.

"Good man. Any suggestions?"

"I'll lead my platoon out to their flank if you'll get the men to give us covering fire. Sir, we need to get behind them, it's the only way to deal with them."

"Good, take your platoon and move out as far as you can go under cover, then wait until we start shooting."

"Yes, Sir."

"And good luck, Schaffer."

I took the ten men of my platoon and we crept along the culvert until we were at the end, near to the railway line. We checked that we had loaded clips, most of the men had two stick grenades, and we waited. Suddenly there was an intense burst of firing, bullets spat towards the enemy positions and ricocheted off the iron of the wrecked trucks, splinters flew off the logs, it would keep their heads down for sure, the weight of fire was incredible.

"Charge!" I shouted to the men, jumped out of the culvert, and started to run. We were halfway towards the enemy positions before they even realized the danger, then bullets started to crack amongst us.

"Keep going, we're nearly there!" I shouted. Two men had already fallen, there were only eight left and I had no idea how many we had to contend with. We were nearly there, only ten yards from the defenses, the tree trunks and broken railway stock. But it was ten yards too far, I knew that if I reached there I'd lose most of my men in the process.

"Down, get down and use grenades!"

I dived to the ground, underneath the hail of bullets a soldier threw himself down beside me. It was Brandt.

"I hope you're good at throwing these things, Scharfuhrer," I said as I ripped out the pin and threw the stick grenade. He followed suit, grunting as he threw it with all of his might.

"Good enough, I think."

We both pulled the pins from our second grenades and threw them, while they were in the air we heard the first ones explode and the screams of the enemy, then there were more explosions as grenades thrown by the other men went off. I jumped up to catch them before they recovered.

"Come on men, we can finish them now!"

I charged forward, not even stopping to look and see if anyone was following me. I ran ducking through the gap between two trucks and suddenly came out next to two Russian partisans, both looked stupefied to see me suddenly appear, they were still suffering from the effects of the grenades. Nearby, several others lay dead and dying on the ground.

One of them recovered before me and lifted his rifle, a battered Soviet Mosin Nagant. I was swinging my machine pistol up but I knew it would be too late, then a short burst of gunfire took him in the stomach and he screamed and fell backwards. I looked around, Scharfuhrer Brandt had come up with me. The second man was cocking his pistol to shoot but I got him first, I pulled the trigger and a burst from my MP38 knocked him over. It seemed to happen in slow motion, his look of anger and determination turning to surprise, then fear, then the agony as my bullets hit him. The surviving members of my platoon burst through and started shooting at the rest of the partisans until they were all dead. I recovered my wits and shouted at them to cease-fire. As we did so, the covering fire from out battalion started to slacken.

"They're all dead," I shouted at them. "We're coming out, don't shoot!"

The firing died away completely and I led the men back out to the battalion. Dirlewanger stood at the front, as ever.

"Any problems, Untersturmfuhrer?"

"I lost two men, Sir, but the enemy are all dead."

"Never mind about a couple of losses, well done to all

of you, a very satisfying action. We can finish of these Jews and then get home for some dinner, I've had enough of this stinking place."

As he spoke, I saw a half dozen prisoners running away to the shelter of some distant buildings. The Einsatzgruppe machine gunner saw them and sent a burst of gunfire in their direction but his bullets went high and the Jews disappeared into an apartment block.

"After them, men, don't let them get away! Schaffer, take your platoon to the back of that building and try and cut them off."

I gathered my platoon and we dashed towards the apartment block. I was still numb, I could think of nothing other than the man I had just killed, the first time I had taken a life. He had only been defending his country against us, the foreign invaders, I had taken my place amongst the descendants of the Teutonic Savages, plundering the civilizations of Europe for loot. We ran around the back of the building, it suddenly occurred to me that there weren't many of my men with me. I stopped and looked around, just Gerd and Karl-Heinz, the rest had stayed back, probably because they'd seen some opportunity for loot.

"We'd better be careful, if our men come blundering through the building shooting we could catch a stray bullet."

There was an outbuilding nearby and we sheltered behind it. I looked at my hands, they were still shaking.

"Still bad, Sir?" Brandt said.

"I've felt better, the poor bastard was a patriot, Karl-Heinz, he was just doing his duty."

"As were you, don't forget that."

"Really? What exactly is our duty?"

Gerd took hold of my tunic. "Look, Sir, you know what your duty is. To survive, that's all, nothing more. But we've got a problem."

"What now?"

"What do we do if those poor prisoners come out this way? Do we shoot them, or take them back to be shot?"

I realized the enormity of the dilemma we were faced with. We were damned if we did and damned if we didn't. There was only one answer.

"Shouldn't we be checking this outbuilding for loot?"

"But it's empty," Brandt protested, then he understood. "Oh, yes, of course. Could be something valuable in there."

There was a flimsy door, we kicked it down and went inside. From there we were out of sight but we could see through cracks in the wall. We stood quietly and waited. From inside the apartments we could hear the occasional shot, the crash of doors being broken down and glass being smashed. Then there was movement in the rear entrance and a ragged group of prisoners appeared, looked fearfully around and talked rapidly amongst themselves. There was loud shouting nearby, two more shots ran out and they made a run for it, straight into our outbuilding. They fell into our laps, we stood there, heavily armed, steel helmets, to their eyes we were battle scarred SS troopers. They were like scarecrows, just the way we had looked so recently, emaciated, clothes in rags, missing teeth, hair fallen out in clumps as starvation and disease took its toll. Their faces were covered in sores, their eyes rimmed with grime and filth. And terror. I looked at the other two.

"No, don't kill them! We're not letting this lot get killed along with the others."

There were five of them, one of them looked at me with a puzzled expression, a man who looked to be about sixty years old but was probably nearer thirty.

"What's going on, you may as well shoot us now. They'll only kill us when they've finished killing our friends."

"You're German?" I asked him, surprised at his cultured accent.

"Of course we are, we're all German. I am Joseph Goldberg, I was a physician in Vienna before the Gestapo picked us up. Look, what are you waiting for, SS man? If you're going to kill us do it now, don't mock us by trying to make it more civilized."

"If you are from Vienna, you will know about Mauthausen, we were inmates there until recently, all three of us."

"You? But you're SS."

"We are now. Joining this unit was the only way to avoid a lingering death in the camp."

"So to save yourselves from a cruel death you have to commit others to that same death?"

There was a loud commotion at the back of the apartments and some of the men appeared in the doorway. There were four of our Dirlewanger men, they'd captured an elderly Jew and were systematically kicking him to death on the ground. I turned to Joseph Goldberg.

"Can you run for it if we cover for you? You'll need to lose yourselves in the town."

"Yes, of course. But what about those men?"

The Jew on the ground was losing blood badly, near death.

"I'll deal with them, you look out for yourselves."

I handed him my MP38. "Do you know how to use it?"

"I was a reservist, yes, I can use it."

"It's got a full clip, I suggest you save a bullet each for yourselves if things go wrong. Good luck."

He shook my hand. "Thank you, my friend. I'll never forget this."

"Just survive, Joseph, one day at a time. We'll deal with those soldiers, as soon as the shooting starts, go quickly!"

He nodded.

"You men, the only chance these men have is if we deal with the troopers beating that old man to death. Is that any problem to either of you?"

The both shook their heads. "None whatsoever," Gerd replied with relish.

"Let's go then."

I drew my Walther and stepped out into the open. The troopers looked up for a moment, then grinned when they saw we were part of their unit and carried on with their game. We got within four feet of them. I could smell the sweat and the booze.

"Having fun, men?"

"Yeah, we sure are, this one's been a real scream."

I shot him between the eyes and he fell backwards. Brandt and Rundheim gave the others a burst from their machine pistols and I walked up to check the old man. He was almost dead, I put my pistol against his head and pulled the trigger to put him out of his misery, but it didn't put me out of mine. That was three men now that I'd killed in a short space of time.

I picked up one of the fallen men's MP38s to replace the one I'd given to Joseph.

"Let's make it look good, we'll pretend to chase after the partisans."

I fired a burst in the direction that was opposite to where the prisoners had run, and then I shouted at the men to follow me. As we ran, more Dirlewanger men ran out of the apartment block and I shouted to get their attention.

"The partisans, they killed some of our men, follow me, let's get the bastards!"

We ran along the row of buildings, stopping to peer into each one. The men caught up with us, incandescent with anger.

"Fucking bastards, I'll rip their guts out!" one burly schutze snarled.

"Check every building," I shouted at them, "we don't want to get ambushed."

My warning slowed them down as we looked carefully into every nook and cranny. After half an hour, they'd lost interest and gave up the hunt, stopping to look for loot. We started back to the railway line, when we were half way back there was a heavy burst of firing that seemed to go on forever. Gerd looked at me.

"I reckon that's the prisoners being finished off," he said.

"At least we got a few of them away," Karl-Heinz said quietly.

"It's better than nothing. And we finished those bastards who kicked the old man to death."

I looked away. They hadn't kicked him quite to death, I'd administered the coup de grace. Before we reached the railway line, the firing died away and when we got there only bodies lay in the middle of the open ground. Rows, piles of corpses lay banked up in heaps, like old, bloody rags. A pall of smoke hung over the area and the troopers were stood down, some of them drinking again, the rest smoking and chatting like workers everywhere that had just completed an everyday task.

"Did you get them?" Dirlewanger asked.

"No, they got away, but we ran into a group of partisans and they shot four of our men."

"Damned Russians, have they gone now?"

"I'm afraid so, Sir, they're well away, they know every nook and cranny in this place."

"Hmm, perhaps we'd better ask the Luftwaffe to flatten it, that'll take away their hiding places. That was a brave action today, Untersturmfuhrer, attacking the partisan position, I won't forget it."

"Thank you, Sir. But you were wounded, how is it?"

"Nothing, just a minor scratch, a leader has to be prepared for these things, but I don't need to tell you that, Schaffer. You've got the right attitude for the Sonderbattalion Dirlewanger, you could go far."

"Thank you, Sir."

He went away to supervise the men being rounded up to return to our quarters in Minsk. I gathered that this was a normal part of the battalion's operations, recovering the men from their missions of rape and pillage. It took two hours to drag them all back to the waiting trucks and get them on board. The troopers of the Einsatzgruppe watched disinterestedly, most of them were already drunk, some of them were picking over the corpses, two men had pliers and were prizing open the mouths looking for gold teeth. One 'corpse' opened its eyes and screamed when they started to rip out a gold tooth, the trooper just pulled out his pistol and shot him between the eyes while the other carried on pulling at the tooth. They were former concentration camp guards of course. Bullies, psychopaths and sadists, they would have been attracted to service in the Einsatzgruppe by the very prospect of loot, rape and pillage, most of which would have not been possible in the closely guarded confines of the camps. With our Sonderbattalion Dirlewanger they were in good company, I doubted there was any aspect of man's brutality, cruelty and sadism they had yet to sample.

We bumped along the track back to Minsk, the men still drinking, shouting and swearing. Some were already gambling away the small pickings they had taken from Mogilyev, the three of us survivors from the camp, Karl-Heinz, Gerd and I sat together, we had little to say to each other. We'd seen it from both sides now, the brutal regime that had infected almost the whole of Europe with its insane drive for conquest no matter what the price in lost humanity. When we got back to base, I scrounged a bottle from Karl-Heinz.

"Don't you want to share it, Sir?" he asked in surprise.

"No, Scharfuhrer. I want to forget."

At least I had seen favor from the CO today for my part in attacking the partisans, that at least would keep me out of Mauthausen for the time being. I had also helped some Jews to escape, but they were such a pitiful few compared with the thousands that had been machine gunned next to the railway boxcars. I opened the bottle and started to drink. Halfway through, I got out my diary and a pen and wrote down the events of the day, it was so little but at least it was something.

During the next four days we had time to ourselves, many of the men went into the city and created mayhem, there were reports of rapes, thefts and murders, none of which were considered worthy of following up. On one occasion, the SS Feldgendarmerie arrived with a packet of complaints from the local military leaders. Their commander, an SS police lieutenant, an Obersturmfuhrer was red faced with anger.

"Damnit, Sturmbannfuhrer Dirlewanger, the local people are on the verge of revolt. The Wehrmacht are threatening to complain directly to Berlin and even the SS are unhappy! You're stirring up a hornet's nest here, you'll incite the locals to trouble and they'll start taking pot-shots at our men and petty acts of sabotage."

Dirlewanger was livid. "Obersturmfuhrer, I couldn't give a damn about the local people. My men are trained to be ruthless, to terrify the locals into submission in the rear areas to prevent them joining the partisans. If they're a little high spirited when they go into town, it's only to be expected."

"But it's not working, Sir, they are joining the partisans,

often it's directly because of what you men are doing."

"We have a simple expedient for that too, my friend. If they won't play ball, we kill them. Just tell me where the trouble is coming from and I'll get a squad down there and wipe them all out. What's the name of the area from which most of this trouble is coming?"

"It's called the Soviet Union, Sir."

The policeman turned and left, leaving Dirlewanger red-faced in fury.

We received more new recruits, it seemed that there were plans to expand our unit into a full regiment and beyond. It all seemed a waste to me, the men could have been better employed fighting at the front, if they could ever find the time between looting and raping. Instead, they roused the local population to rebel by their very barbarity. The locals hated us, of course. We had taken to going into the city centre in large groups, none less than platoon size, all of us with machine pistols. On the fourth evening after we got back from the carnage at Mogilyev, I had to take the platoon into the city to rescue two of my men who had disobeyed orders and gone out on their own. We found them in a backstreet behind a brothel, both of them were naked, their throats slit. Holst and Brubacher, both ex-poachers and experienced and expert sharpshooters that I had needed to keep my platoon up to strength. I'd lost two men at Mogilyev and now this, it meant that my platoon now had a fighting strength of myself and six men. We threw the bodies onto our truck and drove back. When we arrived, Dirlewanger was in a fever of excitement. He took my arm as I walked in.

"You'll have a chance to show off your heroics again, my friend. We're back into action in the morning. Three villages have been identified as harboring partisans, Borki, Zabloitse and Borysovka. After our last action at Mogilyev we're in demand for this sort of work, Schaffer, we're becoming famous."

He caught sight of the two naked bodes being unloaded.

"What happened to your men?"

I told him about finding them behind a brothel. He smiled.

"Let's hope they had some fun before they went, eh? Cheer up, we'll take revenge later, in the meantime we need to get ready to pull out just after dawn."

"I need more men, Sir. I lost two at Mogilyev, now these two dead."

"When we get back I'll find you some more, you'll just have to manage for now. Officers' briefing will be at dawn, get yourself some sleep."

As I was trying to doze off, I wondered about the CO. He was certifiable, of course, would he be taken into a lunatic asylum before the Russians killed him? One or the other was inevitable.

IRON CROSS AMERIKA

CHAPTER FIVE

'Today we are crushed by the sheer weight of the mechanized forces hurled against us, but we can still look to the future in which even greater mechanized forces will bring us victory. Therein lies the destiny of the world.'

Charles de Gaulle

While the men were loading our vehicles, a dozen Renault ASN trucks commandeered after the fall of France, the CO called us to him and held an officers' briefing. He was still flushed with enthusiasm for the coming action, I guessed he had not slept the night before. He rambled on about our chance for glory, to emblazon our names on the Third Reich's Rolls of Honor, whatever they were, then he came to the mission at hand.

"Our first objective is the village of Borki. We have a police battalion there trying to root out the partisans but they have insufficient weaponry and they have requested our assistance. So we drive straight to the assistance of our SS police comrades, once we are finished with the problem in Borki we push on to Zabloitse and then to Borysovka. It will take us two days at least to carry out the mission, I have ordered the quartermaster to issue supplies accordingly. Remember what happened to Schaffer's two men last night, make certain that you deal with these Russian dogs appropriately."

I wanted to point out that these people were Belorussian, not Russian, many of them hated the Soviets as much as we did, but I doubted it would do any good. Mercy was not a word he understood, or would wish to acknowledge.

"Intelligence suggests that we will run into partisan activity along the way, so be very alert. I've managed to obtain a motorcycle from the Divisional transport depot that we'll send ahead to carry out reconnaissance. Make sure that the men are all warned, and they keep their weapons ready at all times. And please…"

He looked around at all of us. "cut down on the men's drinking! It's becoming excessive, we need clear heads for this one, we're heading into bandit country."

The officers laughed and cheered, was it over the mention of drinking or the possibility of action? Probably the former, they hadn't struck me as especially keen to tangle with a heavily armed and prepared enemy.

An hour later, we left the outskirts of Minsk heading north for the village of Borki. There were a hundred and fifty of us, half the unit, packed into ten Renault ASN trucks. The BMW motorcycle combination led the convoy, ridden by an SS Sturmmann, a lance corporal with a schutze in the sidecar operating the mounted MG34 machine gun. Other than their steel helmets, they had no protection, only their motorcycle goggles and their waterproof motorcycle coats to protect them from the elements, not Russian Bullets. Dirlewanger followed in his Kubelwagen, recently repaired following a burst of Soviet machine gun fire that had destroyed the engine. He rode the vehicle standing up in the front, much like the Fuhrer on one of his parades. He didn't even wear a tin helmet, disdaining the necessity to wear a peaked officer's cap instead. Our trucks mounted MG34s in hatches that the mechanics had cut above the passenger seat in the cab. We posted men with machine pistols at the sides and rear of each truck, keeping watch for possible enemy action. It was the best we could do and none of it was of any use against aircraft.

They came roaring in without any warning, two Soviet Ilyushin Sturmoviks, the Russian equivalent of our Stukas, but better, much better. With a maximum speed of over two hundred and sixty miles per hour, they were faster, better armed and carried a heavier bomb load. They were causing massive disruption to our operations in Belorussia and the Ukraine. These two were intent on destroying our convoy.

"Stop the truck!" I shouted at the driver. "Everyone out and get under cover. Get those machine guns firing, see if we can bring down one of those fighters!"

Our truck shuddered to a halt, most of the men leapt out and followed me to the side of the track. There was a low wall marking the boundary of a peasant's field, I jumped behind it and looked for the other men. There had been twenty-five men in my truck, under the command of an Obersturmfuhrer and myself. That officer and at least five of his men were shouting and cursing, hitting out at each other as they blindly tried to save some of their possessions from the truck. It occurred to me that they probably carried their more valuable loot with them, leaving it in our quarters would be an invitation to theft. The rest of the men vaulted over the wall and joined me behind cover. The first Soviet aircraft swooped and fired a long burst that stitched through a group of men bunched together near the side of the road, flinging them to the ground in a bloody, ragged heap of dead and dying. The trooper with the MG34 looked dazed, terrified by the Soviet fighters.

"Karl-Heinz, get that gun firing, I'll load for you!"

He ripped the machine gun out of the man's hands and set it on the stonework. I straightened the belt and made certain it would feed straight, then attached the next belt so that firing would be continuous. I'd done it in officer's basic training before we went into France, I had no idea if I had it right, but I'd soon know. Brandt pressed the trigger and sent a stream of bullets up towards the incoming Sturmovik, the pilot pressed his trigger at the same time and his tracer bullets hammered towards us, hitting a second truck in the convoy and sweeping over our position, blasting chips of stone from the wall. We saw the rockets slung under the wings and held our breath in case he fired them. But he wasn't to have it all his own way, our bursts of fire riddled his cockpit with bullets as he came in low and we saw the pilot, one moment his head pressed forward to look through his gun sight, the next moment he was thrown back as one of more of our bullets struck him.

It wasn't a fatal hit, he righted his aircraft and managed to fly off to the east, the other aircraft broke off the attack too and flew alongside him as escort. The two trucks were burning fiercely, I sent the men to try to put out the fires and salvage any equipment that may still be useable. I looked around my position, there were several corpses lying on the ground, shattered by machine gun and cannon fire.

"Gerd, Karl-Heinz, would you check the trucks and see how many casualties we suffered."

They ran off and I inspected the bodies on the ground near the wall. There were four dead, none were wounded, the cannon fire had done the damage, devastating the stone wall and killing outright the men sheltering behind it. Gerd and Karl-Heinz came back.

"Seven of them including the officer, all dead, most of them burnt to death when the truck caught fire."

That made a total of eleven dead, out of twenty-seven officers and men. Now there were only sixteen of us, myself and fifteen men. Dirlewanger was walking along and inspecting the damage, I noticed his machine pistol was smoking where he'd obviously emptied it at the Russians.

"What's your situation, Schaffer?"

I told him about our casualties.

"That's too bad, but at least now you've got a good sized platoon under your command. Serve the stupid bastards right, they should have taken cover rather than grubbing around to save their valuables. We lost more than twenty men up front, they herded together and froze, that first attack got them all. You'd better take over their truck too."

"What about the dead, Sir, when do we bury them?"

He looked at the corpses. "Throw them all into a pile and pour petrol on them, set fire to them," he looked at me, his eyes were dilated and wild, his expression fierce and intent. "A true Viking funeral pyre, Schaffer, send them to Valhalla, the warrior's heaven. Don't you think the Reichsfuhrer would approve?"

"Yes, Sir, I have no doubt he would."

I would have to be careful. With his doctorate, our Sturmbannfuhrer was no fool. He missed my irony completely, but one day he would notice it and I could find myself in serious trouble, or even back in Mauthausen. I gave the necessary orders to the men and ten minutes later the pyre was ready. Dirlewanger of course had to perform the final act of the ritual, he threw a burning rag onto the heap of petrol-soaked bodies and we stood back as they started to burn. The sickly sweet smell of burning flesh wafted all around us, it was the smell of war and of course the smell of the camps. I waited for the order to stand to attention, some sort of salute to the fallen, but of course, this was the Sonderbattalion Dirlewanger, corpses were its everyday trade.

"Right men, mount up, we're running late."

He strode forward to his waiting Kubelwagen, I ordered my men into the surviving truck we'd been given. This time we were more careful. Like the other platoon officers, I ordered my men to pull off the canvas roof as we were driving along the track. It gave us much better vision and we were able to keep a watchful eye out for aircraft as well as partisans. An hour later, we stopped two hundred yards outside the village of Borki, a large collection of cottages and huts, there were also half a dozen larger buildings, barns probably. A group of SS troopers had established a position on the track and in the distance I could see another armed group at the opposite side of the village. The CO jumped down to greet them.

I climbed down to stretch my legs and the rest of my men followed suit. The cordon consisted of Belorussian and Lithuanian collaborators, led by German SS Police officers and NCOs. I could hear their commander describing the situation to Dirlewanger.

"We followed them here, Sturmbannfuhrer, two partisans both armed with rifles, they saw us coming and hid in the village. They're sheltering in one of those houses and we need to find a way to drag them out."

"Where are the civilians, the people who live in this Godforsaken shithole?" he asked.

The policeman shrugged. "Still there, as far as I know, none of them have come out."

"Many of them?"

"I would guess about eight hundred."

"Any Jews?"

"Sure to be, yes."

"So we've got a village of Jews and partisans, is that correct?"

The policeman scratched his head thoughtfully. "Well, not exactly, Sir."

"War is not an exact business, my friend. We'll call it an enemy held village of Jews and partisans, agreed?"

The policeman was reluctant, we could all see that, but he was in command of about thirty men, faced down by a superior officer with almost one hundred and fifty heavily armed troopers, finally he nodded his head.

"Agreed."

The CO started barking orders, our men cocked their weapons and marched into the village. While the machine gunners covered them, they kicked down doors and ordered the residents out. As soon as they had left they torched the building, sometimes using grenades if they thought there might be others still hiding inside. The villagers were rounded up in a large group, hundreds of them in a field next to the village. As the round up continued, Dirlewanger issued orders to the men to find spades and get the villagers to start digging a large hole, fifty feet square and ten feet deep.

"Anyone that doesn't dig, or is too slow, shoot them!"

He approached me. "Schaffer, some of these people may be useful to us, they could be sympathizers or even ethnic Germans. Start checking them out, anyone that speaks German may well be on our side. There might even be a dozen or so worth saving."

"Karl-Heinz, Gerd, come with me."

I took them to one side.

"You know he means to kill them all?"

They both nodded. "What the hell do we do now?" Gerd asked.

"We're to sort out the ethnic Germans, make sure then we find plenty of them that can say 'Ja' and 'Nein', it's all we can do, I'm afraid. Let's try and save a hundred, any more and we'll be in the shit ourselves."

We went through the terrified group of villagers, questioning them and selecting those who we thought my pass muster as 'reliable'. Anyone that showed a glimmer of understanding we pulled to one side. There were two men who spoke good German, I impressed on them the need to make sure that their fellow villagers understood a few words of German within the next hour. Hour after hour went by, one by one the houses were burned to the ground, some villagers were shot on a variety of spurious pretexts, the rest set to digging the huge hole. I made a rough count, there were around seven hundred of them engaged in digging, did they realize what they were doing, digging their own grave? And if they did, what could they do about it? Dirlewanger strutted up to me.

"That seems like a large number of sympathizers, Schaffer. Are you sure they're all reliable?"

He marched up to the group and snapped out, "Do you support the German cause?"

Six voices shouted in unison, "Jawohl, Herr Sturmbannfuhrer," in the most execrable German I had ever heard, but it was all we'd had time to teach them and enough for him. I suppressed a smile as he nodded in approval, "Good, good," and walked away. But it would have been the only smile on that day. With my two fellow concentration camp survivors I led the 'reliables', there were one hundred and four of them, away from the village with supposed instructions to walk to the next village, find out if there were partisans hiding there and report them to the nearest German unit. Instead, I told them about our next objective, Zabloitse.

"You need to get there and warn them, I believe it's about twenty miles away."

A savage looking Russian, or Belorussian, stared at me intently. He was a slim, wiry figure, his clothes ragged and full of holes but beneath his grimy, bearded face. I detected a strength inside him, a fighting sprit.

"Why are you telling us this, fascist? Are you planning to shoot us as soon as we turn our backs?"

Only Gerd and Karl-Heinz were within earshot, I told him that the three of us were concentration camp survivors. He looked disbelieving.

"What about the rest of our people?" he gestured towards the crowd who were toiling to dig the mass grave.

"I'm sorry, I think you know their fate. If we could stop it we would, but there are three of us and almost two hundred of them. You know it is impossible to save them."

He nodded and reached out his hand to shake mine. I knocked it away savagely, he jumped back.

"I'm sorry, but if they see me being too friendly they would be suspicious. Warn your people in Zabloitse. You must be in touch with the partisans, can you not get them to help?"

"I am a partisan, so yes, perhaps we could organize an ambush to attack your people. You could be killed, though."

"Do it, we'll take out chances, we want no part of this

butchery. Tell me, what's your name?"

"Vladimir Pushkin. Pushkin, like the writer. And who are you?"

I introduced myself. "We're staying at the Karl Marx Hotel in Minsk. You can contact us there if you need to."

"You really want to help us?"

"Yes, I do. Keep in touch, this murderous bunch of thugs needs to be stopped."

"Do you know that we have our own problems in the Soviet Union?"

"I'm sure you do," I replied. "I can't do anything about that, but I can at least try on this side of the lines."

We all jumped as the gunfire started, then the screams split the afternoon sunshine. I looked across, the crowd of villagers stood on the edge of the pit they had dug, many had fallen in, others were falling as they were shot or simply were pushed by the weight of bodies that fell against them.

"You'd better go, my friend, in case our commanding officer changes his mind."

"Yes, I'll do what I can for Zabloitse. Thank you."

"Good luck."

They ran along the track, jogging as fast as they could away from the slaughter of their fellows, as soon as they reached the nearby wood they left the track and disappeared. I prayed for another pair of Sturmoviks to appear and machine gun the Sonderbattalion Dirlewanger together with the police unit they were supporting, but the Devil looks after his own and the sky remained clear. The shooting went on and on and the screams cut through my very soul, I decided that it was too much to bear. There had to be a way to stop some of this fearful slaughter, not here, not today, but I resolved to form a plan to work towards stopping it. There was one awful duty we had to attend to, though.

"Karl-Heinz, Gerd, we need to get down to the burial pit and do some shooting. Over their heads, of course, but we need to make it to look good if we're going to survive. Afterwards, I'm going to find a way to hit back at these bastards, are you with me?"

They both nodded firmly. "Just give the word," Gerd said.

"I'd sooner die that see much more of this," Karl-Heinz added solemnly.

We walked down to the mass of screaming villagers and fired a few ragged shots over their heads. Soon there were only occasional screams of agony from the wounded, slowly they died away as the troopers went about their grisly task.

"I think we should go and check out those barns, Sir, in case anyone is sheltering in them," I said to Dirlewanger. He looked across at the wooden buildings.

"Yes, good idea, Schaffer, burn them when you're finished."

"Yes, Sir."

My platoon had found a store of vodka in the village and had looted a barrel of the fiery spirit. They were already drunk and in no position to come with us across to the barns. We walked towards them, our guns cocked ready to fire. There were three nearby barns, we reached the first one, opened the door and rushed in, but it was empty.

"Gerd, set fire to it, we've no choice, we'll go over to the next one."

We rushed into the second barn but it was equally empty. I waited while Karl-Heinz set fire to it, Gerd joined us and we approached the third barn. It also appeared to be empty, I was about to give the order to torch it when something stopped me. There was a thin layer of straw on the ground, I thought I saw it move.

"Be careful men, I think there's someone here."

"It could be an animal," Gerd said dubiously.

"We'll see. Brush that straw to one side, we'll cover you."

He kicked the straw away, pointing his machine pistol at the ground. We could now see a small hatch set into the floor of the barn, someone must have been about to come up when they heard us enter, the movement I'd seen was probably the hatch dropping back down.

"I'll open the hatch, cover me if anyone starts shooting."

They nodded and took up positions either side. I ripped away the hatch and jumped to one side. They were children in there, perhaps twenty of them, the oldest was twelve or thirteen years old. None of them were armed. They were shaking with fear when they saw us, the German uniforms, the distinctive helmets, the machine pistols.

"Christ, now what do we do?" Karl-Heinz asked.

"Does anyone speak German? We're not going to hurt you."

"I do," a boy said, he was about eleven years old.

I explained to him about the murderous troops outside.

"We've already freed some of your people," I told him.

"They've taken the road to Zabloitse, do you know where that is?"

He nodded. "Yes, I know Zabloitse, my aunt and uncle live there."

"Good, listen to me. Leave the barn from the side away from the soldiers and move towards the wood. If anyone shouts at you or starts shooting, just keep running, ok?"

"I'll try, but some of them are very frightened."

"You're not frightened are you?"

He thought for a moment. "A bit."

"Be brave for the others, they need you. Now go!"

They climbed up out of the hatch and went to the side of the barn away from our troops. Karl-Heinz and Gerd were there, they'd kicked a wooden panel out of the side of the barn to make an exit door for the children. One by one, they slipped out. They were almost all through when I heard someone come into the barn.

"Hey, what's going on?"

It was two of our SS policemen, they were both reeling, drunk with the looted vodka.

"It's ok, we found them in here, we're rounding them up."

We looked suspicious but they were so drunk that they couldn't work it out. Their machine pistols were slung on their shoulders, they weren't expecting any more action. The last of the children slipped out of the opening and the two SS police looked at them stupidly.

"Hey, Untersturmfuhrer, they're escaping."

"Yes, I believe they are," I replied. Then I lifted the barrel of my MP38 and fired a long burst into both of them. Gerd and Karl-Heinz looked stunned.

"Get out, both of you!" I snapped at them. "Start shouting that there are partisans in here."

They dashed out and I heard them start shouting, other men were answering, 'how many of them, where had they come from'. I took the MP38s from the two dead men and found a narrow crack in the woodwork of the barn, pushed the barrels through and emptied both clips in the direction of our soldiers. Warning calls and more shouts erupted from the troops and police, a few shots cracked against the side of the barn. I ran back, threw the guns down next to the corpses, set light to the bales of straw piled at the back and squeezed through the hole where the children had left and exited the barn. There was one thing left to do, I snapped a stick grenade off my harness, pulled the pin, pushed it back through the hole in the side of the barn and ran.

More men had started firing into the barn, shots were going everywhere, smoke and flames were oozing out of the hole in the wall, then the grenade exploded. It seemed to fan the flames, they caught even more fiercely and I had to retreat from the heat. A few more moments and I judged it was enough. I ran to the edge of the barn and shouted to our men.

"I'm coming around, don't shoot, hold your fire!"

They heard me, the shooting died away and I walked slowly and warily into full view of the troops. Dirlewanger pushed through them and ran up to me.

"What's going on, Schaffer?"

"Partisans, Sir, four of them. They got two of the men when they came to search the barn. I was at the back, I think I got two of them, the others got away."

"So they're cooking inside the barn, are they?" he said with satisfaction. "A pity about our men, but we won't need a pyre for them, will we?"

He turned to the men. "Two of our soldiers died here, men. Let's give them a final salute."

He saluted and the rest of us joined him to give a final send-off to the two rapists, thieves and murderers whose bodies burned inside the wooden building. After a minute, he put his hand down.

"That'll do, men, we need to push on to Zabloitse. Kraus, get those SS police into their vehicles, they can follow us."

We mounted the trucks and drove through the evening and into the early hours of the morning, most of the men snored, drunk and asleep on the looted vodka. They were too far gone to mount any kind of a guard, but as light faded and we drove on through the dark night there was little likelihood of being attacked from the air. We were a sitting duck for the partisans, hardly anyone on guard and I couldn't be troubled to push them to do it. The mass murder at Borki was so enormous that I felt that anything these soldiers got they deserved. I almost prayed for the partisans to attack, whether I was killed or not just didn't matter, I could almost welcome death. We arrived a mile outside Zabloitse at two in the morning.

Dirlewanger was still as charged and energetic as he had been the previous day. He cajoled the troops to laager the vehicles, posted sentries and told the officers to instruct the men to get some sleep and wake at five to go into the village. It was laughable, most of the men had been sleeping since we left Borki and it would need a bomb to wake them, but we all nodded solemnly. He left Kraus in command and went forward with Sturmscharfuhrer Mintel and two troopers to reconnoiter the village. I found a spot to doze and lay down to get some rest after the long drive through the night. It was short lived, Karl-Heinz shook me awake almost as soon as I fell asleep, or so I thought.

"It's five am, Sir, time to get moving."

"Thank you, Scharfuhrer."

I staggered out from under my shelter and began the process of getting my platoon ready for the forthcoming action. I formed them up, in a very unmilitary way. They stood around in a ragged, filthy, bleary-eyed group. They looked to me more like a band of cutthroat bandits than a platoon of soldiers, but of course, that was exactly what they were. It was an odd part of Nazi life that the innocent were frequently imprisoned and slaughtered whilst the guilty were given guns and uniforms and free rein to plunder, pillage and murder. The CO shouted for the whole battalion to form up ready to march in. He ordered the police unit to march behind.

"They don't seem to be expecting trouble, I've had a good look around the village in the night."

I felt depressed, hadn't Pushkin managed to warn them before we arrived, to get them away to a place of safety?

"I want the platoons to block all sides of the village, north, south, east and west. Machine gunners set up a blocking position at either end of the track, there's only one way in and one way out. Be careful when you open fire, all of you remember that our troops will have surrounded the village, so aim carefully. There's a large building, the only large building in the place, it looks like a school. If we handle it properly we can herd the prisoners in there and deal with them all afterwards. Usual tactics, knock down the doors, get them out and set fire to their cottages. Clear?"

"How many people are we expecting, Sir?" I asked him.

"Good question, Schaffer. About four hundred and fifty, I believe."

We moved away to our positions. Gerd was stricken, I felt equally sick to the stomach. Karl-Heinz seemed to have frozen into a disbelieving daze. "We can't kill them, Sir, surely? Is this going to be like that last place?"

"Keep your voice down. Let's hope that Pushkin managed to get some of them out. All we can do now is to fire over their heads."

"It won't stop the others shooting them, will it?" Gerd said bitterly.

"No, it won't stop them, I'm afraid."

The troops went in. While we watched they broke into people's homes, dragged out screaming occupants and escorted them to the school, where they were forced inside under guard. As dawn broke, flames and smoke were already licking out of people's cottages and yet still the brutal clearance went on. House after house was smashed into, people dragged away, occasionally there was the odd shot as an unwilling resident was killed, but in the main they gave in and allowed themselves to be dragged off to the school. There was only one ameliorating factor, many of the cottages were empty. It seemed Pushkin had managed to get there first and persuaded a good number of them to run away. Still, it was all sickeningly familiar, smoke, flames, gunshots and screaming civilians. They managed to get most of them locked inside the school.

That was when the partisans attacked.

Two troopers were about to set a cottage alight when they were bowled over by two well-aimed rifle shots. Someone shouted aloud. "Partisans, take cover!"

We dived to the ground, more rifles were shooting at us now, and then a machine gun opened fire. Our own troops were stunned into immobility, horrified at the unexpected attack and unaware of where the shots were coming from. Dirlewanger ran around, shouting, encouraging and threatening them.

"Come on, men, there are only a few of them, they're in the trees, we need to fight them off! Machine gunners, open fire, the rest of you, follow me!"

He charged across a narrow strip of open field towards the clump of trees where the partisans appeared to be hiding, bullets flicked all around him but miraculously he wasn't hit. Twenty men found the courage to follow him, then another ten were shamed into standing up and running after them. Dirlewanger led his squad bravely straight into the trees with all guns blazing, there were screams and shouts, shots, more bursts of machine gun fire, then it went quiet. After a few minutes he led the men out and back over to us.

"Bastards disappeared, they killed three of my men before they left. Damnit, I'd like to have slaughtered the lot of them. Partisans, I'll spit on the grave of each and every one of them!"

He caught his breath and shouted for Sturmscharfuhrer Mintel.

"How far have we got, Mintel?

"All the villagers are in the school building, Sir, the cottages are mostly alight, the men are finishing off the last of them now."

The bloody work was indeed, almost done. Dozens of peasant cottages were in flames, the street was bare of anyone other than soldiers, and the corpses of some of the victims who hadn't moved fast enough for them. Once again, the sweet smell of roasting human flesh was starting to waft around the village as those shot in their houses started to burn.

"Very well. Kraus," he shouted, "where are you?"

"Sir," the adjutant waited at attention for orders, it was almost laughable, in this place of plunder and death, as if to pretend it was a proper military operation.

"You can tell the police unit that they can go in and finish of those partisans and Jews."

"All of them, Sir?"

Even Kraus looked surprised.

"All of them, tell them to hurry up, we've still got one more village to sanitize, Borysovka. It's about an hour away from here so we haven't got all day. You can call in the troops on the cordon first and get them loaded in the trucks while the police are dealing with the prisoners."

"Yes, Sir."

Kraus shouted more orders to a nearby group of officers and sent Mintel to the east side of the village to recall the cordon, then went himself to the west side and brought the men in from there. They started to board the trucks and he ran over to the police commander and gave him orders to deal with the prisoners. The execution squad doubled over to the school and stood in a group outside, cocked their weapons and charged in. The sound of machine pistols firing constantly seemed to cut through to my very soul. They went on forever, the shots, the screams, the shouts. Then it was all over and the police came out and set fire to the building. They doubled back as flames were licking around the school.

"All done, Sturmbannfuhrer."

"About time too, hurry up and board your vehicles, then follow me."

In the back of our truck as it lurched and jolted along the track Gerd was almost in tears. Karl-Heinz bore a frozen expression, refusing to acknowledge the enormity of what had happened. The three of us were on our own at the back of the truck, ostensibly keeping watch to our rear. The other troops were drinking and swapping jokes with each other. Gerd Rundheim put his face close to mine and whispered. "It's got to stop, Sir. What can we do?"

"I wish I knew, Gerd. That partisan knows were we're staying in Minsk, maybe he'll contact us and we can set up some kind of resistance."

"We could join the resistance, couldn't we?"

I laughed. "Yes, we could. How long do you think that hated and despised members of SS Dirlewanger would last in a partisan unit, no matter what we've done for them. They hate us, Gerd, hate us with an intensity that is hard to believe. They'd shoot us down like dogs given half a chance."

He nodded. "You're right, so we fight them from inside, is that the plan?"

"It's the only way, my friend."

We reached the village of Borysovka, another poverty-stricken settlement of peasant cottages and huts. Once again, we formed up outside the village and Dirlewanger strutted around like a warlord from an epic tale from ancient history.

"This is the last one, men. I want this done quickly, straight in, just get into the houses, kill them, torch the buildings and get out. I want to be on the way home to Minsk in time for dinner. Get moving!"

The men were tired from the previous two operations, some half-drunk, many hung over, they staggered into Borysovka like automatons, it was frightening to see the way they conducted the operation. Doors were kicked in, screams, shouts, shots fired, sometimes a short bust of semi-automatic fire, then the wisps of smoke and tendrils of flames started to appear as the squad moved on to the next cottage. Kraus was running behind them with a clipboard, trying to keep up a tally so that the CO could put it in his report. I had managed to keep my platoon away from the carnage, we were mounting guard outside the area, patrolling the outskirts of the village in case partisans attacked suddenly. But it was not to be, the wretched inhabitants of Borysovka were not destined to be saved, the murders went on. Then one of my men saw a family making a run for the wood, they were almost there. He raised his MP38 but I knocked it to one side.

"What the fuck did you do that for, I could have had them all?" he snarled.

"And ruin my fun, Schutze Fischer? I'm going hunting for them, it's called officer's privilege."

He grunted. "That's unfair, I saw them first, I should have some fun with them."

"I promise you the next lot, soldier."

"You'd better."

"Gerd, come with me, Karl-Heinz, you look after the platoon."

We raced after the escapees. "We need to make this look good, Gerd, or they'll rip our guts out."

He didn't reply, just kept running, struggling to draw breath. We crashed into the trees and plunged through the wood. We ran for a hundred yards before we caught up with them, they had stopped by the side of a fast flowing river, the mother appeared to be urging the family to go north, the father for them to cross the dangerous current to the far bank. They saw us and instantly froze, the only movement was them shivering with fear.

"Does anyone speak German?" I asked them.

A girl of about twelve years old replied.

"I learned a little in school."

She looked half-starved, very thin, her clothes ragged. But however bad their existence on the fringes of Belorussian society, she was entitled to enjoy it without Dirlewanger's murderous thugs exterminating the whole village.

"Listen, we can help you escape. Which is the quickest way out?"

She spoke rapidly to her parents. The father started to speak, but the mother cut across him.

"North, but why are you doing this? Is it a trick?"

"There is no time to explain. You'll hear some shots, don't be frightened, we need to make it look as if we've killed you."

I ripped off my pack and rummaged for food, gave them some bread, cheese and a piece of dried meat. Gerd did the same and they held the pitiful pile of food in their hands. It wasn't much, but it might ward off starvation for now.

"Go, now!"

They ran, following the riverbank to the north. We waited until they were clear, and then emptied our MP38s into the river.

"Make this look good, Gerd. We killed them and threw them in the river, right. Five of them."

"Got it, don't worry."

"I hope so, they'll send us back to Mauthausen if they think we let them go."

We returned to my men and went on back to the battalion. The village was destroyed, every building burned to the ground, including the school with its complement of corpses. As we drove back to Minsk, I thought seriously about my next move.

Every time I saw a corpse now it had Lisl's face, I thought I might be losing my mind. At times, I thought seriously about ending this journey through hell, several times I even took out my pistol to look at it fondly like an old friend that would travel with me on my journey to hell.

"We managed to save a few, Paul," Gerd said. I looked up, it was rare to hear him use my Christian name in such a personal way, but he was trying to get through to me.

"It's not enough, my friend, nowhere near enough."

"And if you kill yourself, even those few wouldn't have been saved. Would you deny them their lives?"

I was out of answers, out of ideas, my mind could only picture hundreds and hundreds of corpses and every time I looked closely, it was Lisl.

IRON CROSS AMERIKA

CHAPTER SIX

'Democracy alone, of all forms of government, enlists the full force of men's enlightened will. It is the most humane, the most advanced, and, in the end, the most unconquerable of all forms of human society. The democratic aspiration is no mere recent phase of human history. We would rather die on our feet than live on our knees.'

Franklin Delano Roosevelt

We returned to Minsk and were given five days in which to stand down to repair, re-arm and re-equip the battalion. During that time ten more recruits arrived, all were reprieved murderers from different prisons and camps in Germany. Evidently, the Reich Sicherheits Haupt Amt (RHSA), the bureaucratic organization that administered the Sonderbattalion Dirlewanger, had decided that these people would be in good company, ideally suited to our kind of so-called 'anti-partisan' work. They were probably right. Dirlewanger said casually that we might be moved shortly to Poland, to Warsaw, where the Reichsfuhrer was growing concerned at the numbers of Jews hiding in the Ghetto. Until then, we were to take a rest. The police unit that we had supported in the massacre at the three villages, Police Battalion 310, took over a nearby hotel, the Hotel Heroes of the Revolution. I did my best to stay away from them the reeking, brutal, drunken sadists. Once the platoon's vehicles and weapons were overhauled, I went into Minsk with Gerd and Karl-Heinz. It was slightly risky going into the city centre with fewer men, but I'd had more than I could stomach of the Dirlewanger for a lifetime and the three of us needed privacy to talk. We were all of the same mind. We found our way to a bar in a back street of the city and sat at a filthy table.

"Waiter, three beers," Gerd shouted.

The man muttered something surly and went behind the bar. Soon, we heard footsteps approaching and a voice said, "Gentlemen."

We looked up, I raised a hand to take my glass of beer and stared into the barrel of a sub-machine gun, a Russian PPSh. The man that held it was not the barman.

"Do not reach for your weapons, I could empty the magazine in this place and no one would notice, this area is well known for being wild and unlawful, nobody will come to your aid. Get up, put your hands over your heads and come with us."

I looked around, he wasn't alone. Two other partisans, for that's what they were of course, were standing nearby one either side of us, each held a pistol.

"Where are we going?" I had to ask, in this country of

agony and death I felt it was every man's right to know where his end was going to be.

"Just come with us, we'll ask the questions."

Karl-Heinz and Gerd half rose. "Sit down, both of you," I said to them. "If they're going to kill us they can do it here like men, we're not going to die in some dark, squalid corner." They sat back down. Even as I spoke it struck me that we were in fact already in a dark, squalid corner, would they take my words as an invite?

"We're not going to kill you, fascist. There's someone who wants to speak to you."

I wasn't sure whether to believe him. I had a sudden thought, someone had seen us letting the prisoners go, this could easily be a Gestapo trick.

"Men, we'd better go with them." I got up and the three of us followed the gunman, the two men with the pistols came behind us.

"Watch what you say, they could be Gestapo, it could be a setup, even a test," I murmured to Gerd and Karl-Heinz. They both nodded.

They marched us out of a back door and into a narrow, claustrophobic alley behind the bar. The man in front checked carefully, then beckoned us to follow him further along the alley. We walked a few more yards and he entered the open doorway of a wrecked house, all of the woodwork and windows were missing, even the roof had gone, it was just a shell. An ideal place for an execution, I gave a meaningful look to Gerd and Karl-Heinz and put my hand down near my pistol holster. I'd hoped they wouldn't see, but although it was dark there was sufficient moonlight for them to notice my move.

"Don't touch your pistol, fascist, or I'll kill you."

I took my hand away and we stood waiting. For what, a bullet in the back? But if it was the Gestapo, there would surely be a fake offer to join the partisans, perhaps to sell them weapons or spy for them. A fourth man entered the room from the other side of the building. In the moonlight, I suddenly recognized him. Pushkin, Vladimir Pushkin. He came up and shook my hand warmly.

"SS man, thank you again for saving my people."

We all relaxed. "Vladimir, it's good to see you, I thought this was a partisan or Gestapo trap."

He laughed. "Not this time, SS."

"For God's sake, call me Paul. This is Karl-Heinz and Gerd." They both shook hands with him.

"Do you still wish to help us, all three of you?"

"More than ever," I replied.

I told him about the events at Borysovka, after we'd left Borki and Zabloitse.

"You got some of your people out of Zabloitse, at least we saved a few."

"We did, yes, thanks to your warning. We saved two hundred, the rest were determined to stay, the fools didn't believe us. They thought it was a trick to steal their livestock and possessions."

"What do you want of us, Vladimir?"

"We need information, intelligence on where your battalion is ordered to next, the routes you will be taking and the numbers of soldiers involved. Can you do that?"

I thought about it for a moment, but it wasn't anything too difficult. "Yes, we can do that. I assume you plan to evacuate the villages and maybe ambush our column before they get there?"

He smiled. "All of that, yes. We need to know how to identify your own vehicle so that you don't get killed."

"We'll work something out, do you have any ideas, men?"

"Sir, we could put something bloodthirsty on the side of the truck," Gerd said, "that way they'd think we were really committed murderers. A skull and crossbones would be good, something like that."

"I like it, yes, they'll never suspect. Vladimir, we'll paint a pirate flag, black background, white skull and crossbones, how does that sound?"

The Belorussian smiled. "It sounds fine, but you know that it will make you a target for every partisan that comes across you and doesn't know you're with us? The skull and crossbones is widely associated with your SS death squads."

"I don't care, we've seen so much slaughter, we feel that we're dead already."

"That may be so, but if you are killed we'll lose our source of information."

All three of us smiled, it was backhanded appreciation, but still, it was better than nothing.

"We'll just have to take that chance, I'm afraid. Listen, Vladimir, the word is that our unit may be moved to Poland, probably the capital, Warsaw. Can you connect us with any of your people there?"

"The Communist Party has fighters everywhere, Paul. In fact, I have business to attend to in Poland, I may well go there myself, it would be good to keep our arrangement going on a personal basis. Others may not trust you, any of you."

Karl-Heinz got out a bottle to celebrate our new partnership, it seemed we had now officially joined the partisans. I felt a weight lifted off my mind, we were fighting back, not just passively firing over prisoners heads or allowing a few to escape. If we were careful, we could play our part in defeating the Nazi scourge that had descended over Europe like a stinking plague.

"We have a contact in Warsaw, can you remember Ost House? It's a dressmakers, they make uniforms as well as evening gowns and suits. If you look them up, ask for the owner and give her the password, Borki. Is that clear?"

"I've got it, yes, Borki, that's good."

"When I know that your unit has moved to Poland I'll make arrangements to travel to our partisan cell in Warsaw, if all goes well we can make contact. But until then, contact Ost House. Do you have anything for us now?"

"Nothing at present, no. Except the unit that organized the massacre. It was Police Battalion 310. They're billeted in a nearby hotel."

"We'd sure like to hit them, what can you tell me?"

"They'd be an easy target, my friend. Although they're called a battalion, there are no more than fifty or sixty of them and most of those are permanently drunk. Hit them in the middle of the night and you could take out all of them in one go."

He looked thoughtful. "How would you suggest we do it?"

I shrugged. "I've no idea, I'm not really a soldier, as you know. I'm just trying to stay alive."

"As we all are. Do you have any ideas?" he asked Gerd and Karl-Heinz."

"Explosives," Karl-Heinz said, the old soldier. "Fifty pounds of high explosives on the ground floor should do it, a drum of gasoline next to it. Anything that's not destroyed in the explosion will burn."

"We can't get access to explosives that easily, it could take time," Vladimir said.

"But we can."

They all looked at me. "There are dozens of crates of explosives in the armory, we should be able to make a couple of them disappear together with a drum of gasoline. I'll do a snap inspection at dawn tomorrow, the men will all be asleep with hangovers, we'll just carry two boxes out to the truck. Gerd, you can help me with that, Karl-Heinz, I'll leave it to you to make sure the drum of fuel is loaded ready. Where do you want us to bring it?"

"Do you know the camera store off Barricades Street? Brodskis?"

"We'll find it," Gerd said.

"There's a street behind there with the back entrance to the storeroom of the camera store. Deliver it there, we'll be waiting for you."

We returned to the hotel with a new mood of optimism, we had a chance to remove some of the stench of the battalion from ourselves. Karl-Heinz promised to wake us both early and it was indeed still dark when he shook me awake. I simply walked to the armory with Gerd and went to unlock the door, but it proved to be unlocked already, no doubt the armorer was drunk. In fact, he was fast asleep, snoring like an industrial saw. We removed two cases of explosives and went out to the vehicle park, where Karl-Heinz stood waiting by our truck. He had loaded the gasoline ready, Gerd drove us into the city and we looked for the back entrance to the camera store. We kept a careful watch for Feldgendarmerie and local police, but there was not a single person or vehicle moving on the road. I checked my watch, it was fifteen minutes past five, if everything went well we could be back before the city or the battalion, started to wake up. As we drew up the door opened and Vladimir came out, he had a pistol in his hand held low by his side.

"Any problems?"

"None, but we need to unload and get back quickly."

Two partisans had already come out to the truck and were manhandling the supplies off the back and into the storeroom. We shook hands.

"Until Warsaw, my friend," I said to Vladimir.

"Until then, and thank you, we'll make sure this is put to good use."

I climbed back into the truck and Gerd drove away, we got back to the Karl Marx Hotel and still the battalion slept soundly, there wasn't even a sentry in evidence.

Two days later, we were on a train heading west to Warsaw. Our unit's trucks were loaded on flat cars at the back of the train, our three anti-tank guns lashed down with them, our stores and equipment safely stowed in the boxcars next to them. We had almost the whole train to ourselves, there were only two carriages at the front behind the engine taking casualties back to the Reich. As usual, the men were drunk, shouting, arguing, a couple of fights broke out, many of them were playing cards, gambling away their pay. I was in an officers' compartment with Max and Heinrich.

"Did you hear about those poor bastards up front, the casualties in the front two carriages?" Heinrich asked.

I shook my head.

"That police unit we helped out the other week, you remember the anti-partisan operation at Borki and those other two Soviet shitholes?"

"SS Police Battalion 310, you mean?"

"That's the one. Some of the unit was out on patrol, the rest were in their billet at their hotel in Minsk, the bloody place blew up, then caught fire."

"Really, Heinrich, that sounds pretty bad. So they took a lot of casualties, the men left in the hotel?"

"Half of them were killed outright, the other half are mixed in with those casualties up at the front of this train, most of them were badly burned. Most of the wounded on this train are from the fighting at the front, probably Stalingrad, they say they're taking heavy casualties up there."

I didn't feel at all upset or guilty at the thought of the murderous police unit blown to pieces, most of them, anyway. Maybe the partisans would get a chance to finish off the rest of them before long.

"What's the news on Stalingrad?"

There were eight officers in the compartment, all talking optimistically about the progress of the war. When I mentioned Stalingrad, they went quiet.

"What? What's the problem?"

Two of the officers, both new to the battalion, were glaring at me. One of them snapped, "You don't know what it's like, do you?"

He had a patch over one eye, it made him look very warlike. I shook my head.

"How could I, there are no SS units at Stalingrad?"

"We were both there, the Sixth Army under General von Paulus," he said. "I left my eye in that fucking city, and Hans here left part of his leg."

The other officer tapped his lower right leg with his knuckle, it was made of wood.

"We were both injured in the fighting, we volunteered for this SS police unit rather than go back to the Cauldron."

"So it's that bad, eh?"

He laughed bitterly. "That bad, I'm afraid it's much worse than 'that bad'. No matter how many of them we kill, there are always more to take their place. Kill two men and three more step forward to replace them. They defend every building as if it contains the Tsar's family jewels. They constantly snipe at us, their ambushes are an everyday occurrence and no matter what we do they always seem to have a new trick ready for the next time we attack. Every day they bring more and more reinforcements across the Volga, we can't seem to stop them.

"What about the Luftwaffe, I heard we had complete control over the skies?"

He laughed again. "General Wolfram von Richthofen commands the Luftwaffe for Army Group South, he's a good man, but he only had a limited number of aircraft. Maybe the Luftwaffe do control the skies, but every time a bomb drops and destroys a boat, they bring up two more. Destroy a Soviet aircraft, they put two more up in the sky. Destroy a hundred men and they bring two hundred. God only knows where they get them all from but they always seem to find them. And the winter, my God, we didn't have nearly enough cold weather gear last winter and they've done nothing to supply us with anymore for this winter. When we heard about your unit, we jumped at the chance to get out."

"So it's looking bad at Stalingrad, is that what you're saying, surely not?"

They looked at each other, then at the other officers who were listening intently.

"No, no, we're not saying that. The Fuhrer has said that we will beat them, so of course it must be true. No doubt he will send in his miracle weapons soon and the Russians will be destroyed."

He looked around guiltily. I didn't believe that any of the officers were in any doubt about the real situation. I had a different agenda, a different war to fight but even so I was puzzled. The German armies had not been defeated so far in this war. Did it mean that things were changing? Despite their denials, these two officers from the Sixth Army believed they were. I thought of the piles of bloody, burned bodies, slaughtered by the Sonderbattalion Dirlewanger, it couldn't happen soon enough.

When we steamed into Warsaw, we stopped opposite a long row of boxcars. Our unit began to detrain, I supervised the unloading of our vehicles from the flat cars. Across the tracks the boxcars were surrounded by dozens of SS police, their machine pistols pointed at the containers as if they contained something dangerous. Then I saw something that chilled my blood, a thin, bony hand emerged from a crack in the woodwork of the nearest car. They contained people, prisoners. I walked a little nearer, careful to keep my eyes fixed on our vehicles, I didn't want to be noticed displaying undue attention to a trainload of prisoners. The Reich guarded its security jealously and I had already tasted the penalty for trying to interfere with prisoners. I could smell them now, above the smoky, coal dust smell of the railway station mixed with the dust and filth of decades. It was the stink of humanity, the stench of human waste, sweat, urine, excrement, vomit and fear. There was a constant, low hum, the moaning of pain and despair, I thought of my months in Mauthausen, but this was worse, much worse. I assumed that at the end of the line they were to be taken out and shot, just as I'd seen happen in Belorussia. I turned away and paid attention to the unloading, there was nothing I could do, nothing at all. Gerd was watching me, he gave me a sympathetic glance and a slight shake of his head, the meaning was clear. Leave it alone, survive for this day.

I had another shock as I turned back to organize the unloading of our equipment. A man was watching me, trilby hat, leather trench coat, a face as hard as an Arctic winter. Gestapo, of course, but there was something familiar about him. He came nearer and with a shock I recognized him as Mischer, Kriminalassistent Mischer, the Gestapo man I'd first met in the cellars at Prinz Albrecht Strasse in Berlin. He gave me a thin smile.

"Untersturmfuhrer Schaffer, I see you have been assigned to new duties. How was your stay in Mauthausen, pleasant, I trust?"

But it was different now, I was an SS officer on active service in a war zone, not a cowering prisoner in a Gestapo cellar.

"What do you want, Mischer, we're rather busy fighting the Red Army."

"Yes, I was in the radio room when the report came in on your action at Borysovka. Had some fun, did you?"

"Not really, no, we were just doing our duty."

"Really?" his smiled widened. "Let me tell you, Schaffer, I'm doing my duty too, here in Warsaw. There are too many terrorists and partisans interfering with our operations, Governor Frank has given us a free hand to deal with the problem. You should know that it means we have power over all SS personnel, regardless of rank. But of course, I know I can rely on you to be helpful, can't I? You wouldn't wish to go back to the camp, my friend?"

Just then, a large hand trolley piled with wooden crates was coming towards us, Mischer was standing in its path. It was being pushed by two soldiers, I jerked him out of the way as the two troopers pushed it past us, their vision blocked by the sheer size and weight of boxes on the trolley. He looked startled, his face was pale, frightened by the near miss.

"Mischer, war zones are dangerous places, I suggest you leave me to do my job and you do yours."

He looked after the truck that had almost flattened him and nodded thoughtfully.

"Yes, I will do my job, never fear, Untersturmfuhrer Schaffer. You may be assured of that."

He looked as if he was trying to make up his mind as to whether or not to go after the two troopers, but he evidently thought better of if and walked away towards the station exit.

We completed unloading the vehicles and stores, climbed aboard the trucks and drove away. Dirlewanger as usual stood upright in the front of his Kubelwagen, a dangerous exhibition in an occupied city such as Warsaw, but I now knew that life and death to him were all part of the same game. I doubted that he even understood that there was a line between the two of them. We were once again billeted in a hotel, the Nova Rest Hotel about a mile from the Jewish Ghetto. The RSHA had arranged with the Governor of Warsaw that we would have exclusive use of the building, which featured a spacious gated and cobbled courtyard for our vehicles. As soon as we arrived, the men ignored orders to unload the ammunition and equipment and they ran inside to find the bar. By the time I got to them with three other officers to assist, they'd knocked the barman to the floor where he cowered in terror while they helped themselves to Polish vodka. We looked at each other, shrugged and went back outside. When the men were like this, drinking heavily, they were at their most dangerous. After all, they were the Sonderbattalion Dirlewanger, thieves, rapists and killers. We finally rounded up enough men who were still sober to unload the trucks and I found the room I had been assigned. One benefit of being billeted in a hotel was that it meant having your own room, provided you were an officer. When I'd unpacked my few possessions I went down to the hotel dining room, now serving as Dirlewanger's 'planning room', or so he said.

"My friends, we can have three days to relax and get to know the city, then our work begins in earnest. Obergruppenfuhrer Frank, the Gauleiter of the General Government formerly known as Poland, has expressed his wish for us to go into the Ghetto and start to clear out the Jews. He told me frankly that he believes there are far too many of them skulking in there. That's the job he's given us, so relax and enjoy yourselves, then we roll up our sleeves and get to work. Dismissed."

I picked up my hat and walked to the door of the hotel. Max and Heinrich were standing nearby.

"Leaving us, Schaffer?" Max asked in his usual supercilious tone. I was determined to be pleasant to him, he could be dangerous, but then again he had suffered badly in the concentration camp with Karl-Heinz, Gerd and me so he was entitled to the benefit of the doubt. He was another survivor.

"I'm going to see the sights of the city, Max. They say it has plenty of places worth looking at. While I'm at it I intend to find a good tailor and buy myself a new uniform."

We'd been paid, Kraus, the adjutant had come around with Mintel and we were all given a month's wages and a hefty bonus. I felt guilty accepting it, the money was quite obviously looted, but I needed it to go forward with my efforts for the resistance.

"What a good idea, let us know if you find anything worthwhile."

"I'll do that."

The streets of Warsaw were teaming with people, shabby, hungry looking people. They looked at me warily in my SS uniform, their eyes filled with fear, and hate. I had to remember how much they despised the German occupation with its attendant brutality and be careful I wasn't ambushed in some dark passageway. There were as many partisans in Poland as in Belorussia.

I had to ask nine people before the tenth gave me directions to Ost House, the dressmakers I'd been told to locate. The first people I asked looked at me with hate-filled eyes and shook their heads, two men actually spat on the street and walked on. Perhaps if I'd been with a squad of troopers they wouldn't have been so bold, but on my own I was vulnerable. The tenth person I asked, a woman, gave me directions. She was obviously a prostitute and looked at me hungrily.

"I can show you the way if you like, my apartment is quite near. I can offer you a little hospitality too."

And a cocktail of venereal diseases, no doubt. I thanked her and followed her directions to the store. It was in a quiet, upmarket part of the city, cobbled streets, old-fashioned lamp standards and little stores with bow windows. Half way along the street was a cream painted façade with an ornate sign, 'Ost House, Dressmakers'. I walked through the door, a bell rang in the back and a young woman appeared behind the counter. She was beautiful, possessing that classic, aristocratic face that you come across sometimes, finely chiseled, a cupid mouth, large, dark brown eyes under an urchin haircut. On her, it looked exquisite. Her skin was pale, smooth and alabaster-like, the overall effect of her face struck me as elfin. She greeted me without a trace of alarm, there was only a look of polite enquiry on her face.

"How may I help you, officer?"

"I am in need of a new uniform, I am told you can make me one quickly."

"Of course, if I may take some measurements I will quote you a price."

She picked up a measuring tape and a pad and pencil.

"Please stand with our hands to your sides, just relax, this won't take long. Were you planning to pay me in zlotys or deutschmarks?"

It would affect the price, of course. The German occupying authority had pegged the value of the deutschmark artificially high, it meant that the Polish zlotys were virtually worthless, but Dirlewanger had paid us in deutschmarks. She smiled.

"In that case, I can offer you a good discount."

She finished taking the measurement and filled out a long form describing the order.

"Did you have any particular style in mind? Some SS officers like small modifications to the standard uniform."

"I've heard the Borki style is rather stylish, can you do that for me?"

She looked puzzled. "I'm sorry, I haven't heard of that one."

It had to be her, she was obviously the proprietor of the business.

"I think you know it well, we have a mutual friend, I suspect."

"Who sent you here?"

"Vladimir Pushkin, from Minsk."

She went and locked the front door and put the 'closed' sign on it.

"Come with me, I have an office in the back, be careful what you say, my staff are at work."

I followed her to the back of the store, three women were working at a huge table, one was cutting fabric, the other two were busy sewing with ornate, iron treadle sewing machines. She went up a flight of stairs and I followed her into her office. She closed and locked the door and went to look out of the window. Satisfied, she sat down behind her desk and indicated the chair in front for me.

"Your name?"

I told her.

"Very well, I am Anna Ostrowski, the owner of this business. Are you sure you weren't followed here?

"I'm sure."

"Good. So what can you do for us, Untersturmfuhrer Schaffer?"

"Please call me Paul."

She nodded and smiled. "An SS officer who is a human being, that's something new. Very well, you may call me Anna. Now, what can you offer?"

"Anna, my unit has only just arrived, I've no idea what you want. To be honest, I'm new to all of this."

"We need to know what you can give us if you are going to be useful, Paul. What about information, is there anything planned for the Ghetto?"

"You mean the Warsaw Ghetto, the Jews?"

She nodded, "That's right."

"Yes, there is, we're due to go in to clear out parts of the Ghetto in three or four days."

She looked at me without speaking for a few moments, as if weighing me up. Then she went to a closet at the back of her office, moved a pile of dresses to one side and fumbled with some sort of a hidden mechanism. I could see part of the back of the closet opening like a doorway.

"You can come out now, Jakob."

A man pushed the dresses to one side walked through the closet and came through into the office. He was dressed much like the civilians I'd seen on the streets of Warsaw, shabby jacket, torn, dirty shirt, hair uncut and unkempt, broken shoes. But it was his eyes that captured my attention. They were the eyes of a fanatic, gleaming with an intense fire that threatened to devour everything they rested upon. He glared at my uniform with a colossal hatred, I could almost imagine fire jumping from his eyes, crossing the gap between us and consuming me in a ball of molten fury. He stood near Anna, almost as if to protect her from me, and what I represented. If he only knew, I had only needed one look to know that I was already half in love with this beautiful, aristocratic Pole. He looked strong, too, quite muscular, although somewhat wasted from lack of food. I reflected that he must have once been a huge, imposing man before the war brought so much destruction to his country.

"This is Jakob, Paul, Jakob Koslowski. Jakob, ignore the uniform, Paul is on our side."

I held out my hand and after thinking about if for a few seconds, he took it reluctantly and shook it.

"You heard what we were saying?" she asked him.

He nodded. "I heard."

"Jakob is a Jew," Anna said to me. "Many of his relations are still in the Ghetto. He has lost many already, killed outright or sent to Treblinka."

"Concentration camp?" I asked her.

"Death camp, SS man," Jakob spat out. "You know what that is?"

"I was in Mauthausen, yes, I know what a death camp is."

They both looked astonished. "How the hell did you get out of Mauthausen?" Anna asked.

I explained to her about the Nazi scheme to recruit men for their SS police units.

"They posted me to the Sonderbattalion Dirlewanger, most of them men are either former inmates or camp guards."

"The Dirlewanger does have a certain reputation, you must know that," Jakob said.

"My friend, I've been with them in Belorussia, I know just

what they're like. I doubt that their reputation is even as bad as the battalion really is when they go into action."

Anna intervened, explaining what she had obviously been told about me by Vladimir. It was my passport to their circle, Jakob relaxed and we talked in a friendlier manner.

"Tell me about this Treblinka," I said to them. "I've never heard of it."

"Not many have," Jakob replied. "The camp exists solely for extermination, there are a few work assignments, but the vast majority of people shipped there are murdered on arrival. They have hermetically sealed rooms where the prisoners are herded into. The Nazis have parked several captured Soviet tanks next to them, they run the exhaust smoke directly into the rooms to kill off the people inside. They even have glass portholes so that they can view their victims dying inside."

We were all silent for a while. It was hard to visualize such a horrific invention, surely the most evil invention yet from man's infinite capacity to cause pain and death.

"Did you have anything like that at Mauthausen?" he asked.

I told him about the gas vans, the shootings, the men forced to push their neighbor off the cliff face or die themselves. He nodded, "Yes, they use the gas vans here too. There seems to be no end to their ingenuity when it comes to brutality and murder."

"How can I help, what can I do to stop some of the killing?"

"It will carry on until the war is ended and Germany is defeated," Anna said.

"In that case, tell me what I can do towards that end."

We talked for an hour, discussing the various options open to us. They told me that the Jewish resistance fighters in the Ghetto were short of weapons and ammunition with which to fight the Germans.

"But they can't beat all of our armies," I said with exasperation. "How will it help them live if they have the means to fight back?"

Jakob laughed. "It's not about living, Paul. It's about fighting the Germans. We know we won't survive, most of us, we just want to make a contribution towards finishing off the Nazis, killing as many as possible before we're killed ourselves."

"But that's a death wish, Jakob. You're telling me that you're on a suicide mission."

"Isn't that what you're on, my friend? Do you think you can survive this war? You have the enemy to contend with, the Soviets, the partisans and even your own people if the Gestapo or the SS find out what you're up to."

I nodded. "You're right, I don't expect to survive. But I plan to give it a try."

"I wish you luck, then," he smiled. "Can you help us with any weapons and ammunition?"

I thought about his request. I'd already done something similar in Minsk, why not here in Warsaw?

"Yes, I think I can do something. I'll work out the plan and come back here to let Anna know the details."

"Good, I have to leave to warn my people about the attack. Three days, you say?"

"Three or four, yes, I believe so."

He nodded and left.

"If you come here again, Paul, it needs to be on the pretext of a fitting," Anna said.

"When will my uniform be ready?"

"About a week."

I smiled. "That's not soon enough, you'll have to come out to dinner with me tomorrow night, I'll give you the information you need then."

She didn't look amused. "I do not accept dinner engagements from German officers, Paul."

"In that case I'll come as a civilian."

I could see a slight smile around the corners of her lips. "Do you have a suit, a shirt and tie?"

"I can always buy them, I haven't needed them so far."

"Come with me then, we have a selection of clothing, I'll find something to fit you."

"So you'll come?"

She nodded. "Yes, if that's the only way to get you to give me the information."

It would have to do. She led the way back down the stairs and into the workroom. The three women looked nervous at the SS officer's uniform in their workplace. Anna walked through to a storeroom where there was a rack of suits and shirts.

"Find something here to suit you, these have been left my customers who sent them for repairs and disappeared."

"Jews?"

"And Polish army officers, killed during the invasion."

"You'll have a better eye for cut and fit than me, would you choose something for me?"

"Very well."

She rummaged in the racks of clothes and produced a charcoal grey formal suit. I checked the label, Chanel. The lady certainly had taste. She found me a thick, silk shirt in a muted off white and a tie that looked regimental. She saw me looking at it.

"It's a Prussian cavalry officer's tie, Paul, so you don't need to worry that it's from one of Germany's enemies."

"That's a relief, I have enough people gunning for me in this city as it is."

I tried it all on and found it fitted to perfection, she handed me a pair of shiny leather shoes.

"They're from a bespoke Warsaw shoemaker, he disappeared into Treblinka. His widow asked us to take the clothing and use if towards the resistance. She's gone too, by the way, they took her a month ago."

I checked my image in the mirror, it certainly looked good, I was the picture of a wealthy, successful industrialist or banker. Anna's eyes were shining.

"You look wonderful, Paul, I'm sure you'll be a fine dinner companion. Where are you taking me?"

"Will you choose, I'm new to the city, find somewhere nice, and expensive."

"Good, you have Deutschmarks to spend so it won't be a problem."

"I'll call around tomorrow evening and change into these clothes," I said as I took them off and put my uniform back on.

"Shall we say half past seven?"

She nodded. "That will give us time, yes, I'll see you tomorrow, but if you need to get an urgent message to me before then we have a contact at your hotel. He's working tonight in the bar, his name is Lek Kaminski. Just send it marked 'A'."

As I walked past her and went out through the door, she reached up on tiptoe and gave me a gentle kiss on the side of the cheek, then turned and closed the door. I walked back to my billet feeling as if I was walking on air.

I told Karl-Heinz and Gerd about the meeting.

"They need weapons in the Ghetto, how can we get them to them?" I asked them.

Karl-Heinz, ever the old soldier, had an idea that I was convinced would work. He came with me to find the CO, Dirlewanger was holding court in his 'planning room'.

"Sir, before our action in the Ghetto, I'd like to give the men a few hours training and weapons familiarization. With your permission, I'll schedule it for tomorrow morning, we'll take one of the outlying streets in the suburbs and run some security checks. If we find any resistance activity we can deal with it, but I doubt we will, it will just be a way of getting the men up to fighting readiness."

His eyes blazed with enthusiasm. "Excellent idea, Schaffer! Your mission is approved, I'll suggest that some of the other platoon leaders to the same thing. Carry on, well done."

Karl-Heinz had been waiting by the door, he laughed as we walked away.

"Who does he think he is, Feldmarschal Erich von

Manstein?"

Von Manstein was the architect of both the successful armored invasion of Poland and then the lightning thrust across France that defeated several armies at a single stroke.

"I have no doubt he could offer Feldmarschal von Manstein some good advice, my friend."

We broke the news to my platoon that we would be out on a training exercise in the morning.

"Full kit, men, make sure we have the MG34 and a spare in the truck as well, those barrels are prone to overheat so we'll have one ready just in case. Grenades, MP38s, bring some cases of explosives in case we need to bring down any enemy buildings or strongpoints."

One of my troopers objected. "I thought you said this was a training exercise?"

"That's correct. However, we are at war, would you prefer to go outside without suitable equipment in case we are attacked? What if we come across Polish partisans? Even Jews?"

They recoiled, the Nazi propaganda machine had done its job well. Whilst the Jews were almost all innocent civilians, businessmen, artisans, doctors, teachers, and lawyers, the Nazi had managed to fix them into the German psyche as dangerous subversives, a threat to the state. It was nonsense, but dangerous nonsense.

The platoon loaded the truck ready to leave at first light. I made certain that there were plenty of supplies of ammunition and grenades. They took the spare MG34 out of its crate and made it ready for use, Karl-Heinz suggested a few spare MP38s and I agreed to that too.

"Make sure you have plenty of spare clips, Scharfuhrer."

The rest was easy. The two troopers who were on sentry duty had been enthusiastic participants in the slaughter at the three villages, I had no interest whatsoever in whether they lived or died, they deserved to be hung for their willing participation in the mass murder. The sentries went on duty at ten o'clock, at eleven Gerd and Karl-Heinz wandered out into the hotel car park, now home to the battalion's vehicles, with two bottles of vodka. I watched from the window of my bedroom.

While they lounged against the hood of our truck drinking vodka, the two sentries watched them enviously, an overhead lamp provided some dim illumination and I could even see both sentries licking their lips at the sight of the vodka. Then they walked over, exchanged a few words with Karl-Heinz and Gerd and the vodka changed hands. My two men went back inside the hotel, the sentries sat down and started drinking, chatting to each other, totally oblivious to the fact that they were guarding a truckload of weapons in a military compound in the middle of a war zone. I went down to the bar for a drink, found the barman and left a message for Anna, I only hoped it would get through in time.

In the morning, I was awakened by a series of shouts, a siren sounded, whistles, boots clattered along the corridor outside my room. I got up and opened the door.

"What's happening?" I said to a passing soldier.

He turned, looking at me wildly. "Partisans, Sir, they've been here in the night, they killed the two sentries and stole a truck."

I went back into my room and began to pull my boots on. There was no rush.

CHAPTER SEVEN

*We look forward to a world founded upon four essential human
freedoms. The first is freedom of speech and expression everywhere
in the world. The second is freedom of every person to worship God
in his own way-everywhere in the world. The third is freedom from
want. ... The fourth is freedom from fear.'*

Franklin Delano Roosevelt

Dirlewanger raged over the theft and the murder of his two
soldiers.

"I'll round up every fucking one of those Jewboy
communists and rip their fucking guts out. Damnit, how could
this have happened?"

Kraus stood attentively at his shoulder. "Er, they'd been
drinking, Sir, both the sentries, we found the empty bottles.
Polish vodka."

"Fucking filth, I'll have it banned from our headquarters!"

"Er, there is nothing else to drink if you ban vodka, Sir,"

Kraus said apologetically.

"Go and fucking find something then," he shouted at the top of his voice. "Schaffer, I understand it was your truck they stole?"

"Yes, it was, Sir, it was loaded ready for today's exercise, I've had to cancel it."

"Of course, of course. I'll ask Divisional HQ for a replacement, God knows you might have to have something different, I don't believe they have any decent trucks to spare like the Renaults, probably some Polish piece of crap."

"We'll just have to manage, Sir, it's a blow but not one we can't get over."

"That's the spirit, Schaffer. Make do and manage."

"Yes, Sir."

"Now let's see, today's Thursday, we'll attack the Ghetto on Saturday, isn't that the Jew holiday?"

No one answered, no one wanted to admit any knowledge of anything Jewish.

"I'll take that as a yes," he continued. "Very well, we'll assemble at five am, leave headquarters at half past five and begin the attack at six, it's not far away. Kraus, make sure the anti-tank guns are ready."

"They have tanks, the Jews?" the adjutant said, alarmed.

"No, we'll just use high explosive shells against strongpoints, if necessary."

I spent the rest of the day working out my platoon, we were short of equipment and it was a struggle to get the stores to release more, but I was in favor with Dirlewanger and eventually I had replaced all of our stolen munitions. During the afternoon an old truck wheezed into the vehicle park, our replacement for the stolen Renault, a nearby mechanic identified it as a Polish Ursus 703.

"It must be at least twelve years old, Sir. Probably one of the last ones to be made, the company went bust in the financial collapse of 1929. They were taken over by the state-owned PZInz company and they updated it, called it the PZInz 703 and gave it a more powerful six cylinder motor. This one still has the original four cylinder engine, I'm afraid, but they're not too bad if you don't overload them."

"How do you know so much about these trucks?"

"I worked in the factory, Sir, when there wasn't any work to be had in Germany I came to Poland to find employment. Of course, Germany's a different place now, thank goodness. No need for any German to go looking for work in foreign countries building these crappy trucks."

And yet here he was, back in Poland working on the same 'crappy truck', probably being paid less than the Poles paid him at the time and risking getting his head shot off every time he walked along some dark Warsaw street. I guess that was what they called progress. I asked the mechanic to service the motor as he seemed to know so much about this particular vehicle, particularly its idiosyncrasies. I also ordered two of my men to refuel it and check the oil and tires, ready for the operation.

"It should be an easy one," the schutze said as he pumped gasoline into the tank. "They're supposed to be unarmed so we'll drive right over them, it should be all over by lunch time."

I didn't reply.

At seven o'clock I went out to Anna's dressmaking shop. I got there fifteen minutes early and wandered around the nearby streets. I wondered if she would still go to dinner with me, I no longer had an excuse to see her. It was depressing, I'd heard that Warsaw before the war was an open, vibrant and wealthy city, but now it was dark, shabby and forbidding. People scuttled furtively along the streets, ragged and thin, darting glances around them as if they were frightened that they were in danger of being attacked. Perhaps they were, petty crime was a serious problem in the city where so many people were starving and the law of the jungle had asserted itself. Only the fittest survived. Several vicious looking groups of youths came near to me, but when I put my hand on my pistol, they swerved away and crossed the street. At seven thirty I knocked on the door of Ost House, Anna answered it. She was breathtaking, wearing a floral silk cocktail dress with a complementary scarf. She had little makeup, but she'd fastened a flower in her hair that set off her pure skin to perfection. I wanted to seize her in my arms and shower her with kisses, but instead I gave her a light kiss on the side of her cheek and went in.

"You'd better get out of that uniform, you won't get many admiring looks in this area."

"I've already seen that, I had to threaten to use my pistol once or twice."

"They're only trying to survive, Paul, don't hurt them."

I smiled. "Of course not, I only had to show it to them and they ran off. I'm here to help them, not shoot them."

"You'd better get changed, go through, you know where everything is."

I changed into the lounge suit, fastened the top button of the shirt and the tie and laced my shoes. I checked in the mirror, I was impressed with the change, I looked anything but a soldier. I found the basin in the bathroom and slashed water over my hair to smooth it down, then went to join Anna. Her eyes shone, she was happy with my appearance, that was enough for me.

"You look wonderful, Paul, quite the playboy."

"One day, maybe."

We left the shop and walked to a restaurant that was about a half a mile away. She said she wanted to walk, as she never got enough exercise. I was more than happy to show off the beautiful girl on my arm, we attracted plenty of glances from passers by but they were looks of envy this time, not pure hate. It was a pleasant stroll, we ambled along the cobbled streets, the evening was still quite light. We reached the restaurant just before darkness fell and went inside, Anna had already reserved a table. We sat down and she offered to order for me.

"Unless you speak Polish?"

I shook my head. She conferred with the headwaiter and he went away. The wine waiter arrived and I chose a good vintage, then our first course arrived, the waiter left and we were able to talk.

"I thought you may not come to dinner with me tonight. I assume it went alright, the theft of my truck?"

"I said I would and here I am, Paul. Yes, they were highly

delighted. The guns and ammunition have all gone into the Ghetto and the explosives will be used to booby trap the approaches. But aren't you worried that some of it might be used against your own platoon?"

I shook my head. "I was reprieved from Mauthausen, but truthfully this is no reprieve. For me, Karl-Heinz and Gerd, we're just serving more of our sentence. If any of us die, well, at least it will be out in the open, not inside one of the camps."

She looked into my eyes, it was a very serious, concerned look. "I don't want you to die, Paul. We've only just met, and I'd like to get to know you better. Stay alive for a little longer."

"Anna, there's nothing I'd like more. Let's drink to getting to know each other better."

We toasted each other with the fine, Polish wine. Then I leaned forward to whisper to her.

"They're going into the Ghetto on Saturday morning, at six am."

She looked around to make sure no one was listening, but the waiter had been pre-warned and had chosen our table well, there was no one nearby.

"I'll get the information out to them tomorrow morning. I'm expecting Jakob to call in then to see me."

The main course arrived and we ate the most delicious Goulash, it was unbelievable. I'd tasted it in the States but not like this. When I told her, she smiled and asked me to tell her about my life in America. "It must be very different from this," she said.

I laughed aloud. "It couldn't be more different. We've got no war on our own soil, although of course many of our soldiers are fighting since Pearl Harbor and Hitler's declaration of war."

She looked solemn. "I understand that, but apart from the war, tell me about the US."

So I told her about growing up in Chicago, the skyscrapers, the automobiles, the gangsters, Al Capone.

"Did you ever meet him, this Al Capone, we've all heard of him even here in Poland."

I shook my head. "No, the G-Men, that's the FBI, they caught him and he was sent to prison for tax evasion, he's in Alcatraz, it's an island located in the San Francisco Bay, in California."

"I thought he was a murderer?" she said in a puzzled voice. "Why did they imprison him for tax evasion?"

I shrugged. "I guess no-one would give evidence against him, they were all too frightened."

"So it's just like with the Nazis in Poland, yes? They commit endless crimes and atrocities and everyone is too frightened to complain."

"You're right, that's exactly what it is, except on a much bigger scale. Capone never took over the whole country."

"Lucky for you," she said.

But she was smiling as she spoke, there was no implied criticism of my home country. We carried on eating and drinking, we got through a second bottle of wine. I felt her foot touch mine under the table, her hand came across the table and reached for mine.

"Paul, could I ask you something?"

"Yes, of course."

"I want you to come home with me tonight."

I looked into her eyes. "In that case I'll be the luckiest man in Poland."

Her eyes opened wide. "Only Poland?"

"No, no, Europe, the World, whatever."

But she was laughing. Later, we paid the bill and I walked her home through the deserted streets. We were both quiet, both anticipating what was to come. She put the key in her door with a shaking hand and led me upstairs. We went past her office and up the next flight of stairs to the small apartment she lived in. When we reached the living room we were past caring, we were kissing, hugging, touching, ripping each other's clothes off until we were both naked, then I put her gently on the couch and climbed over her. She looked up at me.

"Make love to me, Paul, give me everything you've got, let's forget the war for a short time and just enjoy ourselves."

"A short time," I smiled.

"As long as you like."

I entered her and she groaned, we kissed, our tongues intertwined and we made love with a passion that completely overwhelmed our bodies and minds. She squealed and wailed in complete abandon, dedicating herself totally to our lovemaking. When we finally climaxed I slumped down exhausted. I glanced at the clock, we'd been back in the apartment for nearly three quarters of an hour. She saw my glance.

"I really wasn't timing it, you know," she grinned.

"Anna, I have to get back, I'll be posted absent otherwise."

"Please, don't go yet." She hugged me with her arms around my neck.

"If I don't go I won't be able to get information to your resistance friends, I'll be locked up in a cell for desertion."

She let me go reluctantly. "All right then, but come back to me soon."

"After the Ghetto operation on Saturday, if I can get away in the evening, I'll come."

I nearly added 'if I'm still alive', but we both knew that already.

"I'll wait for you."

I put my uniform back on and went out into the deserted streets. There was a curfew on, as a uniformed officer I wasn't worried about it. Twice I was stopped by patrols but when they saw my SS uniform and I told them I was Sonderbattalion Dirlewanger it was enough, they were almost amusing in their frantic efforts to get away from me. When I got back to the hotel that served as our HQ, Karl-Heinz and Gerd were on sentry duty, they'd volunteered for tonight to cover for me.

"A good night," Gerd smiled.

"Totally, magnificently and absolutely brilliant."

They grinned, I didn't need to say anything more, but I did. "If I die tomorrow, it was worth it."

Their grins faded. "Try and stay alive a little longer, Sir. We have a lot of work to do now. Besides, we could be transferred to that bastard Max Hofstetter's platoon, now that would be very bad."

Something about the way they said it rocked me out of my

warm reverie.

"What have you heard about his platoon?"

"Only that they're bragging that they're determined to out-rape, out-steal and out-pillage everyone else in the battalion."

I was completely sober now. "That bad?"

They both nodded.

"In that case, we need to let the partisans know that they must be especially careful with Max's band of psychopaths. It's hard to think that any soldier could be even worse than any of the other of Dirlewanger's men, but if it's true, the partisans may want to deal with them separately. Permanently."

"It may not be easy to take out a whole platoon," Gerd said doubtfully.

"I'm sure they'll think of something. Don't go soft on me, Gerd, how would you feel if it was your sister or mother they were raping, your father and kids they were torturing and murdering?"

"I'm not going soft, Sir, don't think that. You're right, we need to get someone to nail those bastards. They're giving the Sonderbattalion Dirlewanger a bad name."

I had to check twice to confirm that he was smiling as he said it, that it really was a joke.

On Friday, the whole battalion was buzzing with activity. The operation required all of our men to take part, they were cleaning and checking weapons, sharpening knives, many of them were experts in the use of blades, they had learned their skills in drunken fights in brothels and bars across Europe. I had little doubt that they expected to use their knives tomorrow, the word was that we were going in to deal with unarmed civilians, the battalion specialty. 'Jewboy communists' was how Dirlewanger kept describing them. I fervently hoped he was in for a surprise. By Friday evening, they'd settled into their usual routine. Half of them were drunk, the other half were out in the streets of Warsaw, looking for whores and fights. I went to the battalion office ostensibly to finalize my platoon's deployment for the next morning but when I came out, I had the information I needed. I then left our HQ and walked to Anna's dressmaking store, she looked puzzled when she opened the door.

"I wasn't expecting you, is anything wrong?"

I went in the shop and we embraced and kissed.

I told her about Max's platoon. "I haven't got much time, but you need to warn them in the Ghetto, Max's platoon is looking for a bloodbath. They're the worst of a bad bunch."

"What can the resistance do?"

"The platoon is due to be stationed at Marszalkowska Street. I would suggest that the resistance hit them hard there, it shouldn't be too difficult to set up an ambush in such an urban location."

"I'll pass on the information, you must be careful, Paul, I don't want to lose you tomorrow."

I smiled. "I survived Mauthausen, my darling, I'll survive this."

There was a hammering on the door and I saw her pale.

"Are you expecting anyone?"

She shook her head, her eyes were wide with fear.

"Have you made any progress on my uniform?"

She nodded. "We've cut out the tunic and stitched one of the sleeves."

"Get it, quickly!"

While she ran off I ripped off my uniform tunic, took off my boots and pull down my pants. Wearing only my underwear, I went to open the door.

"Yes?"

There were four men, two Polish police officers, a uniformed SS trooper and another civilian, a man of about thirty-five, civilian clothes, long, leather greatcoat and trilby hat. Gestapo. Mischer. He pushed past me and the other three followed him. I adopted an angry look and snapped, "What the hell are you doing here, Mischer?"

He looked around the store without answering.

"I'll ask the questions. What's going on in here?"

Before I could answer, Anna bustled into the room carrying my partly made tunic, unmistakably part of an SS uniform.

"Untersturmfuhrer, I thought you were alone, I have your part-made tunic for the next fitting."

They all looked at her. She was so beautiful. "Schaffer, perhaps you should put your uniform on," Mischer sneered. "You wouldn't want to embarrass the lady, would you? Or have you already?"

I approached the Gestapo man in just my underwear and put my face six inches from his.

"You know which unit I fight in, Mischer, we're called the Sonderbattalion Dirlewanger, you also know of our reputation.

Our specialty is taking nasty little shits out of their cozy offices, cutting off their balls and giving them back to them to eat. We're operating in the Ghetto in the morning, why don't you come and see how we work? It could make a change from beating up helpless prisoners in Gestapo cellars!"

He wasn't intimidated by my threatening tone, but my meaning was clear. The Sonderbattalion Dirlewanger didn't play by any rules, that included Gestapo rules.

"Show me your papers."

I laughed. "You know exactly who I am, Mischer, but sure, I'll show you my papers. After you show me yours."

He sighed and got out his metal Gestapo identification disk. I took my documents out of my tunic and showed them to him. I decided to yank his chain a little more for the embarrassment he had caused me. Besides, I doubted that guilty men would play games with the Gestapo.

"I see that it's Kriminalassistent Mischer, you are not an officer."

"No, that's true, but it makes no difference to my authority, as you well know."

I put on a sneering, bullying expression. "I couldn't give a fuck about your authority, my friend. My battalion gives me all the authority I need. Tell me, what are you doing here, looking to buy a frock?"

He looked embarrassed. "We saw the lights on. It could have been terrorists, partisans, black marketers or some other illegal activity."

"In a lady's dress shop? You cannot be serious. Do you think they're sewing silk dresses for the resistance to wear when they attack our troops?"

My tone was bitingly sarcastic, at least they had the grace to blush red.

"We weren't to know what they were doing."

"Now you do know, Kriminalassistent Mischer. Would you kindly leave us alone now so that I can finish the fitting for my uniform? I do have my duties to attend to afterwards."

"Yes, of course," he said quickly.

"We're assembling at dawn, six am at the Sachsischer Garten, why don't you join us and see how we really deal with partisans and Jews."

"I will look at my diary and see if time allows," he said drily.

I gave him a superior smile. "You really should see how the battalion operates, Mischer, you might even learn something. We don't go hunting for partisans in dress shops."

He turned to his men. "Let's go."

I nodded curtly as they left.

When the door closed, Anna breathed a sigh of relief. "I thought we were dead."

I said nothing, I had died a long time before. I was walking through a kind of half-life, a half-life that I didn't feel certain I was fully entitled to.

"I'd better get my uniform back on and go back to the battalion."

"You can't stay longer?"

"I'm sorry, my darling, I have to get back to prepare for the morning."

"When will it ever end, Paul?"

"The war, do you mean? It's not going well for Germany, they've been stopped dead in most parts of the Soviet Union and the Russians are fighting back hard, most people think they've taken on more than they can manage on the Eastern Front. Or did you mean Operation Reinhardt?"

She was puzzled. "What is Operation Reinhardt? I've never heard of it."

"Operation Reinhardt is the code name given to Berlin's plan to clear all of the Jews in the General Government, as you know that's what we call Poland. The deportations to Treblinka, that's part of the ongoing operation, the military governor of Poland, Obergruppenfuhrer Odilo Globocnik has given orders to increase the resettlements until his area is completely Jew free."

"You mean until all of the Jews are dead," she said bitterly.

"Until then, yes, I'm sorry but essentially that is their intention."

"Are they planning to clear the entire Ghetto?"

"I don't know, Anna, when I do find out I will tell you. Tomorrow's operation is just routine, not part of a bigger plan. I have to go."

I put on my cap, straightened my uniform, kissed her tenderly and walked back through the dark streets.

In the morning, I dressed and walked into a hurricane of preparations. Dirlewanger was running around like a lunatic, probably convinced that today would be the day, when his unit's name went into legend.

"Schaffer, your platoon is assigned to Mireckiego, it's a small square on the other side of the Ghetto. Here, let me show you on the map."

He'd already shown me the day before but I politely looked at his map. It suited me, we'd be far away from where I suspected the partisans would place their main force, the ambush that I hoped would eat into the ranks of Dirlewanger's butchers.

"Is that clear, Schaffer? You'll be well placed to deal with any partisans or Jews who try to escape our frontal assault."

"Yes, it's clear, Sir."

"Good man, there'll be some medals awarded for this day's work I'm sure."

"I'll do my best, don't worry."

He was about to speak when someone shouted, "Achtung!"

We whirled around, a long, gleaming black staff car was entering the vehicle park. A General Officer's pennant fluttered from the front wing. It came to a stop and the passenger, himself a middle ranking officer, an SS-Sturmbannfuhrer, leapt out and opened the rear door. Out of the car came an SS Gruppenfuhrer, a full general.

"My God," Dirlewanger said. "Higher SS and Police Leader Friedrich Wilhelm Kruge, this is a real honor."

He rushed over to greet the arriving dignitary while I took the opportunity to look over the new arrival.

He was every inch the image of the Prussian senior officer despite his SS rank, tall and ramrod erect. He wore a field grey SS uniform over which he had a beautifully cut, matching grey leather coat. The collar of the coat was casually undone to reveal his decoration, the Knight's Cross hanging on a ribbon at his throat. He initially ignored our CO, looking around at the bustle of activity as the battalion prepared to move out, then he deigned to notice Dirlewanger, they shook hands and spoke for a few moments. Dirlewanger climbed on a box and shouted for us all to listen.

"Men, this is Deputy Higher SS and Police Leader Gruppenfuhrer Kruger, he is also Reichskommissar for the General Government. He wishes to say a few words to the battalion before we leave today."

Kruger eyed us coldly. His voice when he spoke was cold, he sounded tired, perhaps he hadn't slept well? Maybe the war wasn't going as well as he'd hoped, the news from the Eastern Front wasn't good, our German armies were finding the Soviets a much tougher nut to crack than they'd anticipated. Then again, perhaps he'd just had too much to drink the night before.

"This operation is a major part of our drive to rid the General Government of Jews and partisans." His voice was thin, reedy, as cold as the winds that whipped across the Pripet Marshes in Belorussia. It made me think of the poor devils that had been murdered in that benighted land, murdered by battalions such as ours, inspired by people such as him and Dirlewanger.

"These scum are becoming ever bolder, attacking my men and destroying Reich property. It must stop!"

He was shouting now, we were silent as his voice rose to a rant.

"Remember, when you go in, you kill them, kill them all! You're not going to pussyfoot around. We would prefer not to have too many prisoners to deal with. It's their way, not ours. Stalin himself said, 'Death is the solution to all problems, no man - no problem'. We shall take a leaf out of his book and do just that. I know your battalion's reputation, burn them, bomb them, shoot them, I don't care how you do it but finish them!"

He abruptly got back into his car, the door slammed and they drove off.

"You heard him," shouted Dirlewanger, "you know what to do!"

Men ran around and threw the last of the equipment into the vehicles, engines started, Dirlewanger mounted his Kubelwagen and looking like a Roman Emperor at the head of his legions, he roared out through the gate. We followed at the back of the column, our assigned position was away from the main force. Max's vehicle peeled off first, I noticed the name of the street, Marszalkowska. The rest of us drove for the main entrance to the Ghetto, my platoon turned off and we drove around the perimeter to Mireckiego, arriving next to the peaceful square five minutes after. Our driver halted the truck and stopped the engine, Karl-Heinz dropped the tailboard and my men clattered out and formed up.

"MG34 team, set up your weapon behind the wall, the rest of you find good positions behind cover and keep your eyes peeled for the partisans. Karl-Heinz, take charge, Gerd, come with me, we'll take a look around for any signs of the enemy."

The entrance to the Ghetto loomed in front of us, dark

and forbidding. At this early hour there was no one around, I wondered were they waiting inside, the stolen MP38s and MG34s pointed at us ready to fire. Gerd looked uneasy too.

"Could be an ambush, Sir."

"It damn well is an ambush, Gerd. I just hope the buggers have set it up on the right side of the Ghetto."

A man came out a doorway, thin and ragged. At first I thought it was Jakob Koslowski, the partisan I'd met in Anna's shop, but closer up I saw it was a different man. Just as shabby in appearance but his features were more Jewish, more Semitic, he looked like a college professor from Chicago University, an unemployed one, perhaps, definitely down on his luck. He wasn't armed, but he stood squarely in front of us, forcing us to stop.

"Who are you and what do you want here?" he asked in a voice that resounded with hate and contempt. I suppressed my automatic reaction to feel dislike, guess he was entitled to feel such animosity towards our uniforms.

"Untersturmfuhrer Paul Schaffer, Sonderbattalion Dirlewanger, this is Schutze Rundheim."

Gerd made to lift his MP38 to cover him but the man gestured towards the open windows above us, each had a man with a rifle, covering us.

"Don't touch the weapon, Private, there is no need for it," he seemed to relax. "Are you Anna's friend?"

"Yes."

"My name is Aaron Majewski. I command one of the resistance groups in the Ghetto. I understand that it is you we have to thank for our weapons?"

I nodded. "It was the least we could do. There are three of us, my friend, the other man is my Scharfuhrer, he's outside the gate with the platoon. We were all in Mauthausen together."

He smiled faintly. "Yes, we know of the reputation of Mauthausen. The Nazis have accelerated their death camp programme in Poland, have you met Higher SS and Police Leader Kruger? He's here to crack the whip and make certain that Poland is cleared of Jews."

"I've met him, a nasty piece of work."

"Yes, the nastiest. He is working to make their 'Hunger Programme" work faster too, it's not just the Ghetto that is suffering."

"I've never heard of the Hunger Programme."

"It's the Nazi master plan to starve the occupied Eastern Territories to death. After the Great War, when Germans starved in the streets after the allied blockade, Hitler made a decision not to allow it to happen again. It's a simple programme to deprive conquered territories of foodstuffs to make the Wehrmacht self sufficient, as well as to have food surpluses to send back to Germany. They achieve that ambition by simply starving the population, to death if necessary. We don't know the exact figures, but thousands are already dying of starvation in Poland every week. They've made our whole country one big death camp."

I looked at Gerd, we should have been horrified, but we'd seen so much death and brutality that there was unlikely to be anything that could shock us any further.

"Are you ready for them at the main gate?"

"Yes, we've done our best to prepare a hot reception for them."

"If any of your people escape this way, tell them not to come through this gate, my platoon are waiting outside to open fire on anyone that comes out of the Ghetto."

"I assumed that it was the case, don't worry, I'll warn them."

"In that case, good luck," I said to him. "I won't shake hands, people on both sides may get the wrong idea."

He smiled again. "I have little doubt they would."

I turned back to the gate with Gerd and we went out.

"All quiet in there, Scharfuhrer, but keep alert, they may well come this way when the firing starts."

Even as I said that the firing did start, the loud, explosive cracks of the three anti-tank guns as they started firing shells into the Ghetto. Then the machine guns started and the morning calm was shattered as the battalion on the north side of the Ghetto emptied magazine after magazine into the houses and apartment blocks. The firing increased and it soon became obvious that the Jews were firing back, the echoes of rifle and sub-machine gunfire ripped through the buildings. To the east of the Ghetto there was more firing where I knew Max's platoon was stationed, they were obviously joining in with gusto. Then the explosives went off.

A jet of flame and smoke spurted into the sky, I felt the earth move as someone detonated a mine. It sounded as if it came from the area of Max's platoon, I imagined a good number of his murderous thugs had been blown to their particular hell.

But no people came our way. Some of the men got restless.

"Sir, couldn't we go in and roust out some of these Jewboys, we're bored waiting here," a beefy Sturmann said to me, a lance corporal.

"The CO had ordered that we hold the position here, Geisler. Of course, if you want to get your balls cut off you could disobey his orders…"

He shook his head. "No, no, we can wait."

I smiled as he went back to his position. Dirlewanger could be just as psychotic with his men as with the enemy, he'd been know to shoot more than one man for disobeying him. I looked at the other men, but they were already starting to sip from hidden bottles, presumably schnapps. That suited me, if they got drunk and fell asleep they would hopefully stay out of trouble. The battle raged for over two hours and still no one came near us. Then a Kubelwagen suddenly screeched around the corner, Dirlewanger standing in the front as usual, looking red faced and angry.

"The fuckers, they were waiting for us," he shouted. "Any action this side?"

"Not yet, Sir, no."

"Right, get your platoon together and go in and start flushing them towards the north, I'll send two platoons from that side and we'll squeeze the bastards between us. Watch out for our own men, there's a danger of getting caught in our own crossfire."

He looked around at my men, lounging in that relaxed way that only those that have drunk large quantities of alcohol seem to be able to achieve.

"Are they up to it, Schaffer?"

"I'll make sure they are, Sir."

"Good man, you're an officer I can rely on, my friend. You know about Hofstetter?"

I shook my head.

"Those fucking Jews had a mine buried right where his platoon was positioned. Killed most of them, only three of them missed the blast."

"Is Max ok, Sir?"

"Yes, you two are friends, aren't you? He's fine, a few scratches from shrapnel, nothing too serious. I'll fire a yellow flare over the Ghetto when we're ready, that's your signal."

His driver drove him away rapidly, he had to clutch the windscreen for support.

"Karl-Heinz, I need the men mobile in ten minutes, can you do that?"

He laughed. "Watch me, Sir."

There was a water container set up on the open back of our truck. He found a bucket, filled it and went around the men dousing them one by one with cold water. They shouted, swore and threatened, but in ten minutes my platoon was standing ready to move out. I doubted that their guns were all loaded properly, even less that they would be able to aim them in any particular direction with any accuracy, but it was good enough. The last thing I wanted to do was shoot anyone. We waited for another half hour, and then the flare shot up in the sky. I walked forward.

"Platoon, advance!"

They followed me in a ragged, straggling column, only Karl-Heinz and Gerd were sober. We went through the gate and entered the dark alleys of the Ghetto. I looked up but there were no rifles poking out of windows. We advanced further, and then a movement caught my eye, the unmistakable barrel of an MG34 pushing out of a tiny hole in a roof where a slate had been removed. I looked around for Majewski but there was no sign of him, the Jewish resistance fighter had moved to another area of the fighting. I had to make a decision, and fast.

"Machine gun, get under cover!" I shouted at the men.

They scattered, just in time. Karl-Heinz and most of the men swerved through a pair of opened double doors and I leapt through an empty window. The machine gun opened fire, the bullets hammering down into the street and bowling over two of my men who had been too slow to move out of the way. Probably drunk, it was too bad. They wouldn't be able to slaughter any more innocents, their murderous days were over. A volley of gunfire blasted chips of brickwork around my head, Gerd was next to me, he looked across and smiled.

"Are they using our own machine gun against us?" he asked me.

"Probably. Let's make sure we keep our heads down and not make it easy for them."

I shouted across to Karl-Heinz. "Scharfuhrer, how are things over there?"

"We're ok, Sir, what do we do now? We could work our way up to the roof and take him from there."

"No, find a way out through the back or we'll be late to connect with the other platoons. We'll have to come back and finish this one later."

I hoped to God that the Jew on the roof could hear. If he was shot when we returned, it would be too bad. I'd done all I could.

"Gerd, we'll go out the back and loop around and meet up with the others a couple of blocks in."

"It's not a good idea, leaving that machine gun at the back of us," he replied.

"So what do you want me to do, we made the guns available to them, do we kill them for using them?"

He shrugged. "They're trying to kill us."

"Let's make it damned difficult for them then."

We crawled over to the empty doorway that led out of the room and crept away, there was a renewed burst of firing from the roof but none of the bullets came near. Keeping a wary eye out for more Jewish fighters, we made our way north until we could see the remnants of my platoon on a nearby corner. They spotted us at the same time and waved, we ran forward to join up with them. Karl-Heinz looked grave.

"We lost another one, Sir, that machine gunner got him, the damn fool wouldn't keep his head down."

I'd now lost three men from my platoon, thugs, bullies and murderers. They'd all deserved to die, but Dirlewanger may not take it too well if I lost any more.

"Close up, men, watch out for snipers!"

We edged cautiously through the Ghetto, how could anyone

live in this place? It was so dark, claustrophobic, squalid and filthy, the buildings bearing the pockmarks of war where bullets had struck them, reminders of the constant attacks that these people suffered. Huge chunks were missing from the masonry. I knew that this place had suffered shelling by both the Wehrmacht and the SS and bombed repeatedly by the Luftwaffe. It was a testament to these people's strength, determination and simple ingenuity, that they had survived at all. Yet there were apparently tens of thousands of them in here. Where, I had no idea, the area we were in was deserted.

We crept forward, once a rifle cracked out and a bullet chipped stone from the cobbles. The men instantly looked up in time to see the shooter in an upstairs window, reloading. Seven of my men fired burst after burst at him, two others rushed into the building and up the stairs to confront him but he was already dead, flung backwards by the fusillade of fire that was directed at him. The two troopers hurried back down, clutching a rifle, an old, single shot small bore hunting rifle. He'd never stood a chance.

"Is he dead?" I asked one of the troopers who'd gone after him.

"Yes, already dead when we reached him. Must have hit him with twenty or more rounds, he was shredded, fucking Jewboy bastard."

"Let's move on."

We were getting nearer to the north entrance, sporadic firing echoed through the streets, we were all on edge, peering carefully around every corner. The sounds of footsteps made us all take cover in doorways, but it was the platoons from the other side, led by Dirlewanger personally.

"Any sign of the enemy, Schaffer?"

I shook my head, "No, Sir, we just took out a sniper but that's about all this side."

He grunted. "We've lost too many men in this fucking place, we need to finish them. One of the platoons reported that they've gone to ground in the cellars in the next street, we're headed there now, follow me."

The entrance to the apartment building was guarded by Obersturmfuhrer Kraus, crouching outside looking slightly nervous, clutching an elegant Luger Parabellum pistol. Although largely replaced by the Walther P38 and PPK, many officers continued to use this toggle-locked recoil-operated semi-automatic pistol, first designed by Georg J Luger in 1898. Probably it was a form of snobbery but even so, it was a highly effective and reliable weapon. He had a tough looking schutze on each side of him and as I watched he stood up straighter and forced the nervous look from his face as Dirlewanger ran up to him.

"Any sign of them, Kraus?"

"I've heard noises, Sir, they're down there alright."

"Good, let's go in and finish this!"

He hurtled through the doorway, several shots rang out and almost instantly he crashed back out on the street, blood streaming from a wound in his stomach. Kraus went even whiter than before.

"The CO's been hit, two men, pick him up and get him

some help, the rest of you, fan out and cover us!"

They picked him up, the rest of us trained our guns at the entrance to the apartment building. Dirlewanger looked white, but a closer look persuaded me that it was only a flesh wound. He was trying to shout orders, to make us to continue the mission but Kraus had seen enough.

"We need to get the CO out of here, men, carry him carefully, the rest of you cover us as we fall back to the main entrance."

"Kraus, you bastard, I want you to go in and kill those fuckers," I heard him say, but his voice was quieter, weaker, then he passed out altogether. Kraus continued leading us out of the Ghetto.

CHAPTER EIGHT

'In Italy for thirty years under the Borgias they had warfare, terror, murder, bloodshed - they produced Michelangelo, Leonardo da Vinci and the Renaissance. In Switzerland they had brotherly love, five hundred years of democracy and peace and what did that produce? The cuckoo clock.'

Orson Welles

While we watched, the medics stripped off the CO's filthy tunic and shirt, exposing his bloody wound. They cleaned him up and two things became obvious, the first that it was not a life-threatening wound, the second that he had been hit several times before, his upper body bearing the scars of previous shrapnel and bullets that had wounded him during his many murderous operations. There was no doubt he wasn't a coward, just a suicidal psycho. The morphine sent him into unconsciousness and he was taken away in a field ambulance, leaving Kraus in command.

"I'm giving the order to return to our headquarters," he said. "In view of the CO's injury we need to regroup. I've been promoted to Hauptsturmfuhrer," he said as if it was an afterthought.

We all looked up in surprise. "The CO awarded me a field promotion when I took over the battalion for him."

They climbed into the trucks and the drivers started up, our ancient Ursus was still at the other side of the Ghetto. We forced marched around the outside of the perimeter and half an hour later boarded the old Polish truck. It took almost five minutes to get it running, eventually we pulled away from the Ghetto and returned to our HQ. Almost as soon as our driver had put the brake on a schutze came running out of the building.

"The CO wants you to report immediately, Sir."

"Kraus?"

"Yes," he smiled. "General Ludendorff."

I looked up. "What do you mean?"

"You'll see, he's in there planning how to defeat the enemy almost singlehandedly."

Kraus was already asserting his new command, he was standing at the map table, pointing out how he saw the battalion should deploy for our next operation in the Ghetto. I stood to attention and waited. He looked up, he was normally an insignificant man with ginger hair and a wispy moustache, his watery blue eyes stared at me, slightly unfocussed. I noticed his skin bore the broken veins of the heavy drinker, nothing unusual in this unit.

"Ah, Schaffer. You know that Hofstetter's platoon was ambushed by partisans, he lost most of his men?"

"I heard, yes, Sir."

"They took him to the SS hospital in the city, the survivors from his platoon will make up the losses in your platoon so you'll be back up to strength. We have three days to stand down and rest, then we're back into combat. Next Wednesday we're joining with reinforcements supplied by Gruppenfuhrer Kruger, he wants us to clear an outlying village of partisans and Jews."

"What about the Ghetto?" I asked him.

"The Ghetto can starve, for all I care. They're more trouble than they're worth, those damned Jews. Our policy for the time being is to keep them bottled up until they drop dead from hunger. Either that or we'll get the artillery or the Luftwaffe to blow the place up. We've got more important things to do. Kruger wants us to help him clear out Legionowo, it's about twenty miles from here. The Wehrmacht has a prisoner of war camp outside the town, mostly junior officers and NCOs, but there's been too many escapes. The Gruppenfuhrer believes that the locals are helping prisoners to escape from the camp, hiding them and giving them food. He intends to teach them a lesson they'll never forget. We'll take your unit and three others, four platoons should be enough. Briefing will be at two pm on Tuesday, that's all, dismissed."

"This will be reprisal action then, Sir?"

He looked up, annoyed that I hadn't left. "Yes, of course it is, teach them a lesson. Every prisoner they help to escape, we'll shoot twenty of their civilians."

"How many have escaped so far?"

"Ten."

That evening I had to see Anna. Two hundred civilians in Legionowo was an atrocity that I had to try to prevent. In the early evening I walked through the streets of Warsaw, it was several hours before curfew, the sun was shining in a blue autumn sky and half the population seemed to be out walking. I walked quickly, I was halfway to Ost House when I became aware that I was being followed. At the end of the street two men stepped out into my path, civilians, trench coats, trilby hats, hard faces. I turned around to see Kriminalassistent Mischer behind me, flanked on either side by a Gestapo man in civilian clothes. He still wore his black leather coat, the badge of office for middle ranking Gestapo people.

"Untersturmfuhrer Schaffer, you seem to be in a hurry."

"What do you want this time, Mischer? It's no crime to walk quickly."

"Provided that your intentions do not fall outside of the law," he responded quickly.

"Do you have any evidence that mine do not?"

He shook his head. "No yet, my friend, we're just being careful."

I had to be careful too, he was suspicious about something, I only wished I knew exactly what it was. Unless he already knew, in which case I would shortly be dead. His next words were chilling. "What do you know about soldiers in your battalion selling arms to the enemy?"

"That's rubbish, Mischer. None of our men would stoop that low, we're trying to kill them, not supply them with weapons."

"Really? And yet, my informants tell me that the explosives used in the Ghetto were from the Sonderbattalion Dirlewanger."

"We had a truckload of weapons stolen, but who the hell knows where and when they were used. If you think that our people are selling weapons, find out who it is, and arrest them. But I think you're wasting your time. Look, I need to go, I have more pleasant things to do than stand talking to you."

"Ah, the delightful lady in the dress shop!"

"Mischer, she's making a new uniform for me, that is all."

"Of course it is. It's just that she's so beautiful I wonder how an officer like yourself could resist her obvious charms."

I wondered how much he really knew, it was certainly more than was healthy for Anna, and for me.

"I really have to go," I said, starting to push past them. He kept pace with me.

"We could do with someone inside your battalion, Schaffer, someone to make enquiries for us, perhaps you could help us?"

"To spy you mean, on my own men. Forget it. Goodbye, Mischer."

"Until we meet again then," he said enigmatically.

I carried on to the store, there was little point in trying to hide where I was going, he already knew. Anna answered the door, she looked ill.

"Come in, quickly. You heard about Aaron?"

"Majewski? No, I saw him earlier, what has happened?"

"He was wounded and taken prisoner. Paul, he knows

everything."

"Where is he now?"

"He was shot trying to slip out of the Ghetto when the raid had finished, they shot him in the head. He's still alive, they took him away unconscious with the SS casualties, they want to interview him when he's able to talk. If he lives, of course."

"He could be at the SS hospital, then, if he's badly wounded and they want to keep him alive for interrogation they could hold them there. So they know he's a partisan?"

She nodded. "I think so, yes."

I told her I would try to take care of it. "Anna, it's getting dangerous, has Mischer been around here lately?"

"Yes, he came yesterday and today. He suspects something, he must do."

"Can't you get out of here, Anna? If he gets evidence of your resistance work they'll be in here during the night with an SS Police squad."

"And where would I go? I have my business here, my staff and clientele. Then there is Jakob, of course. Where would he go?"

"He'd go to Treblinka if they came here in the middle of the night."

"I can't leave, I'm sorry, not unless I know for sure that they have found out what I'm doing."

I nodded. "I'll do my best to head them off. I think I should go and visit Hofstetter, he's a colleague of mine who was wounded, the one they used the explosives on."

"Oh, I thought they were all killed."

"Most were, yes, but he survived. It'll give me an excuse to find out more about Majewski."

I told her about the raid on Legionowo, the threatened reprisals.

"How many will they shoot?"

"Two hundred."

"Two hundred, my God, do you think they'll do it, it's as bad as what they're doing in the death camps."

"Anna, I'm sorry, I've seen far worse in Belorussia. Yes, they'll do it."

"I'll get word out to the resistance, I have no idea whether or not they'll be able to forestall it," she said.

"I have to leave, I have a lot to do."

We kissed, holding each other, neither wanting to let go of the other. Then I left and walked away up the street.

It was dark when I walked around the corner, the SS Feldgendarmerie had a post set up, blocking the road. The Scharfuhrer on duty shone a torch in my face.

"Show me your papers!"

I slowly handed him my identity document. "I'm in a hurry, Scharf, one of my men was injured in the Ghetto this morning. Can you direct me to the SS hospital?"

He ignored me, enjoying the absolute power that field police enjoy over the military, both Wehrmacht and SS. I controlled my impatience and answered the litany of questions, where was I going, purpose of business, where had I come from. He kept looking back suspiciously at my identity card, then at a clipboard in his hand. Finally, he handed me back my card.

"The SS Hospital is three blocks north, turn right at the end of this street and you'll see it. But you can't go there now."

"Why is that, Scharfuhrer?" His sneering look was starting to irritate me badly. "Since when do you dictate when and where SS officers conduct their business?"

"Since Gruppenfuhrer Kruger declared a curfew for all personnel in the city, civilian or military. Technically, I should place you under arrest," he smiled as he played his trump card. "But I'll ignore it for now, you'd better hurry back to your barracks. Sir," he added after a pause. I nodded and left.

When I got back to our HQ, the guard had been doubled and lights blazed everywhere. Instead of lounging around in their usual drunken stupor, the battalion was preparing for battle. Karl-Heinz saw me and ran up.

"Thank God you're back, Sir, they're going crazy around here, the Jews have teamed up with the Polish resistance and attacked an army barracks just outside the city on the Ozarow road, they killed dozens of our German soldiers and got away with most of the armory."

"What has the battalion been ordered to do?"

"No idea, Kraus is running around like a maniac, threatening everything including killing every man, woman and child in the city, but so far we're just getting kitted up and ready to go."

"Schaffer!" a voice bellowed across the courtyard. "I want you in here, now, officers' briefing."

I went to the 'planning room', where Kraus was puffed up importantly, threatening retribution against the inhabitants of Warsaw.

"I want a thousand of them, no, ten thousand! We'll show those fucking terrorists we mean business!"

"A thousand of who, Sir?" a puzzled voice asked him. I looked across, it was Heinrich Weiss, looking as if he had just come out of a heavy drinking session before the emergency arose.

"I don't give a shit who, just find them and kill them!" he raved.

"But surely, Sir," I interrupted. "We need to kill the men that carried out the raid, if we just kill innocent civilians won't it leave them free to do it all again? They might even come and raid our headquarters in this building if we don't deal with them."

"Here, you mean? They wouldn't dare, would they?"

"It's possible, Sir, yes."

It stopped him dead, the idea that the Jews and Poles might come to his cozy headquarters and machine gun or bomb the place.

"What do you suggest, Schaffer?"

"Perhaps for now a strong guard around our headquarters, Sir. Any night operation could be dangerous. In the morning we find out if the Abwehr, the army intelligence unit here in the city, has identified the location of the terrorists."

He thought for a few moments. "Very well, you could be right. The guard has been reinforced outside the gate, we'll get some rest and ask for orders in the morning. You can tell the men to stand down. Dismissed!"

I thanked God that Dirlewanger had been wounded,

otherwise we'd have been roaring out into the suburbs to roust hundred of civilians from their beds to be lined up and shot. As it was, at least there was time for Kraus to cool down. I went out, found my platoon, and told them to go off duty, and then I tried to get some sleep. The quiet of the night was constantly interrupted by random shots, the occasional burst of sub-machine gunfire and I thought constantly of Anna, hoping she'd be safe. And, as well, I had Lisl in Berlin to think about, another beauty caught up in the horrors of the war. In her case, it was the bombing, constant raids, the RAF Lancasters by night, the American B17s by day. My America.

The very thought of America jerked me awake, I should never have come here, should never have volunteered my services to Germany, to this brutal regime of death camps and violent conquest, a regime that was brutally tearing Europe to shreds. At the time, it had seemed the right thing to do, although that seemed like a trivial excuse now. Lisl and I had made plans to return to America if we both survived the war, but everything I had experienced so far suggested that it was very unlikely we'd both outlive the hostilities. I should have felt guilty about Anna too, I knew that I was falling in love with her. But I couldn't find it in me to feel guilty at all. Amidst the carnage, the terror and the bloodshed, we all had to take what we could. Each day of life was something unexpected, a day to be surprised about and enjoyed as if it was our last. I'd long since given up expecting there to be many more such days. But what if I did survive, to live and go back to the USA? Would I take Lisl, as we'd planned, or would it be Anna? Thank God there'd never be any need to make such an impossible decision, life here was measured in days and weeks, months if we were lucky. Definitely not years.

In the morning I awoke to the bustle of activity, Gerd was nudging me to consciousness. He handed me a mug of coffee as I sat up.

"We're moving out, Kraus has ordered us to be ready to go in two hours. You'd better drink the coffee, Sir, I'll see if I can rustle up some bread."

I tried to clear my mind. "Moving out, where to? I thought we were waiting to locate the partisans here in Warsaw."

"Orders from Kruger, apparently they've brought forward the Legionowo operation. We're going to take hostages, Kruger wants five hundred of them."

"What are we to do with five hundred hostages, Gerd?"

"We are to shoot them."

I scrambled to get my boots on and rushed outside. The sentries on the gate were two men that I'd done a favor for in the past when they'd reported both late and drunk, as duty officer I'd let them off without charge.

"I'll be less than a half hour, you never saw me if anyone asks."

One of them winked. "Never saw who, Sir?"

"Good man." A church bell was ringing, calling worshippers to early morning Mass. The residents of Legionowo would need their prayers this morning. Anna answered my furious banging on her door, her face surprised.

"Paul, what is it?"

"It's Legionowo, they're going in early, this morning. You have to get a warning to them!"

"Is it a reprisal raid?"

"Yes, I'm afraid so. They intend to kill five hundred of them, civilians. I have to get back, can you get word to them?"

"Five hundred, oh my God. One moment."

She took her coat from the peg inside the door, closed it, and locked it. "I know someone who can get a message through, I'll go there now. When will I see you again?"

I held her tightly, very tightly. "My darling, I just don't know, they're going crazy at the moment, Warsaw is in total chaos. I'll come as soon as I get back."

We kissed and I ran back to Headquarters, she went in the opposition direction to try to get the warning out, presumably to the resistance.

Two hours later we were roaring through the outskirts of Warsaw, headed for our appointment with mass murder. We made good time, after just over half an hour of driving we were about to enter Legionowo. That was when the ground erupted. I afterwards found out that the local partisan group had quickly buried a series of huge mines under the road. When they were alerted to the enemy trucks rolling over them, they set off the charges. I was travelling in the middle of the column and I caught the edge of the blast, the rest of the explosion destroyed the three trucks behind me. I was thrown clear of our vehicle, all I could hear was the chatter of machine guns as the Poles opened fire on the stunned survivors of our convoy. Karl-Heinz was shouting at the men to get under cover and bring our MG34 into action. I dragged myself to my feet and staggered towards them, I was supposed to lead them, not lie on the ground waiting for a medic to happen along. Someone shouted something to me, but I was still stunned and I couldn't hear what he said. That was when the machine gun burst tracked across me and I went down, knocked over by three bullets that smashed into my legs and threw me into the dirt. I lay there for what seemed like an eternity as the battle raged, my legs were numb but not painful, not at first. Then the pain hit me and I had to work hard to suppress a scream. Someone was crouched over me, putting dressings on my wounds, I could see a lot of blood on the ground, my blood. Then the pain got worse, wave after wave of agony sweeping through me, driving all conscious thought from my brain. I saw Gerd crouched next to the medic, holding me down while the other man pushed a morphine ampoule into me, then I blacked out into unconsciousness.

I awoke on a train, it must have been in motion because the jerk as it suddenly stopped brought me back to consciousness. I was lying on a low, narrow bunk bed, there was another bed above me. The noise and stench were appalling, men were groaning in pain, some screamed, others called for doctors and nurses. There was an urgent shout for someone to come quickly and hold a man down, I shuddered to think what they were doing to him. The smell was tangible, a thick but invisible fog, the stench of filth, urine, excreta, body odor and blood. I was on a hospital train but I may as well have been in hell, surely there would have been no difference. Someone lowered a window and outside I heard the hiss of steam from the engine, orders being shouted, more men screaming as they were loaded roughly onto the train and then the doors slammed shut and we lurched forward again. I drifted off to sleep then, my dreams vivid, almost surreal, a line of Polish Jews standing in front of a deep pit in the earth, a volley of machine gun fire and then they all disappeared, they just seemed to vaporize into thin air, but not before I saw that they all had the same face. Anna. It had been dark outside but now the first rays of dawn began to show through the blood-spattered filth of the windows. An orderly came along, probably he was an army medic, he lifted my blanket and looked at my wounds, nodding to himself. Was that good or bad?

"Am I going to lose them?" I asked him.

He turned to look at me. "So you're awake, where were you wounded?"

"I've been awake on and off all night. I was injured in the partisan attack at Legionowo."

He looked puzzled. "Legionowo? That was four days ago. You've been on this train for nearly two days, before that you were in the SS hospital in Warsaw, you lost so much blood they thought you were finished."

Four days? I'd completely lost track of time. "Where are we?"

"About forty miles from Berlin, you've been unconscious ever since you were wounded. It's just as well, we've had a bumpy ride, a lot of damage to the line, some of the wounded haven't made it. We'll have you in the hospital soon and they'll make a proper job of fixing you up. No, you won't lose your legs, unless the sepsis gets hold of you."

"Sepsis, that's blood poisoning isn't it?"

"It's a severe illness in which the bloodstream is overwhelmed by bacteria, blood poisoning about sums it up, but the signs are good in your case, you should be ok."

He left me then and I drifted back to sleep. The train stopped three more times during that last forty miles, each time when the air raid alarm sounded. In the distance, even so far from the capital, we could hear the rumble as bombs exploded. Finally, we reached the Hauptbahnhof, the main railway station and steel-helmeted nurses, helpers and doctors rushed on board to take off the wounded. I was put on a gurney and transferred to an old Mercedes truck, it jolted its way through streets strewn with rubble and finally stopped at the main SS hospital. With other wounded men, I was transferred to a ward. There I was washed, shaved and given clean nightclothes to wear. The doctor was optimistic.

"You'll soon be back on your feet, Untersturmfuhrer, as right as rain. I would estimate a week in the hospital, then another week or two to convalesce. Congratulations, you earned yourself a vacation."

"Thanks a lot," I said wryly, "I don't feel as if I'm on vacation."

"It could have been worse, you could have lost your legs, or been dead," he said sharply.

I nodded, obviously a man with a sense of humor. I lay in that hospital for five more days. In the end the numbers of casualties arriving from the Eastern Front was too overwhelming, and they threw me out with two crutches to support me and a packet of morphine ampoules for when the pain was too much to bear.

"Keep the wound clean," a stern faced SS Helferin said to me, a female auxiliary nurse with a face like and Olympic shot putter. "You could still lose a leg if you're not careful."

I thanked her and left. I checked the time, it was too early for Lisl to have gone to work at the Blue Goose so I began to slowly hobble towards her apartment, I had a clean uniform and a few personal possessions in a canvas bag on my shoulder. Normally I would have called a taxi but as soon as I came out into the street it was obvious that the very idea was ridiculous. The streets were narrow lanes between acres of bombed out buildings. The devastation was incredible, beyond anything that could have been dreamed of. Even Warsaw, bombed and shelled both during and after the attack on Poland, hadn't suffered anything like this much damage. Adolf Hitler had much to answer for to his people, he had led them to the very gates of hell and then on through to the systematic destruction of their families and properties. I stumbled on a badly repaired pothole and almost recovered, but my leg gave way and I fell to the ground. A man ran up to me, dirty and shabby, he looked as far gone as the inhabitants in the Warsaw Ghetto did.

"Here, let me help you."

"Thanks, I'm still a bit shaky."

He reached out his arm and started to help me up, but when I was halfway off the ground he snatched my canvas bag, gave me a huge push that sent me crashing back into the dust and ran off. I was so astonished that I didn't even try to get up, I lay on the ground thinking how much had changed in Berlin, the orderly city that I had known so recently where crime was virtually unknown. Then a policeman ran past me, a pistol drawn. He stopped abruptly, took aim and fired three shots. I twisted around to see my robber had gone down and the cop was walking up to him. He bent to look at the body, shook his head and picked up my bag where it had fallen, brought it to me.

"Are you ok? It's shocking, the things they get up to these days."

"Is he dead?"

"Oh yes, I made sure of that. No time to waste on those scum, he was probably a Jew, or had Jewish blood, maybe. We're ridding the city of his kind, don't worry."

I didn't reply, couldn't reply. I was lying in the dust and rubble of what was once a beautiful and cultured capital, now it was little more than a demolition site, yet he was concerned over the racial origins of a common thief.

"A pity you can't rid the city of the RAF," I said evenly, but as soon as I said it, I knew I should have kept my silence.

"What are you trying to suggest, are you being funny?" he scowled.

"No, I'm sorry, I'm very grateful. I only wish it wasn't part of the Fuhrer's master plan for Germany to have his capital bombed constantly day and night."

Shut up, Schaffer, I was telling myself. Even in the US, a

cop would have had his baton out by now and swung it at me, wound or no wound.

"Yes, well, we don't know what is in his mind, but we put our trust in Adolf Hitler, we know that he will come through in the end. He's a genius, you know."

I gazed around at the heaps of rubble, two young children were burrowing into a nearby ruin, probably looking for food.

"Yes, of course, a normal person couldn't have brought us to this."

"Absolutely not," he said. "You be careful now, with those crutches you're advertising the fact that you're an easy mark."

"Thank you, officer."

He holstered his pistol and walked off, picking his way carefully through the narrow tracks between the bombed out buildings. The corpse of the robber lay on the ground, I could see two rats already gnawing at the flesh. A few feet away a teenage boy, thin, filthy and ragged, was looking at the body, probably wondering if it was worth rifling the pockets. Truly, a normal person could not have brought Berlin to this.

When she answered the door, Lisl was still rumpled and bleary eyed from sleep, but when she saw me her eyes widened.

"Paul, this is wonderful. But you've been wounded, is it painful?"

I gave her a brief summary of the shooting that had brought me to Berlin. When she asked me for how long, I told her that I had about two weeks.

"I trust they didn't put bullets near anything important, Paul?"

I grinned. "Not a chance, everything's in perfect working order."

"In that case you'd better show me."

She helped me to her bed and I lay down gratefully, comparing the soft feather mattress to the iron hard hospital bed I'd just come from. She smelled wonderful, a subtle touch of fragrance that blended with the natural musk of her body to produce something akin to an aphrodisiac. Or maybe I was just very horny, but she quickly pushed me onto my back and lay over on top of me.

"As you're wounded I'll do all the work, my darling, you just lie there and relax."

Relax, she had to be joking, I was bursting with an animal lust that seemed to seep out of every pore, when she guided me inside her I knew I had entered Nirvana. If the RAF dropped a bomb on us later I would consider it a fair exchange. I'd been with a few girls in my lifetime on both sides of the Atlantic but Lisl had a flare for the erotic that literally took a man's breath away.

Afterwards, she lit cigarettes for us and we lay smoking.

"Have you been with anyone else while you were away?" she asked me.

I grinned at her. "Have you, Lisl?"

She snorted. "Of course I have, did you think I'd become a nun?"

"Not with you working in a strip club, no, not really."

She punched me playfully. "It's not a strip club, as you well know, it's a cabaret revue. Are you coming to watch me tonight?"

"Of course I am. I wouldn't miss it for anything."

"That's good, I like to be there every night, the club is in a deep basement, it's one of the best air raid shelters in Berlin. Most of them don't have carpets, good food and drink and exotic dancers."

"I expect the Fuhrer's probably has," I said with a smile.

"The Fuhrer, he's the last person to go near a strip club, he's more into young girls, fucking pervert."

I sat up, surprised, it was an automatic movement, and I looked around the bedroom, but of course we were alone.

"You should be careful what you say, Lisl."

"Not in my own bedroom, besides, it's true."

"How do you know that?" I asked curiously.

"Men talk, didn't you realize that? Some of them come into the club, they like to take a pretty girl home for a few drinks and then screw them. That's when the real truth comes out. He was fucking his niece, Geli Raubal."

"I thought she was an adult when she died, not a young girl."

"She was young when he met her, believe me. When Hitler met Eva Braun, he had her killed. The official version is that she killed herself, of course, but that's bullshit."

"That's unbelievable. Besides, who's Eva Braun?"

"His mistress, they live together. She was a photographer's assistant when he met her, now they live together full time, but he keeps her under wraps."

"But, Hitler makes such a big thing about being married to

Germany."

She laughed. "I could tell you a few stories about the Fuhrer and his people, but it may be best if you don't know."

I heartily agreed. I had no wish to add to my problems.

I went to the club that night and watched her dance but I was exhausted afterwards, my wounds had a long way to go before they were fully healed and I spent the next few days 'rehabilitating' in Lisl's apartment. We had nights of hot sex, after she got home from the club in the early hours, she was truly insatiable. We usually woke at midday. She cooked wonderful food, cooking with the meager rations that were all that Berliners had to live on, as well as a good supply of black market supplies that she bought from her contacts at the club. When we weren't eating or making love, we talked.

"I can't believe that you, an American, are fighting for the Nazis, Paul," she said one evening when we'd just finished a bottle of wine after a fine meal. Perhaps it was the alcohol that loosened our tongues.

"I wish to God I wasn't, Lisl, but if you recall I didn't have a choice. It was that or Mauthausen."

"Can't you do anything about it?"

"What kind of thing?" I smiled. "Write to Adolf Hitler and ask to be released from the SS?"

She hesitated for a few moments. "There are many people in Berlin that are opposed to the war, you know."

"Yes, I was opposed to it too when they started shooting prisoners of war and look where it got me."

"They are trying got put a stop to it."

"Fat chance they have while Adolf Hitler is running things."

She was quiet and just looked at me.

I took another sip from my wine. "What?"

"You're right, they've no chance while Hitler is running Germany."

"Well then." Suddenly it dawned on me. "Oh God, no, Lisl! You're talking about the resistance, they're trying to depose Hitler."

"Or get rid of him some other way."

"You mean kill him?" I smiled at the absurdity. "He's the most closely guarded person in the world, my love. He's got a thousand or more SS troopers guarding him, they'll never even get near to him. You should leave those kinds of things alone, they're dangerous politics. Stick with dancing."

"So are you helping your SS colleagues murder innocent civilians like the rest of them, or are you trying to do something about it? We've all heard about your unit, did you think the reputation of the Sonderbattalion Dirlewanger hadn't reached Berlin?"

I trusted her, but if the Gestapo arrested her, she'd give me up, they'd make her, torture her until she told them everything. The Gestapo cellars in the Prinz Albrecht Strasse were infamous for their cruelty, as I'd found out to my cost. It was said that everyone that wound up there admitted everything sooner or later, whether it was true or not. Then again, I didn't want her thinking that I was no better than a mass murderer.

"No, we're not murdering innocent civilians, not all of us. Some of us are trying to stop the worst of their brutality, we've made contacts with the resistance in Poland."

I didn't say more, it was enough. If she didn't know the names, she couldn't reveal them to anyone.

"I assumed you'd be doing something like that, I know you, Paul and I couldn't see you in the role of SS thug and murderer. I do want you to come to the club again tonight, do you feel up to it yet?"

"Why tonight?"

"There's someone I want you to meet."

"Resistance?"

"No, not exactly. He's a Swede. It's nothing political, but I'd like you to talk to him."

I shrugged. "Fair enough, I'd like to go to the club, it's time I went out and stretched my legs without those damned crutches."

"Are you up to it?"

I'd been walking with a single cane for the last two days, my legs were almost healed. I felt a lot better, except that I was due in four days to report for a medical examination. I had little doubt that I'd be sent back to the battalion shortly after.

We'd enjoyed several nights without bombing raids and when we left the apartment the streets were alive with Berliners walking in the quiet moonlight of the evening. I walked confidently on my cane, it was good to be mobile again, even better to be walking with such a beautiful girl holding my other arm. I was dressed in full SS uniform, field grey coat, medals on my tunic, jackboots polished and my cap set at a jaunty angle on my head.

"You look quite handsome in uniform, my darling," Lisl said with a smile of affection.

I pulled her to me and gave her a kiss but as we walked along, I noticed that not everyone shared her liking for the SS, many Berliners gave me hard looks and more than one crossed the road to walk the other side. We reached the Blue Goose, it was a basement bar just off the Kurfurstendamm in the centre of Berlin. Just visible at the end of the street the Kaiser Wilhelm Church, the Gedachtnichtskirche, the beautiful old Protestant church that was one of Berlin's famous landmarks, stood proudly. Lisl found us a table and a waiter brought us drinks. We toasted each other, then she gave a signal to someone I couldn't see. A few moments later a man joined us, he was middle-aged and wearing uniform, but not a uniform I'd ever seen before.

"Paul, this is Count Folke Bernardotte, he is Swedish and he represents the Red Cross here in Berlin and throughout the Reich."

The man gave a small smile. "Call me Folke, please. I prefer not to use my title in informal settings."

We shook hands. His German was fluent and we chatted for a few minutes about the way things were in the city. Then we came to the real reason Lisl had asked me to meet him. He looked at me intently.

"You are currently with the Sonderbattalion Dirlewanger, Paul?"

I was wary now, after all, he was a foreigner, but he appeared to be a friend of Lisl's so hopefully he could be trusted.

"I am, yes, we are currently stationed in Warsaw."

"Not for much longer, I believe."

I was startled, what could he know about the battalion. His lips formed that small, strained smile again.

"I can see you are surprised. The Red Cross has made repeated requests to Reichsfuhrer Himmler to curtail the activities of your murderous friends."

"They're not my friends, Folke, has Lisl told you why I joined the battalion?"

He nodded. "I apologize. Yes, she did tell me that it was the only way out of the concentration camp. Your battalion is moving east, to Belorussia."

"But why?"

"Politics, my friends. Himmler refused to stand the battalion down, despite the pressures from us and the Vatican."

"You're not serious, what involvement does the Vatican have with our battalion?"

"Not with the Sonderbattalion Dirlewanger, but with the twenty million Catholic Poles that have made loud protests that their parish priests have been making to Rome. It was all they could get Himmler to agree to, to move them away from Poland."

I looked around the club, I'd noticed two men that had just come down the steps and walked up to the bar, one of them looked familiar, I couldn't work out who it was at first. Then he turned his head and glanced casually around. Damn! Kriminalassistent Mischer, the Gestapo man who constantly seemed to dog my steps, he always appeared at the most awkward of moments. What the hell was he doing here tonight? Perhaps he had been re-assigned to Berlin, I hoped so, that it was a coincidence. But I wasn't going to let him ruin my evening out in Berlin, perhaps the last for a long time, so I ignored him.

"Look, Folke, this is all very impressive, you knowing the movements of my unit before I do, but what do you want from me if you're that well informed?"

"I need evidence, proof of some of the war crimes your people have committed in the occupied territories."

I'd told Lisl that I'd been keeping a diary, had she told Bernardotte?

"Maybe I haven't got any evidence," I said.

"Paul, I think that you do have exactly the kind of thing I need, dates, places, numbers of people killed and so on."

Lisl looked embarrassed. "I'm sorry, Paul, we hear so many terrible things, I wanted to help."

By getting my head cut off, no doubt. But she was right.

"The diary you need is in Warsaw, when I return to my unit I'll get it sent to Lisl."

CHAPTER NINE

'We shall go down in history as the greatest statesmen of all time, or as the greatest criminals.'
Josef Goebbels, Reich Minister of Popular Enlightenment and Propaganda

We chatted to Count Bernardotte for a short time longer and then he excused himself and left. I watched Lisl's show, she was as outrageous and erotic as ever, stripping almost naked on the small stage. The club was full by midnight, a cross section of wartime Berlin, uniforms, both Army and SS, a few Luftwaffe. Plenty of civilians, but none with the ragged, half-starved appearance that I'd seen in the daytime. These were the party elite and the war profiteers, the ones who always seemed to know how to turn anything into money no matter how bad the situation for the majority of the population. Women in beautiful gowns, many displaying expensive jewelry, a few were middle aged, like their partners, most were young with bright, calculating eyes. Their men wore new, tailor made suits, not for them the frequently darned and repaired clothes of the less fortunate members of the populace. But it was at least a brief respite from the war, away from the sound of gunfire and explosives, the crack of artillery. Lisl, reduced to a near-invisible G-string, finished her last act and went backstage to change. Ten minutes later and fully dressed, she joined me for a final drink and we decided it was time to leave. We got up to the street and started to walk home to her apartment but after less than fifty yards I realized we were not alone. I looked around, Mischer was walking towards us with another man, obviously Gestapo too unless another state organization had taken to wearing black leather coats and trilby hats as a kind of uniform.

We stopped and waited for them, we might as well find out the worst. He came up to us smiling.

"Untersturmfuhrer Schaffer, how nice to see you recovered from your wounds. And the charming Miss von Schenk, may I say how I enjoyed your act."

Lisl nodded at him coldly.

"May I introduce my colleague, Kriminalassistentanwarter Artur Muller."

The other man just stared at us disinterestedly, he was like a farmer inspecting a pair of animals prior to deciding if they were worth him wasting his time on them.

"What do you want, Mischer?"

"What do I want? What can you give me?" he asked with a broad smile.

"I can't give you anything."

"Really? Perhaps you would start by telling me about your conversation with the good Count Bernardotte."

"It was private."

"Nothing is private inside the Third Reich, Schaffer, especially when talking to a foreigner. What did he want? Or perhaps you'd like to come to Prinz Albrecht Strasse to discuss it further?"

"Please, it was just conversation," Lisl said quickly. "Bernardotte was telling Paul that his unit was being moved to Belorussia at the request of the Red Cross and the Vatican, he thought he might be interested."

He nodded. "Yes, I know about that, they want them to stop killing the Roman Catholics and turn on the communists instead. Stupid, really, they're all Slavs, of course."

I shrugged. "That was it, that's what we discussed. Nothing more."

He stared at me, it was an eloquent look, he was saying 'I don't believe a word of it'. But for reasons best known to himself, he decided to let it go. For now. He handed me a card.

"If you hear anything more, you will let me know, won't you, the telephone number of Prinz Albrecht Strasse is on that card," he smiled again, "or you can always call in to the local Gestapo headquarters."

I nodded. "I'll think about it. We need to get home. Miss von Schenk has been working."

I took Lisl's hand to lead her away, but he ignored my move.

"Tell me what you know of Aaron Majewski?"

I tried hard not to betray myself, but I knew that my eyes

would have given me away. I thought of the thin, determined Jewish resistance fighter in the Ghetto. I recalled he'd been captured, had he talked, given them my name?

"Nothing much, I seem to recall we were looking for him in the Ghetto, I recognize the name. We had orders to kill him."

"I see. What about Jakob Koslowski?"

I was more in control now, I shook my head. "Nothing, never heard of him."

"Vladimir Pushkin?"

Jesus Christ, where the hell was he getting these names from? Someone had talked.

"Sounds Russian, but no, I don't know of him."

"He is Belorussian. When you get back to Minsk you may come across him, he's very active across the Reichskommissariat Ostland, including the General Government too. If you come across this gentleman, you will let me know, won't you, Schaffer? We want him badly."

"I will, yes."

"Good. I shall be returning to our eastern territories shortly, perhaps I shall see you there. I will ask Kriminalassistentanwarter Muller to keep a watchful eye on Miss von Schenk. Berlin can be very dangerous in these troubled times, do you not think? I have no doubt you would prefer that nothing bad happens to her. Do keep in touch, goodnight, Untersturmfuhrer, Miss von Schenk."

He smiled coldly and they retraced their steps back towards the club.

"Let's get home," I said, "before they come back. It shouldn't be a problem, he doesn't know anything."

But as we walked along the sidewalk I knew that I was fooling myself, he knew a lot, far too much. At least he hadn't mentioned Anna, I would have found it difficult explaining her to Lisl. He knew all about her, and that I had enjoyed a relationship with her, the question was how much did he know of her resistance work? Had Majewski talked? I felt guilty as soon as the thought crossed my mind, but I hoped that the Polish resistance fighter had died of his wounds before he was able to tell them anything of value.

Four days later, I reported to the SS hospital in Berlin and was cleared to return to my unit in Warsaw. The bored-looking doctor looked at me briefly.

"How are the legs?"

"Better, still sore though but I can walk with a limp."

"Good, you'll be fine."

He stamped my medical certificate and handed it to me. "Next!"

My train was due to leave at nine-thirty the following morning. We had a last, passionate evening together, at the club I got roaring drunk and suggested that Lisl and I escaped to Switzerland. Fortunately, no one of any consequence was there to listen to me. Lisl kicked me out of bed when the dawn was breaking over Berlin. She made me breakfast and coffee, we embraced and kissed and it was time for me to go. I left her with a warning.

"Watch out for the Gestapo, they know a lot more than you realize. I'd stay away from that Swedish Count too if I were you."

"But Paul, he's Red Cross, he's not a threat."

"Neither was Pastor Niemoller, but he's still locked up in Dachau concentration camp."

Martin Niemoller was a pastor and theologian born in Lippstadt, Germany, in 1892. He was an anti-communist and supported Hitler's rise to power at first. When Hitler insisted on the supremacy of the state over religion, Niemoller became disillusioned and became the leader of a group of German clergymen opposed to Hitler. Unlike Niemoller, the group eventually gave in to the Nazi threats. He was arrested and sent to Sachsenhausen and then Dachau concentration camps, where he was still held prisoner. Lisl looked anxious. "They can't arrest Bernardotte, he has diplomatic protection."

"No doubt he has, my darling, but you do not."

Was it only last year that Germany had almost been knocking on the gates of Moscow? Now, the masters of Europe didn't even seem able to supply a well-maintained train to make the long journey back to the occupied eastern territories. It was filthy, most of the seats were torn, the woodwork scratched and the floor covered in dirt and debris. It stank, reminding me of the hospital train I'd ridden in that brought me to Berlin. My compartment rapidly filled up with soldiers, most of us returning to the east after recovering from wounds or back from leave. Two SS officers came in and sat down, they looked at my own SS uniform and its unit badges curiously.

"Which unit are you?" one of them asked, a Hauptsturmfuhrer, a captain.

"Sonderbattalion Dirlewanger, Sir," I replied. "We're based in Warsaw at present."

They looked at each other, then back at me as if I had suddenly acquired a bad case of body odor. They got up and went out to find another compartment. Obviously, the CO's wish was coming true, his unit was indeed becoming famous and widely known throughout the Reich. Two junior Wehrmacht officers took their places and we chatted throughout the journey.

"Where are you headed?" I asked one of them, a Leutnant.

"Stalingrad, the Sixth Army. We're attached to the 76th Infantry Division, VIII Armeekorps."

I tried to look impressed, but the battle at Stalingrad was turning into an epic and unending struggle.

"I thought the Red Army was threatening to encircle Stalingrad, isn't von Paulus planning to pull the Sixth Army back?"

They both looked sheepish. Eventually the Leutnant said, "A strategic withdrawal has been suggested, but the Fuhrer has refused to allow us to pull back. We'll beat them still, the Soviets, they're almost finished."

I made no reply. There was something about Russia that made all of us uneasy, it was so huge, vast, open steppes, freezing cold winters that we were ill-prepared for and ill-equipped to fight in. In the spring and autumn the unpaved roads and tracks turned into muddy quagmires that were impossible to negotiate. The Russians were well aware of how best to use the terrain, it was their own ground and they constantly seemed able to surprise our armed forces, striking where they were least expected and just disappearing into the endless steppes. Stalingrad was resisting all of our efforts to dislodge the Red Army and the city of Leningrad seemed no less a tough nut to crack. Moscow too was as distant as ever, despite the endless ranting of Dr Goebbels on the radio to the contrary.

"I hope you're right, Leutnant," I replied politely.

I managed to fend off too many awkward questions about the nature of the battalion I was attached to and then I fell into a sleep for much of the journey. When the train pulled into Warsaw, the unit had been alerted to my arrival and Karl-Heinz was waiting outside in a Kubelwagen. After the customary greetings, he asked about Berlin. I raised my eyes to the heavens. "The American and British bombers are destroying it, my friend, block by block, it's not pretty. I gather we're about to move back to Belorussia?"

He nodded, surprised that I knew already. "We only heard yesterday, how come you're so well informed?"

I told him about Bernardotte and his request for my diary. He looked dubious.

"I hope it doesn't fall into the wrong hands, that's all, it could get us all chopped. You know we've had the Gestapo sniffing around."

"What were they looking for?" I asked him. Inside I felt chilled, I knew exactly what they were looking for, evidence of a link to the partisans.

"Who knows? They didn't tell me, they just spent time talking to the CO."

We reached Headquarters, Karl-Heinz drove straight into

the courtyard.

"I'll take your bag to your room, Sir."

"Thanks, Scharfuhrer. I'll report to the CO, is Dirlewanger back yet?"

"Two days ago, he still looks pretty bad but he insisted on getting back into the fight, that's what he said."

I nodded and went into the hotel, to the 'planning room'. Dirlewanger was sitting in an old armchair, his feet on a box of grenades. Karl-Heinz was right, he did look terrible, pale, strained, his face etched with lines of pain.

"Schaffer, it's good to see you back in time for our move. You know we're going back to Belorussia?"

"I heard, Sir."

"Good. They need us there, Untersturmfuhrer, they need a firm hand to keep the partisans in check. We've done a good job here, too good, I expect, that's why they asked for us back in Belorussia."

"I'm sure our reputation is widely known, Sir."

"That's true, yes, they've all heard of us. We leave tomorrow morning, we'll be loading our vehicles onto flatcars, the train will take us all the way to Minsk. Exciting times, Schaffer!"

"Yes, Sir."

I saluted and left him, out in the courtyard I almost ran straight into Max Hofstetter. We shook hands.

"You look well, Max."

"Yes, I feel a lot better, thanks."

I was just being polite, he was very strained and pale, like a man who's seen a ghost.

"Is everything set for the morning, anything I need to know?"

"Paul, I've been looking after your platoon for the past four days, I've no platoon of my own to lead after the ambush in the Ghetto. I don't know what Dirlewanger has in mind for me, but your men and equipment are all ready."

His expression was strange, vacant, I was about to reply when he walked away without another word. What had happened to the old, bombastic Max, confident, brash and always elegant? He looked a shadow of his former self, thin and gaunt, his uniform shabby and unkempt. The bomb blast had taken more out of him than was realized. I found my platoon, he had indeed done a good job, everything was in good order, packed and ready. I shook hands with Gerd.

"You heard about the Gestapo?" he asked.

I nodded.

"We need to be careful, Sir, they know that something's up."

"I know, Gerd, but they don't know about us, so we're safe. Don't worry, they won't get near us."

I didn't tell him about meeting Mischer in Berlin, if he knew that the Gestapo had the names of the Polish resistance fighters and had connected them to us he would probably find somewhere quiet and shoot himself.

I wasn't technically on duty until five o'clock the following morning, there was only one place I wanted to go and I wasn't going to allow the SS, the Gestapo or the Red Army to stop me.

"Paul."

"Anna."

We fell into each other's arms. Words were not needed. We got to the foot of the staircase, past the astonished looks of her seamstresses, I winced as we started to climb. She looked at me, concerned.

"Are you ok, you're not fully healed yet?"

"Good enough for today, Anna, what are you waiting for?"

We raced up the last of her stairs and into her living room, we were already throwing our clothes off, we made love on the shabby rug in front of a tiny fire. She was so different to Lisl, who was very, very experienced, very adroit in the most sophisticated arts of lovemaking. Anna was warm, when we made love it was as much a meeting of minds as of bodies. That she really loved me I had no doubt and I felt the same way about her. I felt guilty about Lisl, that was a difficult one. Did I love Lisl too, I wondered? No, I did not, certainly not in the same way. Was I ready to make a commitment to Anna, to her and to no other? I still wasn't sure, but it was very tempting.

"Can you stay for the night?"

I told her that we were leaving for Belorussia in the morning and her face fell.

"So soon? When will you be back?"

"I don't know, Anna. As soon as I get leave I will return to Warsaw."

"In that case I will be patient. You know that the Gestapo have been asking more questions?"

"Yes, I know. We have to be more careful than ever."

"Sometimes, Paul, I think this war will go on forever. And if it does ever end, we will already be dead."

I argued with her and told her not to lose hope, the Russians were hitting back hard and might even fight the German armies to a standstill.

"Then there could be a peace, a negotiated peace."

She smiled, but I knew she didn't believe it any more than she believed in Father Christmas.

It was after midnight when I returned to Headquarters. I was sure that I was followed, but the streets were dark in the blackout and it was impossible to be certain. I found my bed and tried to get some sleep but I needed to attack my small supply of vodka before my mind stopped racing with all of the dangers and challenges that I faced.

In the morning there was too much to do to be overly anxious about the problems that were closing in on me, problems like the Gestapo. Problems that the war may resolve naturally anyway with a bullet or a bomb, I'd already come very close. We drove to the railway station, loaded our vehicles onto the flatcars and boarded the passenger coaches. During the journey east, Dirlewanger came around to inspect his troops and entered our compartment.

"Schaffer, I'm promoting you to acting Obersturmfuhrer, you will be in command and Hofstetter will serve under you until we can replace his platoon. If you perform your duties well in Belorussia, I will make your promotion permanent. That's all."

He left and I looked at Max. "I'm sorry, Max, it wasn't my idea."

He hadn't spoken a word that day, as far as I was aware. He was clearly carrying some serious mental baggage. Maybe that was the best way to survive in this battalion, to have lost your mind. We steamed into Minsk, the vehicles were unloaded from the flatcars and we drove along familiar streets to the Karl Marx Hotel. It had been unoccupied since we'd left, Kraus had arranged for local workmen to clear the worst of the rubbish and make sure we had some basic lighting and plumbing. We drove into the courtyard, the men unloaded, we posted sentries and then collapsed, exhausted. Kraus disturbed us briefly, coming around to shout, "Reveille at five am, inspection in full kit at six thirty."

I couldn't sleep and I found that I need more of my familiar companion, the vodka bottle, to help me relax. I was caught between two armies, the German Army who would kill me if they found out what I was doing and the Red Army who wanted to kill me anyway. Throw in the partisans, the local civilians who hated us, the troops of our battalion who were mostly unstable drunks and criminals and add our CO who was a suicidal psychotic and it was little wonder that I found myself so badly stressed. The vodka finally did its work and I dropped off to sleep. I woke up to someone blowing a whistle loudly.

"Achtung, Achtung, stand to!"

Sturmscharfuhrer Mintel was sadistically enjoying his task of rousing the sleeping officers. I climbed out of bed, pulled on my boots and sloshed water over my face. I strapped on my belt and holster, adjusted my cap and I was ready. I joined the men for a cold breakfast, bread, turnip jam washed down with ersatz coffee and started to get them assembled for inspection. It was six o'clock, we had a half hour to go when Kraus ran shouting through the courtyard.

"General inspection in fifteen minutes, I've just had a telephone call, the General is coming to look at the battalion shortly, hurry up and fall in!"

I looked around at the men. Worn out troops, worn out vehicles and worn out guns, I doubted he'd be very impressed. I still had a certain degree of pride so I bullied and cajoled my hungover and half-asleep soldiers into some semblance of a military formation. We had just formed into line when someone shouted, "They're coming!"

A half-track came rattling along the road and turned into our vehicle park, a Sonderkraftfahrzeug 251, the familiar armored personnel carrier widely employed by the Wehrmacht and SS. The vehicle had mounted machine guns fore and aft, MG34s both manned by crews in steel helmets, they watched everything carefully. There were four more SS troopers squeezed into the front of the half-track, the sole occupant of the back seat was one man. Then the vehicle came to a halt, the troopers jumped out and formed up while the machine gun crews stayed behind their guns. One of the troops opened the rear door and placed a small step underneath it. Their NCO shouted 'Achtung' and only then did the officer deign to stand up and climb down to the ground.

Higher SS and Police Leader Erich von dem Bach-Zelewski, with the rank of Gruppenfuhrer, he was the General entrusted with the military command of the whole of Belorussia and some parts of the Baltic States to the north. He glanced at us casually, Hitler had designated him as the future Higher SS and Police Leader for Moscow, however, the German armies so far had failed to take the city. Von dem Bach-Zelewski was in overall charge of all anti-partisan units on this front, a special command created by Adolf Hitler that he occupied in addition to his administrative duties. Despite having the personal ear of the Fuhrer, he had enjoyed a mixed career and had many detractors. It was said that von dem Bach-Zelewski's tactics produced high civilian deaths with relatively minor military gains, following the tactics he employed. His forces would encircle partisan areas before closing in, but since deploying the necessary forces was so conspicuous, the partisans would be forewarned and many would slip away, after hiding their heavier equipment and many of their supplies. The remaining partisans would carry out a fighting withdrawal, picking off the German troops as they fell back, often resulting in more German losses than partisans. In fighting these irregular battles, his men wantonly slaughtered civilians in order to inflate the figures of enemy losses, so that his detractors said that far more civilian fatalities were recorded than partisan weapons captured. After an operation was completed and the troops moved elsewhere, the partisans normally slipped back to retrieve their hidden supplies and renew the fight. Even when successful, von dem Bach-Zelewski accomplished little more than forcing partisans to relocate to other areas, their numbers swelled with enraged civilians.

His more enthusiastic followers simply pointed to the

numbers of Slavs and Jews he had killed and forced into the camps. There were indeed tens of thousands of them. He was a tall, fleshy looking man with gold-rimmed glasses, he looked more like a headmaster than an SS general. Dirlewanger ran up and almost kissed his hand.

"Sir, we're honored that you have come to inspect the battalion."

Von dem Bach-Zelewski nodded, a chill, half smile on his face. "I'll speak to them now, Sturmbannfuhrer."

He stood silently for a few moments, looking at our ranks. If he was disturbed by the dirty, disheveled look of the troops on display before him, he gave no sign of it.

"You are here for one reason, and one reason only. Partisans!"

He spat the word out with contempt. "There is only one way to deal with these communist and Jew partisans and I'm told that you men know what to do. Tell me how you will rid this country of these vermin."

"Kill them!" the men shouted with enthusiasm.

He smiled. "Excellent, now, I have awards to hand out. Sturmbannfuhrer, step forward."

He gave Dirlewanger a wound badge to add to the others already sewn on his uniform. I was called forward along with Max and several other troopers and he gave us our wound badges. We stepped back and saluted.

"I also have the honor to present the Iron Cross First Class to Sturmbannfuhrer Dirlewanger and the Iron Cross Second Class to Untersturmfuhrer Hofstetter and Obersturmfuhrer

Schaffer, step forward men."

He pinned the medals on our tunics and we stepped back. He checked his watch.

"I am due to visit the front today, I have to leave. You know what to do, make sure you do it, show them no mercy. Sturmbannfuhrer, here are your new orders."

Von dem Bach-Zelewski handed Dirlewanger a thick envelope, they saluted and he climbed back into his half-track. Dirlewanger dismissed us and we set to the maintenance tasks that desperately needed carrying out if our equipment was to function in the field with any degree of efficiency. As for the men, they were long past the point of functioning in the field with anything other than drunken, murderous rage.

The trucks all looked worn out. They were in need of maintenance, spare tires, oil changes, even spare axles and gearboxes. They crunched and ground their way along the tracks and roads, constantly threatening to break down. Many did break down causing more problems for our overstretched supplies. Kraus came bustling out into the vehicle park.

"The CO wants all officers inside now, we have a new mission due to start tomorrow morning."

He was fidgeting with excitement, more his old self.

"My friends, Operation Frieda launches tomorrow, an anti-partisan operation. We've been tasked with the destruction of a powerful partisan group under," he paused to check his orders, "someone called General Wiejerew. This group normally operates around the forests south of Borissov. Once again, we will be joining with 1 SS-Infanterie-Brigade, our job is quite straightforward, we go in there and kill all of the bastards. Borissov is about forty miles from here, we shall meet the Brigade on the outskirts of Minsk and travel in convoy. I want everyone on the mission, the whole battalion, we need to make a strong showing."

I noticed that his shiny new Iron Cross First Class was displayed prominently on his tunic, he seemed more puffed up than ever with martial enthusiasm. He looked at us steadily for a few moments as if to assess our own commitment, then dismissed us. We went back to trying to persuade our tired, hungover troops and our tired, worn out vehicles and equipment to be ready for the operation. When the men went to the cookhouse for lunch, Karl-Heinz, Gerd and myself found a quiet spot to talk.

"How do we play this one?" Gerd asked me. "I don't think that writing about it afterwards will be enough, do you?"

I shook my head. "No, the poor bastards in the forest are going to be murdered. Those bastards from 1 SS Infantry are worse than our own battalion, they're all former concentration camp guards."

"Is there no one in Minsk that can get word to them?" Karl-Heinz asked.

I shook my head. "I haven't got a clue."

"Maybe it's time we joined the partisans," Gerd said. "We're all fed up with seeing these people killed just for defending their homes from murderous thugs like this lot."

"We can't fight several hundred armed SS, Gerd," I said gently. "They'll just have to take their chances. We'll do our best."

In the morning, we boarded the trucks and drove out into the suburbs. In a clearing just outside the city, the 1 SS Infantry Brigade was assembled ready. We stopped and their CO came across to speak to Dirlewanger. Oberfuhrer Richard Herrmann was every inch the concentration camp commandant. His leering, arrogant expression swept over us, those of us including myself that had been inside the camps shivered. His field grey SS uniform was well cut but sufficiently crumpled to show off the fact that he was a fighting soldier. The Iron Cross First Class hung on his tunic, he had dust goggles pushed back on his forehead to make him look like a caricature of General Rommel. His features were hawkish, yet underlying them there were pouches of flabbiness on his face and his slightly rounded posture was anything but military. In short, he was a poser. The two commanders shook hands, exchanged a few words and went back to their vehicles. Herrmann waved to his men and they roared off in a cloud of blue exhaust smoke. We followed, Dirlewanger had the sense to drop behind so that we were spared the worst of the dust they kicked up. There were no holdups on the road to Borissov and we arrived there an hour and a half later.

On the outskirts, we passed the grim barbed wire of a concentration camp, the guard towers stark against the green landscape and blue sky. Inside I could see the usual poor souls, thousands of them, standing, watching, doing nothing while they starved to death. Borissov was a medium sized town, I estimated that it had about fifty thousand inhabitants, I wondered how many of them were already in the camp we'd passed on the way in. We stopped in a large square in the centre of town and were allowed to step down from the vehicles for half an hour to take a break. Herrmann and Dirlewanger called a meeting of the officers. Oberfuhrer Herrmann had a map on the hood of his half-track.

"Sturmbannfuhrer, you will deploy your men this side of the forest on the edge of the town. My brigade will circle around five miles to the east and enclose them in a pincer. It's a hammer and anvil approach, we will be the hammer and drive them on to you, the anvil."

He continued with a long tirade of technical military terminology. I could hardly believe it. He was using the language of Erich von Manstein, Erwin Rommel, the tactical geniuses of this war. It was as if he was at the head of a huge Panzer army, not a motley collection of thugs and bullyboys. But Dirlewanger reveled in it.

"We won't let you down, Sir, we'll be ready for them. We'll be your anvil!"

"Good man."

Herrmann swaggered away and swung up to his half-track, he shouted an order and they drove away. We were told to leave a guard on the vehicles and set up a battle line five hundred yards away on the outskirts of the town.

"Leave the vehicles under guard, we won't need the artillery either," the CO said, nodding at the three anti-tank guns still connected to the tow bars of three of our trucks. "We will need all of the mortars, the MG34s and make sure the men have plenty of ammunition. Jump to it, men, we need to get ourselves prepared for the coming battle and show these people that the battalion means business!"

Karl-Heinz and I exchanged glances. He was living it, seeing himself as some kind of latter-day Teutonic Knight, probably. As I recalled from school, that particular order of Germanic warriors met a bloody end at the battle of Tannenberg in AD 1410, crushed by a Polish and Lithuanian army, the ancestors of today's Belorussian partisans. It may well be best not to mention that fact to our CO. My platoon began unloading our equipment from the truck and started walking to our assigned position. I noticed men slipping away as we marched across the town, the lure of a bar or brothel was more than most of the battalion could resist. I didn't care if they never returned, Herrmann's brigade of psychotic lunatics was able to do more than enough damage to the partisans, they didn't need help from us.

We deployed on the edge of the forest and sat down to wait. The morning was quiet and peaceful, the townspeople had enough sense to stay indoors, or maybe some of them had left the town completely. The men got impatient, the inevitable schnapps bottles came out and soon the smell of brandy reeked on the breath of many of my men. Kraus, the adjutant came around.

"All set, Schaffer?"

"All ready, yes, Sir."

"Good man."

He marched away and reported to Dirlewanger, who had

somehow acquired a swagger stick that he used for effect, slapping it against his polished jackboot. I looked away as a crackle of machine gun fire sounded from the forest.

"Achtung, stand by!" the CO shouted.

"Do you want me to get the rest of the men out of the bar?" Karl-Heinz asked me.

I shook my head. "Let them enjoy themselves, there are enough killers here to do what's needed."

I ducked as a short burst of sub-machine gunfire raked across us. Five armed men were emerging from the forest, they didn't see us at first, then they opened fire. Our battalion shot back, over a hundred guns blazed at the men and all five went down, shredded by the sheer weight of bullets. More gunfire sounded and we dived for cover as the partisans, alerted to our presence, brought up more people and weapons. We were in a serious firefight now, the battalion blazed away, pouring thousands of rounds into the wood, shredding trees, foliage and men. We didn't get it all our own way, two of the men spun around, hit by Russian gunfire, but once Dirlewanger ordered the mortars brought into operation the end was never in doubt. Shells whistled overhead, ripping great holes in the wood, shouts and screams of agony signaled that they were effective. Soon, the return fire slackened and then died altogether. Dirlewanger shouted for the cease-fire and we cautiously went forward to check the casualties.

The partisans had been torn to pieces, there were the remains of at least thirty bodies in the wood. It was obvious that the main force had got away, but even so they'd been hit hard. Our troops began to rifle their pockets and take away loot and souvenirs. Two of them went around checking that they were all dead, twice they fired shots to finish off the wounded. We pulled back into the town and I sent Karl-Heinz and another trooper to drag our deserters out of the bar so that we would be ready to return. There was a shout as a group of men appeared in the distance, but it was part of Hermann's brigade, pushing out of the forest and into the town, probably to hit the bars. They came nearer and I saw that Hermann was at their head. He looked coldly at Dirlewanger. "How many did you kill, Sturmbannfuhrer?"

"I estimate the body count at a hundred and fifty," he replied with a straight face.

"You'll put that in your report?"

"Yes, Sir."

"Good. Our body count was around a thousand, so it's been a worthwhile mission. It's not enough , though, I suspect the townspeople must have been giving these terrorists aid. I'm going to billet the men here overnight, in the morning we'll take the houses, one at a time and see if we can't find some more of these damned terrorists. I estimate there must be at least another thousand hiding in these buildings, don't you think, Dirlewanger?"

"At least, Sir, perhaps more."

"Good. It's a simple police action so we won't need your men any further. You may return to Minsk when you're ready."

On the way back, I could think of nothing other than the people of Borissov that were to be butchered by Herrmann's

1 SS Infantry Brigade. There was nothing I could do to stop it, but I would make sure it was properly documented and then find a way to get the report to Bernardotte in Berlin. No matter what the risk was, he had to see it. Max sat next to me in the back of the truck and I couldn't discuss anything with Gerd or Karl-Heinz, but I would speak with them later and find a way to contact Bernardotte. Max was morose, nothing like he'd been before. I tried to draw him out on several occasions but he just shrugged and said nothing. We drove into the vehicle park and unloaded the trucks. It was early evening and the three of us walked into town to find a quiet bar and discuss the problem. The waiter brought us drinks and left.

"We need to locate Pushkin," I said to them. "He's the only one I know who seems to have the mobility to go between here and Warsaw. Once the Polish resistance has the diary, they can get it to Bernardotte. The question is, how do we locate Pushkin?"

"I have been asking myself the same question, Obersturmfuhrer Schaffer," a voice said behind me. We looked around quickly, the Gestapo man, Mischer, was looking at us with a sardonic smile on his face and a pistol in his hand pointed straight at us. If he was on his own I would have tried to take him, but he had an assistant with him, also Gestapo, armed with an MP38. "You haven't met Garmash, have you? He's a local man, one of our Belorussian volunteers." The subordinate looked at us blankly, his eyes fathomless, yet the half smile, half sneer on his lips was eloquent enough. He was Mischer's Rotweiler, his guard dog, trained to savage on command from his master.

"What are you talking about, Mischer?" I asked him. "Take those stupid guns out of our faces before someone gets hurt."

He didn't budge. "You were talking about Pushkin," he said.

"That's true, I wasn't aware you were so keen on poetry," I replied.

"You're wasting your time, Schaffer, I know what you've been up to. Tell me, what do you know about the partisan leader named Pushkin? He is in command of the entire partisan network in the occupied territories, we have to find him."

"Stop fucking around, Mischer, he's a poet, that's all. I don't know anything about a partisan of that name or any other name. Now fuck off and leave us alone!"

I thought bluffing it out was worth a try, but he didn't even blink.

"I will count to five, Schaffer, either you will tell me what you know about Pushkin or I will place you under arrest and have you interrogated at the local Gestapo HQ. I have already sent a file to my assistant, Muller, in Berlin. When he has finished collating those names with terrorist activities, we will make the arrests. Your name is on that file, Schaffer, together will all of your known associates."

My mind whirled, he would arrest Anna, she would be tortured and killed. He saw the look of distress on my face and correctly interpreted it.

"Yes, the girl is on the file too, that one in Warsaw, the dressmaker. I'll have some fun with her, perhaps I'll hand her over to Garmash here for his personal attention."

I made a move towards him but he angled the pistol at my stomach.

"In fact, I may have to take your men into custody too, the Mauthausen survivors you joined up with, you think we don't know about the weapons you supplied to the Jews in the Ghetto? You've all been conspiring against the Reich, haven't you? You have five seconds to start talking if you wish to avoid going back into the camps. It's not too late to make a deal, Schaffer, only Muller in Berlin knows about the file, if you tell me what you know it goes no further. All I want you to do is give up this partisan leader."

We waited, frozen into immobility. To give up what I knew about Pushkin would mean giving up what I knew about Anna. That wasn't going to happen, I would sooner die. He counted down, five, four, three, two, one..."

There was a short burst of sub-machine gun fire. I shuddered, waiting for the bullets to slam into my stomach and hurl me to the floor to die an agonizing death, but none of it happened. Mischer and his assistant were hurled to the ground, their bodies lying torn and bloodied by the burst of gunfire. Behind them stood Max, Unterfuhrer Max Hofstetter, Swiss playboy, holding a smoking machine pistol.

"Max! What the fuck are you doing?"

"What I should have done a long time ago, Schaffer. We were all in Mauthausen together, we saw what it was like. These Nazi bastards are turning the whole of Eastern Europe into one big concentration camp. I've had enough, Mauthausen, Belarus, the Ghetto, it's all they can think of, torture, reprisals, death and imprisonment. I've stopped supporting these people, never again. I'd sooner die!"

I was staggered. "We'd better hide these bodies quickly, my friend, otherwise you may get your wish sooner than you think."

"Schaffer, you don't get it, do you? I don't care, not any more. I can't take this anymore!"

While we watched horror struck, he turned the machine pistol around and pointed it to his head.

"Max, no, don't, no!" I shouted. I made a lunge for him but it was too late, for the second time the quiet bar erupted to the sound of sub machine gun fire. Max collapsed, the gun fell to the floor and he lay beside it, blood oozing out of his head.

IRON CROSS AMERIKA

CHAPTER TEN

'They have given their sons to the military services. They have stoked the furnaces and hurried the factory wheels. They have made the planes and welded the tanks. Riveted the ships and rolled the shells.'

President Franklin D. Roosevelt

Two weeks later, Dirlewanger finally got his wish to write his name in the glorious annals of warfare, the chance to fight a real enemy. Since that evening in the bar when Max had taken his life, we'd carried on in a more subdued fashion. It was too embarrassing for Himmler's RSHA to mount an in-depth investigation, after all, it was essentially an internal matter, one of his own SS officers killing two of his Gestapo officers and then committing suicide, so we were in the clear. I worried constantly about Muller in Berlin, if what Mischer had said was true he could still use the file in his possession have us all arrested and executed. Hermann's murderous 1 SS Infantry

Brigade continued their campaign of rampage in Belorussia and in the process managed to more than treble the recruitment to the partisans.

I discovered that they had so for managed to murder more than twenty thousand people in and around Borissov and still they carried on raping, pillaging and murdering the population. One of my men had been forced to return to Germany for emergency treatment after he almost died from pneumonia. I persuaded him to take the diary and only hand it over personally to the Red Cross office in Berlin when he had recovered. At least that would not involve Lisl von Schenk. It was still a risk, but it was worth taking. Casualties had increased dramatically in Belorussia, both at the front and in the rear areas as the Russians began to hit back hard. If the Gestapo did get their hands on the diary, the chances are that I would be dead already. Partisan activity in the city had worsened and we had already lost eight of our men, left hanging from lampposts, their bodies mutilated and signs hung from their chests. 'This is what happens to Germans who invade our homeland'. They had used a typical German anti-partisan tactic against us, hanging our soldiers from lampposts with placards and I was sure the irony was not lost on our men.

The alert sounded at two o'clock in the morning, I'd only just got to sleep, after drinking almost an entire bottle of vodka to help me forget.

"Achtung, Achtung, alarm!"

I pulled on my boots, strapped on my belt and went outside, the whole place was in chaos. Heinrich Weiss was shouting orders to his platoon.

"What's up?"

"It's the Russians, they've made a breakthrough at Velikiye Luki, they've got our people surrounded. Part of the 83rd Infantry Division is holding out against at least two full Soviet Armies, they're sending out a relief force, they're calling it Gruppe Woehler. It's a mixed forced, we're joining up with the 291st Infantry Division, the 8th Panzers, the 20th Motorized infantry. Christ, they've even got a Luftwaffe outfit roped in. Orders are to go and break the siege and get those men out if we can. It's great, we're finally going to kick some real Russian ass instead of these bloody partisans."

I thanked him and went to find the CO. He was barking orders at his men, sending them running to prepare to go into battle. He saw me and called me over.

"Schaffer, get your men ready to go, we're moving out to join with the other units of Gruppe Woehler. By God, we're going to kick their red asses this time, we've got Panzers, man, a whole regiment. But we need to move fast, time is short, if they bring up another two or three shock armies the Russians could swamp the city at any time."

He was crackling with adrenaline-fueled fury, his eyes burning with excitement. At long last he would be getting his wish to take his battalion into action with real soldiers and give the Soviets a bloody nose. I wondered if the Red Army would follow his script.

It was a long, boring and tiring drive through the barren, plundered Belorussian landscape. We were driving into Soviet

Russia proper, not one of their outlying satellites. Here, there were not likely to be any faces turned to welcome us from the boot of Russian communist oppression. This was Stalin's Russia, not one of their reluctant colonies. The only faces turned to us would be cold and brutal, their sole ambition would be to take revenge. We drove all through the day and into the evening, eventually we teamed up with Gruppe Woehler at Novosokolniki, about twenty miles outside Velikiye Luki. They were deployed alongside the railway, defending it against Soviet attacks to cut the railway line and destroy the river bridges, part of a long logistical chain that fed our Army Group North and Army Group Centre. We parked in a field outside of the town and hurriedly went into a staff meeting. It was held in a large, unheated barn, lit only by paraffin lanterns. I went inside with my compatriot Heinrich Weiss and waited while the group of officers talked loudly amongst themselves. We stopped as the door opened and a senior officer, a full Wehrmacht General swept in with three of his staff trailing behind him. Lieutenant-General Theodor Scherer, Commander of the 83rd Infantry Division. Unusually for a senior officer he wore a beard, as well as spectacles, he also displayed a Knight's Cross around his neck complete with Oak Leaves. It was quite clear to us all that this was a professional fighting soldier, not one of Himmler's murderous partisan hunting thugs. He didn't waste a second getting down to business.

"Gentlemen, we have a straightforward problem, the garrison is trapped inside the city, a total of seven thousand men including some troops of my own 83rd Infantry Division.

The city is under the command of Lieutenant-Colonel Eduard Freiherr von Sass, who reports that his situation is becoming desperate. The Soviets have attacked with at least two of their shock armies, the Third and the Fourth, currently they have encircled Colonel Sass' forces and they have no way to extricate themselves. Our mission is to break through the Soviet lines and reach the city before the Russians reinforce the siege with more of their troops. Once we have broken through, we will mount a counter-offensive and destroy the Soviet armies. Questions?"

The cold, dimly lit barn went silent. His description of what we faced was eloquent, direct and anything but simple. We were vastly outnumbered, outgunned and at the very end of our overstretched supply lines that could be severed at any time. Even if we broke through, we would still be at risk of a further Soviet encirclement. I put up my hand.

"Sir, can the garrison not evacuate the city completely? It seems to me that merely breaking through won't prevent the Soviets bringing up further armies to keep battering the city, in which case we'll be doing this all over again."

He gave me a wintry smile. "You are an SS officer?"

I nodded.

"Waffen SS?"

I shook my head. His expression darkened.

"You must be Einsatzgruppe, then, you're all former concentration camp guards and released prisoners, unless I miss my guess. In which case, you have only been fighting the partisans until now. From where do you get your tactical and

strategic understanding of the Red Army-=
?"

I was annoyed with him, I had no doubt he was a brave soldier but a little less of his arrogance wouldn't have gone amiss, after all, we were supposed to be on the same side.

"I was just suggesting we tried to avoid another Stalingrad, Sir. I'm not sure where General von Paulus learned his strategic understanding of the Red Army before the Sixth Army was encircled. I just thought it would be a good idea to stop it happening again."

He flushed bright red with anger. "Listen to me, the Sixth Army will be rescued, von Manstein will see to it."

But even as he shouted, it must have been running through his brain that he'd just agreed with my argument. If von Paulus' Sixth Army, the largest, best-equipped army in the German Order of Battle needed to be rescued from the Red Army, something had gone badly wrong.

"The Fuhrer has directed that the city must be defended at all costs, there will be no retreat!"

There was a sudden murmur of voices. The Sixth Army had been given exactly the same order at Stalingrad and now they were cut off from German lines and battling both the Red Army and the Russian Winter, desperately fighting for survival.

"We move out at first light, that's all. You," he pointed at me, "which unit are you attached to?"

"SS Sonderbattalion Dirlewanger, Sir."

"Sturmbannfuhrer Dirlewanger, yes?" I nodded. "Very well, your unit may have the honor of leading the attack tomorrow morning. That's all."

The CO and Kraus were waiting as I exited the barn. "Not clever, Schaffer, to upset the General, but it ended well, him giving us the lead in the attack. We'd better make certain we're fully ready to go in the morning if we're taking the point."

"I'll ask the men to cut down on the booze, Sir."

"Good idea, Schaffer, see to it."

Did the stupid bastard really think that we'd been sent to lead the attack for anything other than a way to slap me in the face for daring to criticize the Wehrmacht? An upstart band of SS cutthroats daring to upstage the Prussian military aristocracy? Probably he did and Kraus would agree with anything he said. I was cold, tired, hungry and fed up. If the Russians had only half the numbers our intelligence had predicted I could quite possibly be dead by this time tomorrow and I couldn't give a damn about the battalion, the General or Adolf Hitler and his bunch of sycophantic psychopaths. I just wanted it all to end.

Dawn abruptly broke through the inky sky. In the distance we could see the city of Velikiye Luki. The railway line ran straight to the outskirts where there were huge marshalling yards. There was a nearby road, which was to be our route forward. As a concession to commonsense, Scherer had allocated a squadron of Panzer III tanks to take the lead and destroy any enemy opposition. Even mounting the larger 7.5 centimeter gun, the tank was obsolete. It had been re-assigned to serve alongside the infantry as an armored support vehicle, together with the similarly outdated Panzer IV, since the arrival of newer Russian tank designs made it vulnerable to enemy fire. But there were no heavier tanks available, we would have to manage with what we had.

The four Panzers clanked along the road, Dirlewanger followed four hundred yards behind, standing erect and looking every inch the fighting warrior he longed to be, in his Kubelwagen 'command car'. Behind him we followed in our trucks, I was in the passenger seat of our ancient Ursus. I was convinced that we would be moving into a situation that needed quick decisions. Decisions like 'get out fast'. I'd instructed our MG34 gunner to be ready to open fire the moment the enemy was sighted, he was standing with his head through the roof hatch, manning the gun. In an emergency, I would stand and serve the weapon with fresh belts until the loader came forward. The morning was quiet, too quiet. The only visible signs of movement were our four Panzers and the battalion transport vehicles. We were only five miles from the city, still there was no sign of any kind of a siege or encirclement, no artillery barrage, nothing, just us. It seemed too good to be true, just as I was beginning to think that the Russians might have pulled out I heard the loud crack of an anti-tank gun. The lead Panzer III slewed to one side as the shell struck one of its tracks, smoke poured out of the stricken vehicle, flames licked around the engine compartment and the hatch was flung open as the crew leapt out to avoid being incinerated.

"Get off the road, into the trees!" I shouted to our driver. The trooper swerved the wheel over, his skin was pale, he was shaking in terror. He drove fast into the trees, all around us vehicles from our unit were coming to a stop and troops jumping to the ground, some taking cover, others preparing the machine guns to defend us.

Dirlewanger sent a trooper to find Scherer, "Ask him for orders, does he want us to keep pressing forward or find another route into the city?" He caught sight of me, "Schaffer, pass the word, until we hear orders to the contrary, we'll keep going forward and knock out those Russians. Get the men formed up, I'll lead them myself, hurry, man! Where's Kraus?"

We formed up in a small clearing, there were almost two hundred of us, the whole battalion. Dirlewanger gave orders for the gun crews to deploy our artillery, they would need to be unhitched and manhandled back out into the open to be able to fire on the enemy. I didn't envy the crews, they looked at each other in terror as he gave the orders, they only had flimsy shields on the guns to protect the crews from incoming fire. Dirlewanger barked more orders and they raced to unshackle the guns from the trucks and push them one by one back into the open to find targets. The firing became intense, rifles, machine guns and the occasional explosion of a mortar shell as the Russians sought us out in the wood. The CO led us off towards the Russian positions, marching proudly upright at the front of his men as ever. He strode along confidently while the rest of us shuffled nervously behind him. For the first few hundred yards there was no opposition, then shots rang out, a burst of machine gun fire cut down several of our men and we flung ourselves flat.

"Bring up the machine guns, it's just an advance post, the MG34s will send them running," he shouted. "Keep going, keep going, kill the bastards!"

We crawled forward in a wide, hesitant group, bunched together for mutual support, I could see men's eyes darting nervously around for signs of the enemy. In the thick wood we couldn't see the Russians yet and they evidently had lost sight of us. Their shooting became sporadic, a short burst of machine gun fire, the lighter sound of sub-machine gun fire, the crack of a rifle. Where the hell were they? We'd gone forward almost two hundred yards, and nothing. Then yes, inside a dark thicket about forty yards ahead I saw the distinctive shape of a Russian helmet moving. Dirlewanger saw it too.

"That's it men, they're in there. Charge!"

He leapt up and ran forward, expecting his men to follow. Most of us did, a few shrank down to shelter in shallow depressions in the forest floor, the rest of us charged after him. Miraculously he wasn't hit, two of our men went down to a burst of fire but the rest of us ran on, several troopers caught up with Dirlewanger and they were still with him when he burst into the Russian position, a tree trunk that had fallen inside a clump of bushes. They leapt over the trunk and poured fire into the soldiers sheltering behind it.

"That's it men, we're clear, forward!"

The CO waved to us heroically, the Wagnerian hero embarking on a voyage to glory and immortality. He did deem to be immortal, too, more shots rang out, another trooper next to him fell, but he was unscathed. We were running again now, we'd cleared one Russian position and the troops had their blood racing, overcome with some kind of suicidal 'joie de vivre' that cleared all reason and thinking from men's minds.

I ran too, I had no choice, Karl-Heinz and Gerd were alongside me, the rest of the platoon behind. It was the sniper who got me, he'd cunningly allowed us to run past, then a series of shots were fired from a position behind us. I felt a blow to my back, there was no real pain, it was just as if I'd been pushed hard in the back as a battering ram hit me. I could hear someone shouting 'he's behind us, he's hiding in that tree' when the pain came. My stomach was on fire and when I put my hand behind my back it came away covered in blood. Gerd knelt down beside me.

"You've been hit, Sir, stay still, I'll put a dressing on it."

Someone, Karl-Heinz I think, was shouting "Hilfe, hilfe." I heard more shooting, the louder explosions of artillery shells landing, then the pain knifed into me like a red-hot poker, slicing through my guts and I blacked out.

I came to on a train. I remembered that I'd been on one before, were they taking me back to Berlin, back to Lisl? Had the past weeks all been a dream? The morphine made me drowsy, I had erotic dreams, Lisl, naked, her crotch exposed, inviting, but when I looked at her face it wasn't her, it was Anna, her voice thick with lust, saying 'Paul, it's ok, I won't hurt you'. My blood was swirling with exquisite arousal and I reached for her, stroking her tits, kissing her, touching her between her legs and seeing her body respond, squirming with sexual need. Then I entered her and we were both groaning with the ecstasy of our lovemaking, I heard myself saying, 'Anna, I love you, I'll never leave you'. I reached for her again, but instead of her bare flesh

I felt cloth, how could that be, she was naked?

"Herr Schaffer, how do you feel?"

I opened my eyes. It wasn't Anna but a nurse, a Red Cross Helferin, the auxiliaries recruited to help tend to both civilians and military since the war had increased in intensity. I felt a keen sense of disappointment, I'd wanted Anna. In every way.

"I'm ok, I think. It hurts a lot."

"Yes, you will for some time. You're lucky, the bullet missed your kidney and passed through into your stomach, they had to open your abdomen to remove it, you won't be able to get out of bed for another week at least."

"Where are we going?"

"Berlin, to the SS hospital."

So I really was going back to Lisl, yet again.

The train rolled slowly through Belorussia, into Poland, we stopped briefly at Warsaw and I thought uselessly about Anna, then we were heading towards Germany. After two days of constant stop and start we were nearing the German border. I felt well enough to get off my soiled gurney and try to restore the blood circulation through my legs. I almost fell when I put weight down, but the sight of so many helpless, wounded men spurred me to push myself so as not to be like them. I could barely manage to keep upright, but there was a crutch on the floor underneath a nearby berth, I picked it up and used it to support me. I walked along slowly and carefully and felt strength returning to my legs, as well as a mass of pain, but I could live with that. Indeed, it was itself a celebration of life when so many of the men on this train would never be able to feel pain ever again. In the next compartment, I was very surprised to find Karl-Heinz laying on a gurney, his legs bandaged and splinted. He saw me at the same moment.

"Karl-Heinz, what the hell happened to you?"

He grimaced. "After you were hit, we got you fixed up with a medic while Dirlewanger pressed on with the attack. We went forward to join him, but it was sheer murder. They'd led us into an ambush, those first few Soviet positions were sacrifices to lead us onto their main defenses. We broke out of the trees and they opened up on us, fixed machine guns, mortars, artillery, the works. That was it, the battalion broke and run."

"Did Dirlewanger get hit?"

He laughed. "He took a bullet that went straight through his arm, no damage really, the Devil looks after that one. We lost about half the battalion, though."

"Half? My God, it really was a slaughter."

"Yes, slaughter is a good word. Gerd managed to pull me out when I was hit, he got the other troopers to help carry me. Plenty of the others weren't so lucky, when we got back under cover we could hear them shouting for us to put a bullet through them to keep them from being captured by the Russians."

I shuddered at the horrific scene he painted, a vision of hell. Any of the Dirlewanger troopers captured by the Russians would receive a taste of what they'd dished out to innocent Russian civilians. Perhaps it was only their just desserts but that didn't make it any more edifying.

"Do you need me to fetch you anything, Karl-Heinz?"

"Water would be good, schnapps even better if you can

rustle up a bottle," he smiled.

"I don't think there's any on the train, but if I come across some you'll be the first to know."

I brought him a mug of fresh water and left him and returned to my gurney, I felt my legs were about to collapse under me. I heard someone shout excitedly, 'It's the Reich, we're home'. Through the window I could see that we were crossing a river bridge, the Oder, we were indeed home, at least to my temporary home. I wasn't sure where I would prefer to call home. It certainly wasn't Berlin. Chicago, the USA, for sure, Warsaw maybe, to be tucked up in bed with Anna, that was an attractive thought, but not here, in this dark, brutal war-torn city. Twelve hours later, they transferred us into ambulances and took us to the familiar SS hospital, a few hours later Lisl had heard I was there and was sitting at my bedside.

"I don't think you're cut out for war," she smiled at me. "Every time you go near the front you get shot."

"It's just fate, bringing me back to you, my darling Lisl. Tell me what has happened since I left."

"Just more of the damned war. The bombers come over constantly and destroy our beautiful city."

"I'm sure our own bombers are doing the same to their cities."

"But I don't live in their cities," she whined. "I live in Berlin and I want them to leave me alone."

"We'll need the war to end for that to happen."

She looked thoughtful. "Bernardotte has spoken to me, he knows you're back, he wants to see you."

"No problem, tell him to visit me here."

"I will, he says it's urgent."

She stayed for another hour until the nurse in charge of the ward threw her out. The following morning, Bernardotte arrived at the hospital.

He was in Red Cross uniform, looking serious and stern, although I'd not really seen him look any different.

"I got your diary, Schaffer," he said without any preliminary words of sympathy. I looked around the nearby beds, I couldn't see anyone listening.

"Can you act on it, Count?"

"We're doing our best, but it's not easy."

"It wasn't easy to get those documents to you, my friend, but what they describe are war crimes. It's simple and clear cut, so why don't you take up with the German government and ask for a formal Red Cross investigation? Just don't tell them where the information came from."

He grimaced. "We have made many such complaints, shooting innocent civilians, the concentration camps, the gas chambers, you don't need me to tell you about those. Do you know that Himmler's RSHA has set out to murder every Jew in Europe? I'm talking about many millions of people, innocent civilians."

"So make it public, why don't you shame Hitler's government into stopping the slaughter."

"Shame?" he laughed then, but it was a bitter, regretful laugh, without humor. "They have no shame, how much shame can people have who slaughter the innocent in their millions?"

"So what do we do, Count?"

"We keep on, we keep documenting, reporting and hoping that this war will come to an end before much longer and the guilty can be held to account. You know that Stalingrad is on the point of surrender?"

"Surrender? Surely not, I know it's bad but von Paulus would never give up. The word at the front is that von Manstein is mounting another rescue bid that is certain to succeed."

He was silent for a moment. "There will be no rescue, the Red Cross understands that the death toll in Stalingrad could surpass that for every other battle since this war began. Casualties on both sides are predicted at a half a million, maybe many more. They will surrender, Schaffer, they are starving, freezing to death and almost out of ammunition. The Russians are refusing to allow the Red Cross access, but we have our sources. Perhaps it is the beginning of the end for Hitler's war."

I thought of those officers who'd been travelling to reinforce the Sixth Army. Were they still alive, freezing, frostbitten, starving, waiting to go into a Soviet prison camp? Or were they already dead in the Russian hell that had become known as the 'Cauldron'? Perhaps they would be better off dead, the Russians dealt harshly with German prisoners of war and who could blame them? They'd learned their lessons well from the Germans themselves.

"Whatever happens, Count, the war won't end anytime soon. Our armies in Russia are formidable, I doubt they'll easily be defeated."

"I prefer to look to the lessons of history, Schaffer. Didn't

Napoleon try the same thing in the last century, and wasn't he beaten by the endless territory and vast resources of the Russian Empire?"

"The German armies have tanks and aircraft this time, Count."

"So do the Soviets," he replied, "in far greater numbers than the Germans."

He urged me to keep the information coming to him whenever I had the opportunity.

"The time will come when these criminals will answer for their crimes, believe me."

I didn't really believe him, but I promised to do my best to keep the information coming, at least I would be doing something to mitigate my guilt. After he'd gone I managed to find Karl-Heinz, they said he would be hospitalized for longer than me due to the nature of the wounds to his legs.

I managed to persuade the hospital to discharge me four days later and I went to stay with Lisl. I was still very shaky and it would be some time before I could be posted back to the front. I lay on her couch, covered by a blanket, drinking real coffee that she'd managed to obtain, there was a knock at the door. Lisl went to answer it and came back with a face I recognized. Muller, Mischer's Gestapo assistant. I'd forgotten all about Muller since I'd been wounded. He was as bitter and sardonic as ever.

"I see our brave soldier is recovering, no doubt you will soon be fit to return to the front. The SS will be pleased to have your services again."

"What the hell do you want, Muller?"

"What have you got to offer me?" he leered.

"Nothing, nothing at all that the Gestapo would find interesting."

"I'm not sure that's true. Tell me about Kriminalassistent Mischer, his death seemed strange."

Mischer, of course, he'd talked about a file that was now in Muller's hands, a file that could send me and everyone I knew to the Gestapo cellars and then back to the death camps. I was very wary and tried to keep my voice neutral.

"It was nothing unusual at all, one of our people went crazy, shot him and shot himself. You know that, surely. It happens all the time on the Eastern Front."

He inclined his head. "I know the official version, yes, but Mischer was a good friend. You know exactly what he was investigating when he was shot, don't you?"

"I have no idea."

"But you must have," he persisted. "He was investigating you, Schaffer. You and your friends, you've been giving aid to the partisan leader Pushkin. I have it all in the file he sent me."

"Muller, believe me, he got it wrong. I know nothing of this Pushkin person."

"I have heard there was a high ranking partisan in the bar, possibly Pushkin himself, at the same time as Mischer was killed."

I shrugged. "There were several people in the bar at the time, how would I know who was a partisan? They don't wear a uniform."

He looked at me intently. "Listen to me, Schaffer. I carry the file from Kriminaloberassistent Mischer on my person, it is a personal project that I do not wish to have taken over by one of my enthusiastic superiors looking for quick promotion. But I shall not wait much longer, Schaffer. If I do not get the information I need in the next few days, I shall be forced to pass the file on and I have little doubt you will be arrested. I warn you, my patience is wearing thin."

He waited. Then, "If there is anything you wish to tell me you can contact me before it is too late, Untersturmfuhrer Schaffer."

He handed me his card.

"Kriminalassistentanwarter Muller, before you go, it's Obersturmfuhrer Schaffer nowadays."

"Really. I am now Kriminalassistent Muller, like you, I had promotion. And I intend to make sure I use my new rank to safeguard the security of the Reich from traitors and saboteurs, Schaffer. That goes for their friends too."

He gave me an eloquent look and left.

Jesus Christ, he must know most of what I had been doing, though not all, if he did he would have arrested me before now. Except that he desperately wanted Pushkin, the major thorn in the side of the German armies in Russia. He expected me to either give him up or lead him to capturing the Russian and the certain glory and promotion that would shower on him after he had made the arrest. I had to be more careful than ever. Lisl looked grave.

"What is that man talking about, partisans and their friends?

You're much more deeply involved that I realized, Paul. What have you been doing, have you become a partisan yourself?"

"You don't want to know, Lisl. As far as you're concerned, I'm not involved in anything, just leave it at that."

She argued, but I refused to tell her anything and she gave in and sulked. I wasn't even sure I could trust her. After an hour of talking she calmed down, I knew she'd forgiven me when she came back to the living room completely naked and started to gently brush my lips with hers, putting my hand on her to play with her tits. My stomach was still very sore and lovemaking was impossible but she took me in her mouth and blew me to a heavenly orgasm.

"That's one you owe me," she said afterwards. "When I decide how I want to collect, I'll let you know."

Two nights later, she helped me dress and I limped to the club where she worked. Her show was more outrageous than ever, I'd little doubt that the sex on the stage was simulated but from where I sat, it wasn't immediately apparent how they'd managed it. The following day I went to visit Karl-Heinz. He was still in a lot of pain but his legs were healing quickly. Too quickly. They needed soldiers back at the Eastern Front, wounds were dealt with rapidly and soldiers sent straight back into the meat grinder.

When we were alone, he whispered to me. "I've been visited by the Gestapo, they came this morning."

"Muller, a Kriminalassistent?"

He nodded. "He knows something about the death of that Gestapo officer in Minsk. He's got a notebook packed with information on us, he showed it to me. Names, dates, places, he's got the lot."

"He doesn't have enough to arrest us, Karl-Heinz. If he did, he'd have done it by now, besides, there's something he wants from us."

I explained about the Gestapo's desperation to capture Pushkin. Brandt looked skeptical. "I hope you're right. He knows an awful lot and he's got it in for you. He said he was going back to question your girlfriend, Lisl von Schenk, this evening. He's got it in for her too. I think he might arrest her to get to you."

"I'll go around there as soon as I leave here."

"What do you plan to do then? If he does arrest her we're finished, we'll be back in Mauthausen, or dead!"

"I don't know, Karl-Heinz. I'll confront him when I go around there."

He looked at me. "Confront him?"

"Look, if necessary, I'll kill him, it may be the only way to protect ourselves. He said that no one else has seen the file and he keeps it on his person, so I should be able to destroy it."

He nodded. "It's a risky business, killing a Gestapo agent. Especially here in Berlin."

"It would even more risky if he used the information in that notebook, I need to get to him before he does that, Karl-Heinz. Don't worry about it, we'll get over this."

"And then?" he smiled.

"Then we recover, they ship us back to the Eastern Front and they'll shoot at us all over again. What else is there?"

"We could escape."

I looked around quickly, but no one was listening.

"You're crazy, the Gestapo and SS are watching everyone, especially us. Don't forget, we were once prisoners ourselves, we're not totally trusted. I don't think we have much chance of slipping away without them noticing. There's another problem too."

"What's that, haven't we got enough problems?"

"Gerd, he's still in Russia. We've been together for all this time, how could we just leave him there?"

He nodded thoughtfully. "You're right, we're in it together. When we get back we could consider going over to the Russians."

"Karl-Heinz, you're not thinking straight. How would the Russians greet deserters from the Sonderbattalion Dirlewanger?"

"They'd string us up from the nearest tree, I guess."

"Yes, after they'd cut our balls off. We know that we've been trying to help them, but they don't all know it."

"Pushkin does," he said softly.

Vladimir Pushkin, of course. "You're right, if we can make contact with him we may be able to get out."

"And if we can't make contact with him?"

"Then we keep going, my old friend. We pretend to fight for the battalion, we do our best to help the partisans and try to survive the war."

He grimaced. "It'll never end, this damned war, and if it ever does end it'll be long after we've been killed and forgotten on some Godforsaken Russian battlefield."

There was a murmuring along the ward, patients were talking excitedly.

"Turn up the radio," someone shouted, I can't hear."

I recognized the voice of Dr Goebbels.

"The tragic battle of Stalingrad is a symbol of heroic, manly resistance to the Jewish Bolshevik threat posed to all civilized nations. It has not only a military, but also an intellectual and spiritual significance for the German people. Here for the first time our eyes had been opened to the true nature of the war. We want no more false hopes and illusions. We want to look the facts in the face, however hard and dreadful they may be. The history of our party and our state has proven that a danger recognized is a danger defeated. Our coming hard battles in the East will be under the sign of this heroic resistance. It will require previously undreamed of efforts by our soldiers and our weapons. A merciless war is raging in the East. The Fuhrer was right when he said that in the end there will not be winners and losers, but the living and the dead."

"So Stalingrad has fallen, finally, the poor bastards," Karl-Heinz said.

A patient, who was covered from his chest to his feet in soiled bandages shouted, "Turn that fucking nonsense off, I've heard enough of that windbag little dwarf for ten lifetimes."

His neighbors whispered to him to shut up. A nurse hurried in to give him an injection, probably a sedative to stop him from incriminating himself. There were many ways to protect their patients, the Gestapo could be every bit as bad as or worse than the enemy could ever be.

"Paul, you know that the Russians have started getting supplies into Leningrad across the frozen lake?" he continued. "It looks like they're going to beat us there too."

"No, I didn't know."

"The Soviets managed to open a narrow land corridor to the city two weeks ago. It wasn't on the radio, of course, but a nurse had whispered it to be the truth. A friend of hers, a girl who slept with a colonel on leave from the Colonel-General Georg von Küchler's Eighteenth Army had murmured it to her during a lovemaking session," he smiled. "Perhaps things are moving in the right direction."

I had a sudden idea. "We couldn't make any kind of a deal with the Russians, Karl-Heinz, but what about the Poles? I've got contacts there, maybe we could talk to them."

"What, really join the partisans?"

"Sure. I'd sooner fight for them than for Dirlewanger and his murderous bunch of thugs. Besides, we're doing it already."

He nodded. "I'm game, when we get back we'll talk to Gerd, but I know what he'll say, he hates the fucking Nazis, Dirlewanger more than any of them."

The sirens started to wail, patients looked up as if to see the RAF bombers flying over the city.

"I need to get back, Karl-Heinz. We'll try and make a deal with the Poles."

"Agreed," he laid back to rest.

Even as I walked back to Lisl's apartment, trying to hurry before the bombing started in earnest, I knew the reason for my suggestion that we join the Polish resistance. Anna Ostrowski.

I was nearly home when the first bombs landed, about a mile away in the Charlottenburg-Wilmersdorf district. A Luftschutz, an Air Raid Warden wearing a shabby, torn uniform and steel helmet shouted at me, "You fool, you'll get killed, come down to the shelter. Hurry, man, it's down here!"

He was standing next to the dark, basement entrance of an apartment block, in front of the entrance was a wall of sandbags. I thought for a few seconds, I wanted to get back to Lisl, but another load of bombs exploded much nearer, the ground shook beneath my feet and I was convinced. I hurried through the thick, oak door and went down some steps into the shelter while the Luftschutz closed and barred it behind me. About two hundred people were already in there, most sitting on coats and blankets on the floor. Children were sobbing quietly, when another stick of bombs exploded. Dust and chips of brick and mortar rained down from the ceiling, some children started to scream in terror. I waited for the raid to end, it must have been an hour before the all-clear siren wailed and I was able to run up the steps and back out into the street. At first, I couldn't see any new bomb damage, then I turned the corner into the street where I lived with Lisl. Instead of the apartment block there was a new heap of rubble to deface the Berlin skyline. The building had gone. Lisl had gone. And of course Kriminalassistent Muller had gone too, together with his incriminating evidence.

Two weeks later, I boarded the train with Scharfuhrer Karl-Heinz Brandt to return to Belorussia. I was glad to be leaving

Berlin, all that was left for me there was the terrible memory of the mound of rubble that lay where our apartment block had once stood, where I had spent so many wonderful times with Lisl von Schenk. I had spent the whole of the next week in every squalid bar I could find, getting drunk and trying unsuccessfully to forget. Karl-Heinz found me and cleaned me up, dried me out and got me on the train back to the front, back to the Sonderbattalion Dirlewanger.

I didn't feel bitter about the RAF, or even my own USAAF or whoever had dropped the bombs that killed Lisl, they hadn't started the war, hadn't embarked on a programee of mass murder. I'd lost everything, all I had left was an insane determination to get back into action and do everything I could to obstruct the German war effort in general and the Sonderbattalion Dirlewanger in particular. I'd already died more than enough for several lifetimes, death held no terror for me anymore, I knew it was inevitable that I would not survive this war. I also knew that the war was ripping away everything I cared about, honor, decency and virtue as well as the people that I loved and cared about.

I was lost in my thoughts, Karl-Heinz brought me back to the present and reminded me that there was another casualty of that bomb, Muller, the Gestapo man.

"I know that, Karl-Heinz and it's good news, but if the RAF hadn't got him, I would have killed him anyway. Is that what Lisl had to die for, just to protect me from the Gestapo? I would sooner have died myself, a hundred times over."

"I'm sorry, Paul, I meant no offense. She would have been

proud of what you're planning to do."

I nodded. "You're right about that, she hated them all."

I had no way of knowing if Anna still lived and no way of finding out. Did I owe it to Lisl's memory to mourn before I looked to renew a relationship with another girl? But in my head I heard Lisl's tinkling laugh, 'of course you should', she would have said, 'take what you can get, Paul, I certainly would'.

I would do my utmost to return to Anna as soon as possible. But as the train rolled east I reflected that I was just a ghost walking, a ghost who was tainted and smeared with the stench of death. Yet I would to my utmost to bring death to Hitler's savages who had befouled this continent with their particular brand of evil. I'd tried surviving and it wasn't enough, never enough. I'd tried passively giving aid to the partisans, that wasn't enough either.

It was time to begin fighting, this particular American had decided to go to war on the real enemy, at long, long, last.

ALSO BY ERIC MEYER

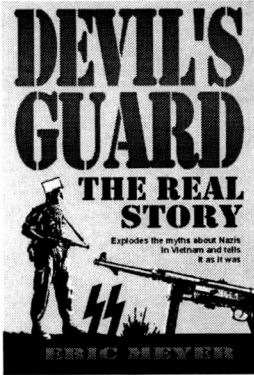

DEVIL'S GUARD: THE REAL STORY

Following the myths and legends about Nazis recruited by the French Foreign Legion to fight in Indochina, Eric Meyer's new book is based on the real story of one such former Waffen-SS man who lived to tell the tale. These were ruthless, trained killers, brutalised by the war on the Eastern Front, their killing skills honed to a razor's edge. They found their true home in Indochina, where they fought and became a byword for brutal military efficiency.

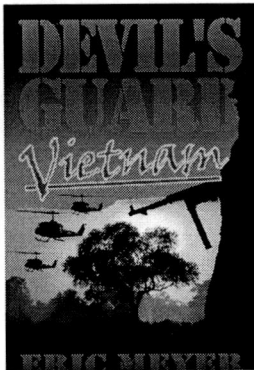

DEVIL'S GUARD VIETNAM

The sequel to the acclaimed 'Devil's Guard - The Real Story'. Once again the Waffen-SS veterans are called upon to battle against the communists of the VietCong. To defend themselves Hoffman and Schuster are compelled to use their brutal fighting skills to once more wage war in the steaming cauldron of Vietnam. The Devil's Guard is on the march again.

IRON CROSS
AMERIKA

ERIC MEYER

First published in the United Kingdom in 2011 by Swordworks Books

ISBN 978-1-906512-80-4

Typeset by Swordworks Books
Printed and bound in the UK & US
A catalogue record of this book is available from the British Library

Cover design by Swordworks Books
www.swordworks.co.uk